Image and Likeness:
Literary Reflections on the Theology on the Body

Edited by

Erin McCole Cupp

and

Ellen Gable

Full Quiver Publishing

Pakenham, Ontario

Image and Likeness:
*Literary Reflections on the
Theology of the Body*
Collection Copyright Erin McCole Cupp and Ellen Gable

Published by
Full Quiver Publishing
PO Box 244
Pakenham, Ontario K0A 2X0
www.fullquiverpublishing.com

ISBN Number: 978-0-9879153-5-1

Printed and bound in the USA

NATIONAL LIBRARY OF CANADA

CATALOGUING IN PUBLICATION

Published by FQ Publishing

A Division of Innate Productions

Table of Contents

Foreword by Damon Owens — 5

Venus if You Do by Arthur Powers — 7

Thou by Gerard Webster — 23

No Turning Back by Leslie Lynch — 27

Purple Hearts by Tony Kolenc — 53

Cries of the Innocents by Karina Fabian — 83

Victorious by Katy Huth Jones — 89

Movements by Michelle Buckman — 91

Full Reversal by Theresa Linden — 103

In the Death of Winter by Arthur Powers — 129

Guess Who's Coming to Sunday Brunch by Erin McCole Cupp — 131

Nice by Gerard Webster — 137

My Pot of Gold by R Elaine Westphal — 151

Claudio by Arthur Powers — 153

This is My Body by AnnMarie Creedon — 163

Good For Her by Erin McCole Cupp — 181

Pear Trees by Dena Hunt — 195

The Walk by Anne Faye — 203

Two Kinds of People by John McNichol — 219

Hard Choices by Barbara Hosbach — 249

MS by Arthur Powers — 263

Made For Love by Theresa Linden — 265

The Death of Me, The Life of Us by Ellen Gable — 293

Foreword
Damon Owens

The power of stories on people is a fascinating phenomenon. A poem, anecdote, short story, biography or novel can engage our imagination, intellect, emotions, and memory in transformative ways. We truly are "hard-wired" for story. As a Catholic speaker and evangelist for over twenty years, I have witnessed how a well-told story can build rapport, engender trust, and influence even the most reluctant listener.

In the early years, my wife Melanie and I would travel most Saturdays telling our conversion story to rooms full of couples preparing for marriage. Our talks covered the most challenging (and challenged) topics for couples: cohabitation, contraception, pre-marital sex, and natural family planning. We recognized very early on the power of sharing our journey from unbelief to passionate teachers. I've often thought our witness to the demands of love — the agony and the ecstasy — moved more hearts to conversion than the decades of theological and philosophical content I try to shoehorn into my talks these days.

It is an ironic challenge to teaching theology of the body (TOB). It is a catechesis *par excellence* on the origin, history, and destiny of man and woman made in the image and likeness of God. It is a story. And not just a story, but *the* story. Our story and His story: the story of Creation, the Fall, and the Redemption of humanity and known as beloved children of a Father who *is* Love.

Ironically, there is so much beautiful teaching contained within the audiences themselves that it can distract teachers from its narrative power. How often have I begun an introduction to a TOB talk with *"...Pope John Paul II's 129 weekly addresses given from September 1979 to November 1984 delivered to the visitors in St. Peter's Square...Original Man, Historical Man, Eschatological Man..."*

Now all of this is true, factual, and extremely interesting — as are the dozens of sublime insights to bodiliness, masculinity, femininity, sacramentality, spousal union, celibacy, and human and divine love. No question about their profundity.

The challenging question in my mind is *how* can we convey these deep relational truths of our being in a way that honors their inherent *power as a story*? How do we teach more as master storytellers and less as didactic instructors of concepts and ideas? The TOB is a proposal that, if true, transforms and redeems every aspect of our lives — the good, the bad, and the ugly. But the sad truth is that too few of us want to journey with others from their ugly to their redemption. We can only take so much of other people's ugly before skipping to their victory.

I am indebted to the authors and poets of *Image and Likeness* for their gifted storytelling of real life "ugly." This book isn't afraid to hold our gaze into the darkness of sin, doubt, and brokenness *before* the resolution of redemption. Some of these stories are heartbreaking to read precisely because I know this is true. Some of them I will never forget because of their unexpected turn to redemption. Through and through, this is an artistic instruction in TOB that shows us the wounds needing the balm, the balm applied, and the health and wholeness of men and women healed. And, like every well-told story, its penetrating TOB truths will influence even the most reluctant reader.

VENUS IF YOU DO
Arthur Powers

I

You explain it. Hubris? Simple chance? Superstition worming into a strangely vulnerable mind?

***

1959. The last Saturday in March. Our band was playing at our school – Hartmann High's – annual "March Home" dance. We were an eclectic group: trumpet, piano, drums, clarinet, sax, based on friendship and whatever talent we could scrape up in our little high school. But we were good. I say that even now, looking back with unbiased, old eyes. We were good.

It was Matt Thompson who made us good. He was our leader, trumpeter, and vocalist, (a better vocalist than a trumpeter) and a charismatic leader. I had known Matt since second grade, and he was the kind of guy who other kids just naturally followed, always one step ahead, thinking of new games or new ways to play old ones, outgoing, self-assured. Breaking rules, but with a smile and charm that always got him – usually all of us – out of trouble. In high school he was our star quarterback, editor of the school magazine, a straight A student. The next year he would be valedictorian of our class. His intelligence was creative, overflowing, incisive. Those teachers who weren't intimidated by him were delighted by his responsiveness, his questioning, the challenge he presented them. He was cocky, of course – as successful young men often are – but his half-smile and his friendly hand on your shoulder made each and every one of us feel we were his special friends.

His stated goal then was to go to law school, enter politics, and be governor of Illinois by the time he was 30. Not one of us doubted he could do it.

The night of the March Home dance he led with all his skill. Frankie Avalon's song, "Venus," topped the charts all month, and Matt had us practice until we mastered it. In the song, the singer asks goddess of love Venus to send him a little, bright-eyed, "lovely girl with sunlight in her hair." Matt crooned the words, *"Venus, if you do..."* promising always to be true, to give her all his love, as long as they both lived.

The crowd loved the song, and we sang it through twice – then once again at the end of the evening.

"He sang it as well as Frankie Avalon," I said to Bart Duffy, the drummer, as we were packing up.

"Better," Bart said.

***

It was Monday morning, and she was there.

Matt and I walked out of our first period class, and she was there, standing alone in the hallway outside the front office. Sunlight flowing in from the high windows touched her golden hair. She was petite, bright eyed, marvelously made. She was – is, always has been – beautiful.

"Billy boy," Matt said, touching my elbow, "it looks like Venus answered my prayer." He flashed me his half-smile, then walked over and started talking with her.

Her name was Sheila O'Conner, and she had just moved into town from Ohio. She was a sophomore – we were juniors. Within a week she and Matt were "pinned" —going steady. For the next year-and-a-half, until Matt left for college, they were almost inseparable.

As part of Matt's group of close friends, I got to know Sheila well. She was every bit Matt's match in intelligence and creativity. She could keep up with his wit, and even sometimes beat him at it; she could be very funny. But – I slowly came to realize – she was more grounded than Matt. Whereas Matt's flights of creativity had an airy, surreal quality – in retrospect, slightly manic – Sheila's playfulness and comic sense were deeply grounded in a love of life. She also had a genuine caring for people; could look into their hearts, whereas Matt seemed to look at people to see his own reflection.

The one place I saw Sheila without Matt was at church. Her family and mine were parishioners at Saint Patrick's, and she and I were often thrown together in Confirmation classes and youth events. I realized then that her essential qualities did not in any way depend on Matt, that she was definitely who she was even when he wasn't there.

Matt never revealed to me anything about their sexual relations. As I found out later, there wouldn't have been much to reveal. But even if there had been, he would not have spoken of it. He and I – all the guys in our group – had been taught by our fathers to respect girls. I sometimes think our fathers' generation was the last flowering of chivalry. There were guys our age who bragged about their sexual exploits – or, more often than not, bragged about sexual exploits they never had. Our group scorned such guys. In my case, such talk made me uncomfortable; it denigrated girls who could have been my sisters. In Matt's case, such talk would have been beneath his dignity, beneath his pride.

***

Matt was accepted into Princeton and went off to college in the fall of 1960. A group of us saw him off at the train station with great fanfare.

I was attending Quincy College, which was close

enough to commute. My family – I was the eldest of five – didn't have the money Matt's family did, and, frankly, I didn't have his academic record. In any case, I had no desire to be away from home.

I saw Matt the day he came home for Christmas holidays. He was upbeat and cheerful in his wry, ironic way – filled with Princeton. He was confirmed in his decision to major in political science. He didn't ask about my studies or Quincy College, but talked about the wonderful courses at Princeton, the world-renowned professors, the kids with famous parents.

"But it must be nice to be home again," I said.

"Oh, this podunk town." He waved his hand dismissively. That rankled me – I loved – have always loved – our town. But then he smiled his half-smile, and I let it drop.

What with one thing and another, I didn't see Matt again until after New Year's. I did see Sheila, though, at church on Christmas Eve. Our families were coming out of Mass. I spotted her on the steps of the church and went over to say hello. She was beautiful as always – a beige coat, a white scarf flowing from around her neck, a small white beret, her face glowing in the cold. But underneath her smile, she seemed sad.

"Is anything wrong?" I asked.

"No, Bill. Everything's okay." She reached out and put her gloved hand on my arm. "Have a Merry Christmas." And she turned and walked down the steps to join her family, waiting by their car.

***

Early in January, I headed over to Matt's house. He would be leaving to go back to Princeton the next day, and I hadn't seen him except for that one time. His mom answered the door and welcomed me with a smile.

"Matt – Billy's here," she called up the stairs, then told me to head on up. I must have been up those stairs hundreds of times since we were kids. The door to Matt's room was open, and he was placing neatly folded clothes into a suitcase on the bed; he was always fastidious about things like that.

"Oh, hi, Billy," he said.

I walked into the room and plunked myself down on his captain's chair – I must have sat in that chair hundreds of times.

"Getting ready to go?" I asked.

"Obviously. Can't wait to get back."

"Oh," I said.

Silence descended on the room, except for Matt humming under his breath – the Princeton fight song, I think – as he continued to pack. Silence between guys isn't usually a problem (I've spent hours in companionable silence with friends) but this silence was uncomfortable. I stood up and walked to the front window, overlooking the street, then turned back to the room.

"How's Sheila?" I asked, just looking for something to say.

"Oh," he said, again waving his hand dismissively. "Sheila."

I was startled. "What do you mean, 'Oh, Sheila'?" I asked.

He had been leaning over the bed, precisely folding a sweater, and he straightened up and looked at me. I was standing with my back to the open door, and I remember the scene clearly, as though it were etched in glass – the maroon bedspread, the beige carpet, the light tan walls, the two windows, one on each wall. Downstairs I heard Matt's mother call his little sister's name, and the smell of cooking wafted up from the kitchen.

"Listen, Billy boy," he said. "Out east there're some real women. Bryn Mawr, Vassar – even the townie girls. Sheila…" – his lip curled – "would never give me what I want."

What happened next seems, when I remember it, to be in slow motion, though it could only have taken a second. Rage flashed through me. He was clearly talking about sex – and what he said was so dismissive, so denigrating – not only of Sheila, but of everything we believed in, everything we stood for, life itself. I felt my hand form a fist, felt my arm pull back and move toward him, felt my fist hit his chin.

Then he was sprawled on the floor – a surprised, half-sitting clown, one arm angled back, the other reaching up to nurse his jaw. A bemused, then wry smile flitted across his face.

"My God, Billy," he said. "It's the thunderbolt of Zeus. She said that it would happen."

I had no idea what he was talking about. I turned, walked through the hall. As I headed down the stairs, I heard Matt laugh, an incongruous, unhappy laugh. I walked out of the house, firmly closing the front door behind me.

II

I rarely saw Matt over the next several years, and then only in group settings – weddings, funerals, and such, where we might, at most, exchange a few polite words. As I remember, he traveled in Europe the summer following his first year at Princeton, and he was almost never back in town for any length of time in later years.

I had news of him occasionally through his sister

Penny. She had been three years ahead of us, so I didn't know her that well as a kid, but she stayed in Hartmann and I would bump into her from time to time. It was from her that I learned, to my surprise, that Matt had dropped political science and switched into reading the classics – Greek and Latin. I also learned that he had seriously started writing poetry – he had been a pretty good high school poet – and had poems published in several reviews that neither Penny nor I had heard of, but which were apparently prestigious.

Matt was not much on my thoughts. Sheila was. She had started at Quincy College the year after I did, and we got to know each other better – often driving the thirty miles from Hartmann to Quincy. We enjoyed being with each other and increasingly did things together – movies, dances, church, parties. I'd been in love with her since the first day I'd seen her – and finally, toward the end of my sophomore year, got up the nerve to tell her so. She smiled, held out her hand, and touched my cheek. It was a cool spring evening. I leaned down, and we kissed.

About a year before that, Matt's name had come up in conversation with friends. "He's a bum," Sheila said, a look of distaste on her face. The summer after that first kiss – when we were secretly engaged and knew we would someday marry – Matt's name came up again, and Sheila showed mild interest.

"I thought you disliked Matt," I said, as we walked away from our group of friends.

She thought for a moment. "I suppose I don't like him much," she said. "But mostly" – she turned and smiled up at me – "he's irrelevant."

Her answer was clear and simple and transparent. For me, that ghost had been laid to rest.

Sheila and I were married the summer after I graduated from Quincy. We moved up to Chicago, where I had been accepted into medical school, and started those busy young couple years. Often now, we wonder how we did it, living in a tiny, but much-loved, apartment, Sheila working part time while taking nursing courses, me struggling with studies, then residency, and our first son, Paul, being born. Finally we realized our dream and moved back to Hartmann, where I took over the general practice of an aging doctor – Sheila working with me when she could, especially after the kids – two boys and a girl – were in school.

We heard about Matt from time to time. Penny and her family (she had married and had four sons) were my patients, and she would fill me in during periodic visits to the clinic. I got other bits and pieces from friends. Matt had become quite well known; I was in medical school when his first poem appeared in *The New Yorker*, and he had several slim volumes published over the years that won prizes and were very favorably reviewed. Out of old loyalty or curiosity, or both, I bought all of them. I like poetry. Matt used words extremely well and had many very striking images. His poems were complex in language and structure, somewhat reminiscent of Eliot, but they lacked something. They didn't have the faith that illumines Eliot. But more than that, they didn't seem to grow. There was a surface quality without human depth – expected, perhaps, in some young poets; but depth didn't emerge as Matt grew older, as though the poet never matured.

The personal side came through Penny. Matt was married at least twice, neither time working out. He was hired to teach at prestigious schools, would stay a few years, but would not be awarded tenure, then he'd move on to another school. "The trouble is," Penny said, "he can't keep his hands off women." The worst came when Matt would have been almost fifty: he was fired from a small university in Pennsylvania for sleeping with a nineteen-year-old student. For about a year he disappeared, then surfaced again in New Mexico, where – according to Penny – he was working for UPS and teaching occasional classes at a community college.

***

About five years later, I went to Albuquerque for a medical convention. Penny had given me Matt's address.

"Don't tell him I'm coming," I asked her. "I'm not sure whether I'll have time to see him."

"I won't," she said. "We seldom talk, anyway."

The convention turned out to be more boring than I expected, so I took off the last afternoon and drove the rental car to the dingy suburb where Penny said Matt lived. I pulled up in front of a small, neat but in-need-of-paint ranch house. I sat in the car for a couple of minutes, then reluctantly got out and started up the sidewalk. I was hoping Matt wouldn't be home, but the door opened and he appeared – white haired, scrawny, but definitely Matt – in the front doorway.

"Billy boy." His voice was falsely hardy. "I've been expecting you."

I was surprised. "Penny told you?"

"Penny? No. Saw it in the shells."

He stood aside and ushered me directly into a living-dining area with an open kitchen at one end. The rug was worn and the furniture tattered, but the place was immaculately neat. On the dining room table was a cloth – about a foot square – with small shells scattered on it, mostly scallops but a few others.

"The shells," he said, pointing to them.

A shiver ran up my spine.

"You...?"

"Divination. One learns a lot from the old Greeks and Romans. It told me an old friend would be coming this afternoon. There aren't many of those, so some simple yes-no questions told me it was you."

He touched my elbow as he had in the old days. He was clearly proud of himself.

"My oldest friend," he said.

He was facing me now, and I could see his eyes. He was drugged on something, his eyes unnaturally dilated. There was a tumbler of what looked like whiskey on the table, and he picked it up.

"You shouldn't mix..." I started to say, almost instinctively.

He laughed.

"The good medical doctor. Well, my good Watson, what will mixing do? Kill me?" He laughed again. "Let me get you a drink."

I accepted a whiskey, not really knowing what else to do. We sat down – he on the sofa, I in the only armchair. Out the picture window I could see the front porch, the unkempt lawn, my rental car. I wished I could get in it and drive away.

We talked about old things – growing up, high school, folks back in Hartmann. His interest was clearly only on the surface. He had the whiskey bottle beside him on the floor and would refill his glass whenever it became half empty. Once or twice he offered to refill my glass, which I was sipping as slowly as possible. When I refused, he seemed relieved.

After about half an hour, he lapsed into silence. I sat looking out the window. I was thinking of how I could detach myself and get out of there, when he spoke.

"You still a Catholic?"

I was startled. "Yes."

I half-expected a sneer or a snide remark, but he simply pondered a moment.

"So you can be forgiven."

"Forgiven?"

"If you've offended your God, you can go to Confession and be forgiven."

"Yes. Of course. If you're truly repentant. All Christians believe that."

"The Greek gods – the Roman gods – aren't like that."

"What?"

"The old gods. There're no rules. Just their whim. If you offend them, they can forgive you tomorrow, or in fifty years, or never. Depends how they feel, their whim. They play with us – 'As flies to wanton boys are we to the gods...'"

He was silent, lost in thought again. After a minute he looked up.

"Have you ever wondered about my damned screwed up life?" he asked.

"Occasionally."

"*She's* behind it."

"She?"

"Don't you remember?" He suddenly broke into song. 'Venus if you do, I promise that I always will be true...'" He stopped. His voice was a ghost of its former self.

"You mean your life's screwed up because you weren't true to Sheila?" I was incredulous.

He nodded.

"My God, man. You're not the only guy in the world who ditched his high school girlfriend. That was ages ago. Sheila's fine – she couldn't care less about all that – it's ancient history."

He laughed. A dry, empty laugh.

"You damn Christians," he said. "You think I feel *guilty* about Sheila?"

"Isn't that what you just said?"

He shook his head. "I've never felt guilty about anything in my life."

Puzzled, I looked at him. "But...."

"It's not Sheila. I don't give a damn about Sheila." He was clearly drunk. "It's Venus."

"Who?"

"Venus...Aphrodite. The goddess of love." He pronounced the word 'love' bitterly, scornfully.

"Are you joking?"

"I scorned Venus' gift – 'Hell hath no fury...' I broke my promise to her. She tortures me..."

"Tortures you?"

"Through her own weapon. She makes me fall in love – time after time after time – love so overwhelming I have to have it, possess it – then throws me out of love as quickly. But the damage is done. She is a cruel and capricious mistress."

"Mistress?"

"Ah, not in that sense. Would that she were. Would that she would embody herself and come down and let me grasp her, hold her, penetrate her. *Then* maybe I'd be satisfied."

His face had taken on an ecstatic, almost animalistic

appearance. I felt repelled, but I had to try.

"Matt. You need help."

"Help?" The empty laugh again. "Who can help against her? She who would see all Troy massacred for her whim. The mother of Phobos and Deimos. Do you know who they are?"

"No."

"Fear and Terror. The goddess of love is mother of Fear and Terror."

"Matt," I said quietly, standing up. I had to give him something to hold onto, something that would hold him until we could get him the psychiatric help he needed. "Matt, Christ is stronger than all that. You don't have to fear the old demons."

"Christ?" He said it as though he were swearing. "Your love is all *agapé*." His voice dripped with disgust. "Ours is *eros*."

"There's nothing wrong with *eros*," I said, "as long as it's subservient to *agapé*."

He looked up at me then, seeming surprised I had said what I did. But his eyes closed.

"Sleep," he muttered, and let his head fall backward. It took me a moment to realize he had passed out.

I stood there, indecisive. Matt needed help. But I had to get to the airport to catch my flight home. Years as a doctor, I told myself, had taught me that you can only help people when they want help. If I stayed? But I was reluctant. Finally, I found a paper and pen and wrote a note, telling Matt I'd help him, giving my phone number, and urging him to call. I set it on the table, next to the divining shells, and walked to the front door, opened it, glad to leave.

On the front porch I glanced down and saw a small

circle of objects. I swear they were not there when I came. I looked closely. There was a small silver hand mirror, a dozen or so scallop shells, a small charm shaped like a dolphin. Who had put them there? I had been sitting, looking out the front window, and had seen no one come or go. Nervously, I stepped around the circle and headed out to the car.

***

Matt never called. I wasn't surprised. From time to time I'd feel pricks of guilt, thinking I hadn't done enough. I told Penny, of course, and I believe she tried to get some type of intervention. But nothing worked.

Two or three years later we learned that Matt had been badly hurt. He'd been playing around with a truck driver's wife; the truck driver found out, got mad, and hit him. Matt's head, as he fell, hit a rock. Penny flew down to see him; he was unconscious but opened his eyes once, smiled, and said something about Zeus's bolt.

When Matt died, the truck driver was charged with manslaughter. Penny flew down for the trial.

"It was pathetic," she told me. "The poor man kept saying he didn't mean to kill Matt. He said what really made him angry was the way Matt talked – 'he talked about Helen' – that was the trucker's wife – 'like she was some kind of whore.' I testified at the sentencing along with Matt's sister, and asked that the sentence be light. They gave him two years in prison."

***

They had brought Matt's body home and buried him in the Presbyterian cemetery, which – I assume – is hallowed ground.

Several months later, I was driving by the cemetery and turned in. I got out of the car and walked over to Matt's

20

grave. There were a few dried remains of flowers. On top of the tombstone, someone has placed a silver hand mirror, a dolphin charm, and a dozen or so seashells.

Whoever had done it, I thought it was in poor taste. I turned away from the grave and headed back toward life, toward home.

THOU
(a poem to Anne)
Gerard Webster

In the spring of my days
    When I was young and free
With the wonder of thy ways
    Thou didst enchant me.

With the beauty of thy form
    And eyes that lured me hence
Thy laughter sang a sweet song
    That taught my heart to dance.

While I was still a younger man
    Unschooled in love and life
With earnest beseeching I took thy hand
    And thou consented to be my wife.

And as we joined in sacred union
    Thou set my flesh aflame.
And as we two formed one communion
    My passions thou didst tame.

The depths of thy soul I had yet to fathom;
    The borders of thy love I had yet to learn.
The frontiers of thy heart still uncharted,
    Thou didst teach my own heart to yearn.

As our lives entwined together
    They then begot yet another.
Just as I ventured to know thee better
    In thee I beheld the love of a mother.

Thy hand to guide, thy look to guard,
    Thy words always gentle to heal,
'twas in thy motherly ways,
    thou didst teach my heart to feel.

Thy touch had power to loose my firm grip,
	Thy look to unfurrow stern brow.
Tho patience oft failed me and compassion slip,
	To be a kind father, thou didst teach me how.

From teetering first step to stride far bolder,
	From infant to child, ruddy youth to full grown,
We watched our children turn wiser and older,
	Thou taught me to care without having to own.

As they build their lives and weave their world
	With wonder I watch and see
In them and theirs, mirror-like reflected
	The love 'twix thee and me.

Beauty's fabric with time grows older,
	It wears and tears and rubs thin.
But love falters not, only grows stronger
	As youth fades to reveal true beauty within.

Throughout all these many years
	Through pain and joy and sorrow
Love's constant rock allays all fears
	Yesterday, today, and tomorrow.

As fire and stone
	Into lava are smelted,
To one substance by love
	Our two elements are melted.

Just as lava flows
	From fiery source to vast sea,
So our love reaches
	To the shores of eternity.

There battered by tides,
	Assaulted by thunder,
It turns solid rock
	And breaks not asunder.

Love tested by tempests
	Is not weakened but improved.
Storm's surges only serve
	To make rough edges smooth.

When one of us loosens
	The bonds of failing flesh
And escapes earth's harness
	To seek eternal rest,

There patiently 'twil wait
	'til joined by the other,
two souls bound in love
	eternal, forever, together.

Thou has set my soul to music,
	Thou hast made my spirit soar.
Thou taught me what true love is,
	For now and ever more.

	Thou!

"Don't tell me what to do, Mom! I'm an adult, you know." Annie Moore stormed out the door, letting the screen slap shut behind her. "I don't need your permission for a belly ring, anyway," she muttered, and thought about the butterfly tattoo she wanted to get on her ankle but hadn't mentioned.

Outside, her lungs filled with the heavy humid air, and her sleeveless blouse, light blue and so cute in the air-conditioned dressing room at the mall, began to wilt immediately. The sun hung above the trees, the promise of relief from its heat a few treetops away. Louisville's rush hour traffic rumbled down the interstate a mile away.

Her mom appeared behind the fine mesh of the door, her mussed blond hair a nimbus backlit by the kitchen's light. She wiped her hands on a towel from the set Annie'd given her last Christmas. Flour dusted her worn blue jeans and the front of the neon pink *St. Anselm Parish Picnic – Food, Fun, Fellowship* t-shirt that fit just snugly enough to reveal her pudginess.

"A number doesn't make you grown up," she said. "Don't make a foolish decision, one you can't undo."

Her voice rose at the end, because Annie had stalked the length of the sidewalk to her car. Layers of dust and ragweed pollen dulled the white, used Ford Taurus her Dad had helped her buy.

"Not everything is so life-and-death, Mom," Annie called over her shoulder.

She jerked the car door open and slung her purse to the

passenger seat. Without waiting for a reply, she got in and fired up the engine, then maneuvered away from the curb. She didn't look back. She knew what she'd see: a frown and tight lips, snappish movements of the towel. Well, her mom needed to understand things were different now. Annie was eighteen, off to college in five weeks. Tired of being the perennial good girl, the geeky wallflower at her parochial high school. Ready to make her own decisions in life. She goosed the accelerator, and the car lurched forward. But it scared her just a little. All the warnings from her dad while she was learning to drive rose in her mind: you never know when a kid might dart out from between the cars, chasing a ball or losing control on a bike. She let up on the gas and ran away a little slower.

Ten minutes later she pulled up to Callie's house for their planned sleepover. Rather than having let go of the argument, Annie had gotten even more upset. From the steps to the wraparound porch, she saw Callie and her parents sitting outside, large plantation fans moving the air above the painted wicker furniture. Her dad, still in slacks and a white short-sleeve shirt, peered at a newspaper through tortoiseshell glasses. Her mom, more stylish than Annie's with her asymmetrical haircut and wearing a flowered sundress more appropriate for someone Callie's age, picked up an ice cube from a dish on the side table and passed it across the skin of her neck. An open bottle of red wine and two wide-bottomed glasses sat on the table. Callie was sprawled on the porch swing, her thick, dyed-blond hair swaying with the desultory rhythm of her foot as she toed the swing into motion. A stripe of light brown roots the same shade as her tanned skin created the illusion that her hair was floating above her head.

Annie pasted a smile on her face, and said, "Hi, Mrs.

Herndon, Mr. Herndon." Then she leaned over and whispered in Callie's ear, "Let's get out of here before I scream."

Callie flicked a curious glance at her, then said, as if they'd been planning this all along, "We're going to the mall. I need to look at school clothes, remember, Mom?"

She flashed a bright smile at her parents, and Annie wondered how they could be oblivious to Callie's manipulation. *Her* parents would never let her get away without a raft of questions. But Callie's did.

"No problem. Have fun, girls." Mrs. Herndon shooed them on their way as she poured a glass of wine.

"Oh," Callie added, "if we run into friends, we might go hang out for a while," her tone nonchalant.

Annie glanced at her, a little surprised, but made her face go all innocent, wondering what Callie had up her sleeve.

"Call if you'll be past midnight."

"'Kay, Mom." Callie grabbed Annie's arm and herded her down the steps to the garage. "Get in."

"Where are we going?"

"Kegger. Down at the river."

A thrill chased its way up Annie's spine. "You know people who go? And where?"

Of course, Callie did. Their unlikely friendship, begun when Callie needed help in freshman English, had allowed Annie to live the cheerleader and "in crowd" life vicariously. Tonight, it wasn't going to be through Callie's overblown and after-the-fact stories. It would be through Annie's own eyes. In person. Without waiting for Callie's answer, she got in the car.

"Do I look okay?" She smoothed the blue blouse and

tugged on the hems of her denim cutoffs. Callie wore low rise short shorts that made an upside down heart of her derriere and a crop top that revealed her silver belly ring. With a real amethyst in it.

Callie shot her an assessing look as she backed the car out of the driveway. "Sure. You should undo the top two buttons on your blouse, but that sweet, naïve look might get you some great action."

Annie undid them and spread the lapels apart to make a deep vee toward the pink embroidered heart in the cleft of her bra. She felt bold and a little risqué. Then she watched landmarks and street names, in case Callie wasn't in any condition to drive on the way back. By the time they'd bumped down a rutted lane and parked among a dozen other cars where the track petered out, she'd decided to prove Callie wrong. On the sweet, naïve part, not on the *getting some action* part. Although, having a guy like her and kiss her would be neat.

"I'll be around if you need anything, but the best thing to do is just dive in." Callie got out, locked the car, and grinned at Annie. "Go for it!"

Before she could chicken out, Annie turned to survey the party. Tall trees, some of them sycamores, cast long shadows in a recently mowed clearing. The air was redolent with the fragrance of nearby forsythia and overlain by the scent of new-cut grass. Twenty-five or thirty kids hung around in groups, some near a pickup truck where some really cool guys were handing out plastic cups of beer. A wi-fi speaker set on a tree stump blared music, its attendant cell phone balanced half on, half off the edge of the rough-cut wood. One couple was dancing. A guy squatted at a rock-rimmed fire pit, his hand extending a lighter with a tiny flame toward the kindling and paper inside the ring.

"Hey, Annie, is that you?" A guy's boisterous cry came from the group gathered around the keg. He waved. "C'mon over. Have a beer."

Heat rose in Annie's cheeks. She couldn't decide if it was her trademark blush of shyness, which she had sworn to put behind her now that she'd graduated, or if it was a flush of pleasure at being noticed. She opted to believe the latter. She hadn't expected to run into too many kids she knew, not this far from home, but she knew this guy. Scott Nichols. From her school. Varsity basketball, recruited by the University of Kentucky in Lexington. She resolved right then: no more shrinking into her turtle shell. It was time for a change, time to grow up and be self-assured. Even more so because of the fight with her mom a few hours ago. She had something to prove, if only to herself.

She waved back. "Hey, Scott. Sure," she called, agreeing to the beer, though she preferred a can she could nurse without someone trying to refill it before she was ready. When she reached Scott, he threw an arm around her shoulder and leaned into her, already tipsy. Maybe drunk. She laughed, even though his assumed intimacy made her uncomfortable, then spied the galvanized tub beyond the keg, filled with ice and stocked with cans. "Hey, I'll have one of those."

He grinned and unwound himself, walked to the tub with loose-limbed grace and grabbed a can, tossed it to her. "Thanks." She popped the top, caught the foam with her lips, the bubbles bursting in her mouth and releasing beery air into her sinuses. She hadn't been sure she'd like the taste, but it wasn't bad. Scott saluted her with his plastic see-through cup, sloshing golden beer over his bony wrist.

"What are you going to study at UK?" What the heck did people talk about at these parties?

"Study?" He guffawed. "As little as possible. I'm gonna join a fraternity, party. Play ball." He chugged half his beer, swaying like a willow in the wind. He finished, slung his bare arm across his mouth to wipe it dry, then belched. He reached for her. Missed, then tried again. "C'm'ere, babe. Let's go in the trees and have some fun." He waggled his eyebrows.

Annie hadn't bargained on this. Her thrill at being singled out by a star athlete faded. He seemed sort of pathetic now. Sloppy. No way did she want to go make out with him. She looked around for Callie and found her in the group clustered around the small bonfire. "Gotta go talk to somebody," she said, sidling out of Scott's reach. She raised her can in a similar toast, but Scott's eyes had roved to a girl wearing a shirt cut low enough to display a ladybug tattoo on the swell of her breast. A laugh burbled up. What a short attention span. Just like a jock. She took a swig of beer, discovering that it *did* hit the spot, just like her dad always said when he came in from mowing their two-acre lot in the summer.

More cars drove up and parked, disgorging more kids. The sky was red at its western edge and deep blue above. The temperature had finally dropped into a comfortable range. She wandered the grassy field, saying hi to kids she knew and several she didn't. It wasn't that she'd been a loner or misfit in high school. Not at all. She'd belonged— to the science club and orchestra. She'd even been a leader. But not popular. A klutz, not an athlete. The more beer she drank, though, the more it made up for all those deficiencies. Made Annie feel worldly. Sophisticated. Grown up. Well, eighteen and old enough to sign contracts, open her own bank account, vote, and join the military. Marry, have kids. But not old enough to purchase or possess the beer in her hand.

Once, just once, she wanted to let loose and have the kind of fun her classmates had been having for years. They all went to Mass with their parents on Sunday mornings, too, but their Saturday nights had been the fodder for hushed Monday morning conversations since they'd graduated from middle school, their whispered exchanges punctuated by coy giggles and secretive, knowing looks. Annie could only talk about concerts and operas and PG13-rated movies.

She hovered at edges of the makeshift dance area, hoping someone would ask her to dance. She finished her first beer and looked for a recycle container, but there was only an oversized plastic trash can. Shrugging, she tossed the aluminum can in and grabbed another from the tub, then wandered over to Callie and her friends, found the conversation boring—who was with who, who'd broken up, what was the latest news about the Kardashians. She noticed a guy who stood out from all the rest. Annie straightened and stared at him, wondering what made him different. One, he wasn't drunk—a plus—and didn't seem to be at the party for the sole purpose of getting trashed. She liked that. And he looked at the girl he was talking with, not scoping out the rest of the crowd for someone more interesting, someone better. She liked that, too. She tipped the beer up and downed a long gulp. It made her feel relaxed. No, more like...wild. Like she wanted to do something crazy. Annie had no idea what that might be, but right now it didn't matter.

She sauntered over to the dance area again. Grinned. Let her hips swivel to the beat of the music, the motion feeling easy and natural for a change, not clumsy. With her free hand, she lifted her long hair off her damp neck. Blond—without chemical help—and curly. The humidity had made her hair thick. Heavy. The Ohio River flowed silently about a quarter mile away. Or maybe the water's murmur was drowned out by the blaring music. With her pinky finger, she pulled her blouse away from her skin and pressed the beer can to her chest.

"Wanna dance?"

A guy moved into her view. Not just any guy, *him*. The one who paid attention to who he was with. She let her hair drop. Took in his height, the shaggy light brown hair with a stubborn wave to it, and his kind eyes, though she couldn't tell exactly what color they were in the dusk of the evening. He seemed older than the other kids, though he didn't look any older. Maybe that's what had intrigued her. He was more mature. Like her.

Annie wanted some of that focused attention. She smiled and tipped her head to one side in a pose she hoped was alluring. "Sure. I'm Annie. What's your name?"

"Chris Hasselback." He took her beer and set it on the stump next to the wireless speaker.

Alarm flashed through her at letting the drink out of her hand—she'd heard stories and warnings about date rape drugs, and she wasn't stupid—but she could just get a fresh one from the ice-filled tub in the bed of the pickup truck after they danced.

He pulled her to the edge of the dancers, and they danced. Fast ones, his eyes roving over her as she moved, appreciation in them, his smile saying he liked what he saw. Then slow ones, during which he held her close like she was precious, swaying, their chests, hips, and thighs creating delicious friction and sparking feelings she'd only heard about.

Emboldened, she went up on her tiptoes to kiss him, aiming for his jaw in case he didn't want to kiss her back, but he did, and Annie forgot about the music, the kids, the river. Her parents. Mass.

It was the most wonderful kiss she'd ever had, maybe because Chris was a man, not a boy. *That* was it, the quality that drew her. He certainly knew what he was doing, not like the fumbling attempts her pity dates had ended with. It felt so good, so right, that Annie leaned into him, asking, silently, for more. He slid a hand beneath her shirt and touched her skin, and it was unexpected and exciting and *right*.

When he tugged her into a copse of trees, she didn't resist. He undid the buttons of her pretty blue blouse and slid it from her shoulders, one at a time, and kissed them. He told her she was beautiful, the distant bonfire reflected in his eyes, along with something that looked a lot like worship. Nobody had ever looked at her that way. With Chris kissing her neck and touching her in places she'd never been touched, her resolve to hold herself back from the forbidden began to crumble. Desire and the beer made her feel wanton. When the image of the small group of Purity Ring wearers from school popped into her mind, she pushed it away.

At this moment, she didn't regret being ring-less. In fact, the more clothing-less she became, with Chris happily accommodating her exploration of his skin—she'd never touched a guy's chest—the more wonderful it all became, and the more her world shrank to him. Just him, and the fire he ignited within her. She felt dizzy with it. She wanted more. His touch made her drunk, higher than the beer had. He made her feel beautiful. Desirable. Loved. Not alone.

"Are you sure?" he murmured at one point.

"Yes," she breathed, sluggish with an overload of sensation, straining for some completion she couldn't articulate.

"I have a rubber." He fumbled in his back pocket.

"I'm on the Pill." Which she was, to her parents' distress, and not for birth control. For acne. Mama had sat her down for a come-to-Jesus talk when the doctor had suggested it.

"This isn't a license for you to be promiscuous," she'd said, her eyes boring a hole into Annie's heart. "Sex is a gift from God. It's sacred. It's a blessing and only to be used within the Sacrament of Marriage. Do you understand?"

Right now, sheer need eclipsed the memory. Desire thrummed through her.

If it hurt for a moment when he finally did it, well, she'd heard about that, too, but after that, it was so glorious and new and blissful that she cried out his name.

"Oh, Chris! Christopher..." She clutched him close, not wanting the moment to end.

He buried his face in her neck, his rapid breathing telling her the experience had affected him as much as it had her. "Christian. Not Christopher."

"Oh." His name poked a hole in her haze of contentment. "Okay."

He held her until she began to worry that someone might stumble upon their nakedness. The fact that they had...had done *that* and she hadn't been the least bit concerned about someone stumbling upon them while they were *doing* it niggled at her. He stood, shielding her from view with his body, then gathered their clothes and let her steady herself on him as she dressed. They emerged from the trees, and suddenly the party seemed banal and noisy.

Suddenly Christian Hasselback seemed like the stranger he was, and Annie wanted nothing more than to hide. He extended a hand to her and tipped his head toward the dancing, eyes inviting, the edges of his lips turned up in an unabashed smile.

"I—no, I'd like to go home." Was there a wobble in her voice? She hoped he didn't hear it.

His smile dimmed. "Want me to give you a ride?"

"Uh, no thanks. I'm with a friend." Annie knew she was being a turd, but in spite of what he'd made her feel, she was confused, maybe even a little ashamed at having done something so intimate with someone she'd just met.

Maybe her mom was right.

Annie turned, but Chris stopped her with his warm hand on her arm.

"Hey." The word was soft, not angry like she deserved. "I'm leaving for the Army in three weeks, but here's my phone number if you want to call me."

"I'm starting college in August." She told him which one, the one for which she'd earned a full ride scholarship.

"Well, then, hey, have a good life." He pulled her into his embrace, held her for a long moment, then kissed her. It felt like good-bye.

The last she saw of Christian Hasselback was a wavering image in the flickering lights and shadows before she whirled and fled.

***

"Callie, I'm late." Annie whispered into her phone even though she was alone in the den and both her parents were out on the patio.

"What do you mean?" Before Annie could get the words out past the lump strangling her throat, Callie gasped. "*You?* Late *that* way?"

"Yes." Tears rolled down Annie's face, and she swiped them away, trying to hide their evidence.

"Who? No, let me guess. That guy at the kegger! Had to

have been him. You guys disappeared for a while. What's his name?"

The words *Christian Hasselback* nearly rolled off Annie's tongue, but the memory felt too private to share, and she stayed silent.

"I'll take that as a *yes*, then. Not bad, girlfriend. Congratulations on not being last virgin standing anymore." Callie laughed, delighted at her sleuthing ability. Then she sobered. "Did you do the test?"

Callie's reaction bothered Annie. Laughter? And kudos? It all felt wrong. "No. Not yet." Misery filled every cell of her body. "I haven't been able to get away from Mom. She's more excited about me going to school than I am."

"I'll come over and drag you to the mall. She'll let me. We can do it there. Don't worry. I'll take care of you."

True to her word, Callie showed up twenty minutes later, buzzing with purpose.

"We won't be long, Mama. I promise." Annie grabbed her purse and jogged to Callie's BMW, painfully aware that she'd already broken her mother's trust. One time didn't mean she was promiscuous, but there were no words for saying that to her mother without it sounding vulgar and shallow. With Chris, it *hadn't* been vulgar. It had been beautiful—but Annie couldn't get around the fact that she felt shallow, because she couldn't offer up any reason or rationale for having allowed it to happen. A time or two, she even tried on the idea that he'd pushed her into it, but that was a lie, a lie she couldn't live with.

Instead of the mall, Callie pulled into a superstore that boasted a pharmacy, strode in with Annie in her wake, plucked a pregnancy test kit from the shelf, and paid for it with confidence that brooked no raised eyebrows from the cashier. Heading directly for the restrooms, she had the package open by the time they got to the door.

"Go pee on the stick," she ordered.

"I thought you had to do it first thing in the morning." Annie wasn't quite sure she was ready to face reality and sure didn't want to do it in a public place.

"There's a backup in here if this one's ambiguous. Besides, you don't really want to do this at home, do you?"

Dread clutched Annie's chest. No, she didn't. Not where anybody could find it by accident. Mutely, she shook her head. Took the kit from Callie. Went into the stall and closed the door. Stared at the plastic wand, felt hope shrivel within her, then gathered her courage, shucked her pants, and did it.

"Timing," Callie said from outside the stall.

Annie tore a piece of toilet tissue, laid it on the only flat spot in the stall, and placed the test stick on the paper, handling it like a short-fused firecracker that might explode in her hand. She deliberately turned her back on it while she flushed and adjusted her clothes, her palms going damp even as her fingers went cold and clumsy. Her heart began to pound and a rushing sound filled her ears.

"Okay, Annie. Look at it."

Slowly, Annie rotated.

Two bright pink lines shone in cheerful accusation from the pristine plastic wand. A moan rose from deep within, and she covered her face with her hands. She'd known the truth in her heart, had known since the morning after her fling when her prayer of repentance had clunked against the ceiling of her room instead of floating into God's heart. She'd known yesterday when she'd blamed anxiety over school for the nausea that had steamrolled her at the odor of breakfast's fried eggs.

But she'd refused to believe it until now. The Pill was supposed to *work*.

"Annie! Open the door." The gray metal door rattled with Callie's knocks.

Fumbling with the latch, and hoping no one else had entered the restroom to witness her fall from grace, Annie finally managed to get it open.

"Don't worry, Annie. I'll help you through this." Grim determination on her face, Callie folded Annie into an embrace. "Tell your parents you want an overnight Friday night, and I'll take you to the clinic Saturday morning. You'll be back home that evening, and no one will ever know."

Annie's heart chilled. An abortion. She hadn't thought that far. But could she do *that*? What option did she have? Tell her parents and risk their censure, maybe worse? Mama and Daddy would be so disappointed, so angry. What if her parents kicked her out? They were big on tough love; they took their responsibility as parents seriously. An ache took up residence behind her eyes. Adoption? Dear Lord, she couldn't even think that far. What about school? What would people think of her? God seemed to be awfully far away, and she had no skills, no way of offering a child a good home.

"It's only a clump of cells," Callie said, patting her on the back. "I've done it twice. It's no big deal."

Annie pulled back, shocked. "*Twice?*" No wonder Callie had known exactly what aisle to go to, had made the purchase with such an air of experience. Reality shifted beneath Annie's feet. She didn't even know her best friend. Suddenly, she felt even more alone.

"Yes. The sooner you do it, the better. But you need money. Four hundred dollars."

Thoughts and emotions swirling in her head, Annie allowed Callie to lead her to the car, explained away her reddened eyes and sniffles as allergies once she got home. Mama fussed over her, making Annie feel even more traitorous.

How was she going to come up with the money? She had it, but she couldn't explain away that kind of expenditure to her parents. Their oversight of her bank account had never been an issue before, rather a collaborative effort to teach her financial responsibility. More to the point, had she already decided that was the only thing to do? She thought of her cousin's baby and holding him last summer. So sweet—and such a hellion already at fourteen months. How could she manage a child when she was barely more than one herself?

"Are you okay, honey?" Her mom sent Annie a concerned look at dinner. "You've been so quiet the past few days."

"I'm fine, Mama." Annie forced a note of cheer into her voice. "Just preoccupied with school. It didn't seem real until a few days ago."

Her mother's face softened. "Of course. I remember how I felt. Grown up, but not quite. Ready, but anxious." She patted Annie's hand. "You'll be fine."

The few bites of mashed potato she'd swallowed congealed in her stomach. Annie took a breath through her nose, hoping nausea wouldn't follow. What a betrayal she was perpetrating on her parents!

When she felt solid enough to talk, she toyed with the food on her plate, and as casually as possible said, "A friend of Callie's is pregnant and doesn't know what to do."

"Oh, honey, is it anyone we know?" Her mom stopped eating and looked at her expectantly.

"No." Annie scrambled for an evasive answer. "I doubt it. She goes to Waggener."

Her dad snorted. "Public schools," he said with disgust. "She—well, both of them should have thought about the consequences before they got carried away." He stabbed his fork into a stack of green beans, then added, "That's the problem with kids today. The music, music videos. Abortion. It's an attack on the sanctity of life. Nobody takes sex seriously anymore. They treat it like it's recreation." He fell silent, but frowned.

Heat flooded Annie's cheeks, and she couldn't lift her gaze to meet her father's. She hadn't viewed it as recreation—it had been too glorious and momentous—but she had certainly gotten caught up in the passion. If he was that unforgiving with her imaginary friend, what would he say if she told him it was her?

Her mother chimed in. "Her parents must be so disappointed. Was she headed for college?" she asked in a tone that assumed college was no longer possible. "What a shame."

"Uh, yes." Annie's heart plummeted. Then a bit of courage she didn't know she possessed prodded her into asking, "So, just hypothetically, what if that happened to me? I'm not, of course, but since my friend's family is really angry at her, it made me wonder. What you'd say." What was one more lie on top of the pile of sins she'd already racked up?

Could she take a year off from school, have the baby and give it up for adoption? Would her parents raise the baby as their own? Would she lose her scholarship? What was pregnancy like? What about labor? Even with all her science studies, she couldn't imagine how a baby came out from *there*.

Her dad's frown turned into a glower. "The law says you're an adult, Anne Marie. If you're adult enough to make the decision to engage in sex, then you're adult enough to deal with the consequences. You'd get a job, then stay here and pay rent or get an apartment." He sat back and put his fork down. "No different than anything else we've discussed over the years. That's why you are going to college instead of taking one of those entry-level, dead-end jobs. So you can have a future."

"John!" Mama placed her hand on Annie's forearm. "I know it sounds harsh, the way your daddy says it, but he's right. We don't want you to ever get in that situation, so we're making the consequences clear ahead of time."

Annie knew exactly how much money she could make at one of those jobs, because her parents had sat down one morning with the classifieds and had her look for jobs, then apartments. It didn't take a perfect SAT score to understand that ends would never meet.

"I'm pretty tired"—it wasn't a lie; she was—"and I'm not hungry. I think I'll go to bed early tonight." She pushed back from the table and went to her room. Panic closed in on her as dusk grew closer. She sat on her bed in the darkening room, imagining scenario after scenario and feeling more trapped as she discarded each one as being either utter fantasy or terrifying. All of them were impossible.

By the time full dark came, she could only see one way out. She went to her desk and pulled out the scrap of paper with Chris Hasselback's phone number. Waiting until everyone went to bed wasn't an option, so Annie took the phone into her closet and pulled the door shut. Fingers trembling, she dialed.

"H'lo?" His voice sounded so solid, so real, her knees gave way, and she sank to the floor.

"Chris?" She knew her voice was thick with tears and

fear, but she didn't have it in her to strengthen it.

There was a pause, and then he said, "Annie?" in a voice that sounded like he hoped he had the right name.

"Yes," she whispered.

"What's wrong, babe? Speak up." The words could have been abrupt, but his tone was focused and concerned. Just like he'd been at the kegger.

"I'm"—her breath caught on a sob—"late. I can't tell Mama and Daddy. They'll be so mad at me."

"What do you mean, you're late? You need a ride? I'll come get you."

A bubble of hysteria rose. Annie clamped a hand over her mouth to contain it, then, when she had it under control said, "No! I'm late! The test—" She couldn't stop a moan and, her voice strangled, added, "Two lines."

There was a long pause. "Two lines." He sounded like he wanted to understand, but had no clue what she was talking about.

"I'm pregnant!" The words burst out more loudly than she meant them to. She repeated them, softer but with no less despair.

"P-pregnant?" He pitched his voice lower, a near-whisper like hers.

"Yes." Incongruously, a blanket of calm settled over her now that he knew.

There was another pause, this one longer. "I hate to ask this, but are you sure it's mine?"

Annie gasped. She gripped the phone so tight her fingers hurt. "Yes," she said. "You were my first time! My only time." She wanted to hit something. How dare he? She wasn't a slut. She wasn't!

He sucked in a breath and held it. Then, each word

dropping like a stone into a battered metal bucket, he said, "Then we'll get married."

Annie's mouth dropped open. Married? That wasn't what she expected him to say at all. She didn't want to get married! Not to him, not now. He kept talking, and she finally began to make sense of his words again.

"—don't know how all the Army stuff works, but I think I get a few days of leave after basic. I'll come home and we'll do what we need to do."

"Chris—"

"We'll make it work. Somehow. You need to get started with the doctor stuff—"

"No!"

"No?"

"I can't marry you!" Oh, now she'd done it. Disappointed her parents, humiliated and alienated the only person who really seemed willing to help her... "I mean—" Her voice broke. It would only compound their mistake if they married, but she couldn't make the words come out.

He went silent. Finally he asked, his voice flat, "Then what do you want from me?"

"I'm not ready to be a mom." Her voice wobbled.

"I'm not ready to be a dad, either, but we are, Annie. A mom and a dad." He sounded blindsided, and maybe a little angry.

"I want"— a full-fledged tremor shook her voice into an uncontrolled vibrato, because she didn't want to say it, didn't want to face the only option she could see, didn't really want to do it —"I have to...an abortion. There's no other way."

"Adoption," he countered without hesitation.

"I can't! I can't tell my parents."

"Annie, you're overreacting. It'll be tough for a little while, I know, but I promise I'll do what I can to help."

He was breaking her already-shattered heart. How she wanted to believe him! But Annie wasn't as strong as he thought she was.

"I'll take the baby, raise him. Or her." Desperation filled his words.

"Oh, Chris..." Tears streaked her face. "How? You're going to be in the Army!" She swallowed the lump in her throat and forced out, "Four hundred dollars. That's what it costs. I can't take it out of my savings without my parents finding out."

"Please, Annie." His voice dropped to a whisper. "That's our kid you're talking about."

"It's not a baby yet, just a clump of cells." Annie desperately tried to believe what Callie said, what all the cool kids at school had said.

"Not a clump of cells. Don't you remember biology class, Annie? You must have taken it. An embryo. A zygote, then an embryo, then a fetus, then a"— his voice cracked — "baby."

She did, but she was trying hard to forget. Her traitorous scientific mind perked up and flashed the letters D and N and A. All present and made complete the moment the spermatozoa penetrated the ovum.

"It's m-my body, Chris." She parroted the sentiments Callie had spouted over and over since the pregnancy test, though they felt hollow. And selfish, if she chose to remember the pictures in her biology text. Never mind the parade of pro-life speakers at school. She turned a blind eye to the memories. "M-my choice." Annie gave up on trying to staunch her tears and grabbed a t-shirt from her dirty laundry to mop her face.

"Will you at least think about it for a while? A week, two maybe? Let yourself think clearly before you decide for sure?"

"The sooner the better." The lump in her throat came back. "That's what they say."

"They don't know everything. *Please*."

"I have to. I'm sorry. We made a mistake. We don't have to ruin our lives over it." Annie hardened her heart, trying one more time to believe what she was saying. The problem was, she was lying to herself and she knew it.

In the end, he agreed to send the money to Callie, and Annie hung up, feeling irredeemable.

Christian—it pained her to recall his full given name— Hasselback was a nice guy, nicer than she'd expected. In fact, he was honorable. Annie allowed herself a moment's fantasy, a little house in a nice neighborhood, kids and a dog, Chris happy to come home to her, but knew she would wonder if he married her out of duty or love until the day she died.

The real problem was that Annie couldn't see a way to love herself anymore, no matter what she did.

She wished she could undo that night with Chris. More than that, she wanted to change her mind, wanted to ask for help, but everything had spun out of control.

The next few days passed in a blur. Her prayers for guidance or deliverance kept hitting the ceiling and clunking back to her lap. A hundred times, she reached for the phone to call an adoption agency, but her breath strangled at the prospect of hurting her parents. She knelt at Mass, her mind a frozen mess, her body going through the motions, pretending to be normal. Dreams filled her sleep, nightmares of still-blind and mewing kittens snatched from her arms, leaving her empty and weeping inconsolably.

Then Callie called. "The money came. This Friday night."

Annie's heart felt hollow and heavy as she agreed. She went to Callie's on Friday. They watched movies, and Callie ate popcorn, the odor of which triggered Annie's nausea, but that didn't slow Callie down.

Saturday morning came. Callie drove. Annie was silent. Callie parked on a side street and they got out, the car doors closing with doom-filled thud-thuds.

Annie trudged behind Callie, then sensed a charge in the air and looked up.

People—so many!—lined the sidewalk to the clinic in downtown Louisville. Not blocking it, but forming a gauntlet of opposing camps, one with breastplates of red safety vests, the other wearing white vests with glittery reflective tape. Murmurs rippled through the early morning tranquility when they spotted Annie and Callie. Annie faltered, one foot around the corner, the other mired in sudden doubt. The heavy sweetness of lilies in a nearby planter competed with car exhaust and the faint scent of muddy river water. *Nausea—*

Callie grabbed her hand. Tugged. It was enough to tip her over the fulcrum into renewed movement. Across the street, kids like her, kids in designer jeans and in private school uniforms, kids who didn't understand how two pink lines had ripped the fabric of her life into before and panic, stood, their backs pressed to the buildings, murmured prayers of the Rosary rising and falling in the air.

Annie ducked her head, letting her hair swing forward to hide her face. She followed Callie, her view limited to the lower legs and shoes of those she passed. No one touched her, nor did anyone chant or accuse her, but dread gripped her like a vise and squeezed with each step.

"You don't have to, you know." A man's voice came from her left, and, surprised, she swung around to look at him. About her dad's height, a couple inches shorter than Chris, hair graying and pulled back into a ponytail. Clad in jeans, sandals, a t-shirt proclaiming *Give Life a Chance*. Kind eyes, also like Chris. This man's eyes were a warm brown. She didn't know what color Chris's were. Her cheeks heated.

The man's words rang true, like the clear sound of handbells at a Christmas concert. She paused. The myriad potential solutions she'd considered over the past days tumbled through her mind. Annie still couldn't see another answer. Then another thought—one she recognized as *not mine*, but ringing just as true as the man's words—zinged its way to her heart. Maybe it was her fear she couldn't see past, fear holding her hostage. If she went through the doors, would she be giving in to those fears or facing them? She didn't know. Maybe he had a point. Maybe she didn't *have* to do it today.

"Come on, Annie. Don't talk to him." Callie grabbed her hand again and pulled.

"You have a choice. You don't have to do what you came for, not today." He stood relaxed, hands thrust into his pockets, an aura of peace emanating from him.

"Come *on*." Callie yanked, pulling Annie off balance.

Annie got her feet back under her, then looked back at the man. Deep sorrow flickered across his face, and she imagined a force drawing her to him, drawing her away from the clinic. She squirmed her hand out of Callie's grip.

Hope flared in his eyes, though he didn't move.

"Mister, you leave my friend alone." Callie stepped in front of Annie, her manner both protective and aggressive. He ignored her, his stillness a small oasis of calm in the tension-filled moment.

Annie stopped. "What do you mean, I don't have to do it today?"

"Just that. Nobody can coerce or pressure you into signing that consent form, but it's a lot easier to walk away now than it is once you go through those doors." He lifted his lips in an enigmatic smile. "Think about it for a few more days."

A few more days. That's what Chris had asked. Could she? A few more days wouldn't make that much difference. Annie could see that now. It was a small shift, but compelling enough that she could now recognize it as evidence that fear had skewed her ability to think.

Callie grabbed her and swung her around. "If you don't come with me now, I'm out of here. After all I've done for you..." Her features twisted into an expression Annie had never seen on her friend's face.

Annie recoiled. Glanced at the man. Looked at the red and white gauntlet, saw a woman in a white lab coat coming out of the clinic, her lips tight and her gaze focused on Annie.

She felt like a pawn in a war. No, not a pawn. The prize. Who would win her?

Something she couldn't define began to grow in her, a certainty that she wasn't going to allow anyone to define her as a trophy in some battle. No. *No.* The sense of doom that had plagued her since the fateful night lifted, just a little. For the first time, she could see she had the right to fight for her own choice, to claim her own direction. Not someone else's. Not Callie's, not anyone in red vests or white vests.

None of that changed anything about her situation. None of it made her feel strong or courageous or grown up. She still felt small and confused. Not a pawn or a prize, just a kid who'd made a mistake. Annie felt the stirrings of empathy for the "clump of cells" within her womb.

"I'm sorry, Callie," she said. But she wasn't. Maybe she owed her friend credit for being there, being a support in her time of need, but if their friendship depended on Annie letting Callie think for her, then it wasn't a true friendship.

"You have a future. Let your baby have a future, too." The man spoke again, his words gentle and soft but crystal clear.

She turned and faced him. "I don't know what to do." The panic that had dogged her over the past few weeks didn't materialize like she expected. Maybe an answer to her prayers would come to her after all. Maybe she wasn't abandoned or as alone as she felt.

"You will figure it out. There are people who want to help you *and* your baby." A smile brought sunshine to his face. "But you don't have to do this today."

Annie took a step toward him, toward the kids who couldn't understand what two pink lines had done to her life, then another step, and a third.

Callie spat at the man's feet and flipped him the bird. He ignored that, too. "Bastard," she shouted, then let loose a lurid curse and stormed to the car.

Annie didn't look back.

She still didn't know what she was going to do, but the man was right.

She didn't have to do this today.

PURPLE HEARTS
Antony Barone Kolenc

Darryl trudged toward the courtroom, his newly pressed Air Force service coat adorned with his Purple Heart medal, a silver badge, and a rainbow of ribbons on his chest.

"Major?" The reporter from the *Times* — her walnut hair wrapped tight in a bun— held out a business card. "When this is over, will you have time for a quick interview?" She wore a button with the Purple Hand on it: similar to one Darryl had worn at a gay pride parade when he was twenty. "I know what you're going through, sir."

"Thanks. Maybe." He kept walking — past the photos of President George W. Bush and the Secretary of Defense — and shoved her card into the pocket of his powder-blue dress shirt, next to the folded scrap of paper with the King James Bible verse he'd copied that morning.

An airman with an unfamiliar face knocked into his shoulder as he passed: "Good luck, Major Witherspoon." But before Darryl could say "thanks," the airman muttered something under his breath: "you faggot."

Darryl nearly collided with his defense counsel, Captain Stanley Miles, who pushed through the courtroom's double-doors. "How you doing this morning, Major?"

"I think that punk just called me a fag."

"Who?"

"Some airman." Darryl glanced back and then shook it off, rubbing the close-cut hair on the back of his head. "Forget about it."

He proceeded down the aisle and settled into his seat at the cherry oak table reserved for the Respondent. Captain Miles clasped hands with their arch-enemy, Captain Brad Jones — the prosecutor who was tasked to be the board's Recorder.

Moments later, Lieutenant Colonel Ken Harrison entered the room as six rows of uniformed spectators and eager journalists snapped to attention. Short but muscular, the colonel took his place at the judge's bench, between Old Glory and a sapphire flag with the Air Force Seal and thirteen white stars. Like all the other participants, Harrison wore his blue service dress uniform, not a black judge's robe.

"This board of inquiry will come to order," Harrison announced. "Let the record reflect that the board members are absent. Before we bring them in, are there any questions from either the Respondent or the Recorder?"

Captain Miles rose and faced Harrison. "Yes, sir. The Respondent wishes to renew his motion to dismiss these allegations brought under DADT—the 'Don't Ask, Don't Tell' policy—as being a violation of his rights under the First Amendment as well as a violation of both Equal Protection and Due Process under the Fifth Amendment. It's a travesty that a war hero like Major Witherspoon is facing discharge merely because of his status as a homosexual."

Harrison stuck out his palm. "As I said yesterday, Captain, I'm not a judge; I'm a JAG serving as this board's legal advisor. My position doesn't authorize me to dismiss allegations. And I should also point out that, ever since President Clinton and Congress passed this law over a decade ago, federal courts have upheld the DADT policy as constitutional. Of course, I recognize that you're simply trying to preserve the record here, so consider it preserved.

Now if there's nothing else, let's recall the Members. When we adjourned last night, the Respondent had just testified on direct examination; this morning we'll let the Recorder, Captain Jones, conduct his cross-examination."

Captain Miles stepped back to Darryl at the counsel table and squeezed his client's shoulder. "Showtime, Major. You ready? Are you okay, sir?"

Darryl had heard those words before...

***

"Are you okay, sir?" The sergeant's hand reached out to him as he lay stunned on the dusty road next to the rumbling Humvee. The sweat and grime streaking the sergeant's face couldn't blot out the man's intense gray eyes under the rim of his helmet. "Sir, I said, 'Are you okay?'"

Darryl grasped the sergeant's hand and pulled himself to his feet. He plopped into the front seat of the Humvee, painted in the shade of desert sand. "What the hell happened?"

"An explosion about three vehicles up, sir. Looks like the bastards buried another IED."

"Only one bomb this time?"

Before the sergeant could answer, gunshots rat-tatted around them. The sergeant shoved him to the ground again as bullets tore a hole through the leather seat where he'd been resting. Darryl rolled to the edge of the vehicle, drawing his Beretta into his palm, and spotted the shooter crouching behind a boulder fifty feet away—a lone Iraqi in a tattered robe and sandals.

"He's reloading!" the sergeant hollered.

Darryl charged his enemy's position, firing off eight rounds in rapid succession. The Iraqi collapsed to the ground, discharging three shots of his own before falling into a heap. Darryl felt the sting in his side before he saw the crimson staining his battle dress uniform.

Suddenly, Darryl — the world whirling in nauseous circles — lay on a blood-soaked gurney with airmen surrounding him, including the ruddy sergeant who'd saved his life in the Humvee. "You're gonna be okay, sir," the sergeant said, his dimples beaming.

As they loaded Darryl into the back of the van to transport him to the base hospital, he reached for the sergeant's hand and fought to push the words out. "What's...your...name?"

The sergeant grinned and squeezed Darryl's fingers. "Jeffrey, sir. Jeffrey Hunt."

***

Captain Miles tapped Darryl's shoulder. "Major, it's showtime. Just like we discussed."

The Board Members—four officers in tidy service dress—had already returned and taken their judgment seats in the jury box. They stared on with poker faces as Darryl wandered to the witness stand and raised his right hand like an automaton.

"No need to do that, Major; you're still under oath," Harrison said, as Darryl sunk into the leather chair. "Captain Jones, you may conduct your cross-examination."

"Thank you, sir." Jones — tall, slim, and hungry-eyed — straightened his papers at the stout podium before prowling into the well of the courtroom to face Darryl head-on. "Major Witherspoon, you testified last night that you're a homosexual, correct?"

"That's my sexual orientation, yes."

"But you say you're not a 'practicing homosexual,' whatever that is."

"Exactly. I follow my faith." Darryl could see the *Times*

reporter in the back row scribbling on her pad, as if taking down his every word.

"Right, you told us all about that yesterday. And so your faith led you to join the military even though you knew the DADT policy prohibited homosexual conduct?"

Darryl cleared his throat. "The policy says my orientation is a 'personal and private matter' unless 'manifested by homosexual conduct.' I comply with that policy."

"And you testified that you've never engaged in homosexual acts?"

"Not while I've been in the military, no."

"But you did engage in such acts prior to joining the Air Force?"

Captain Miles pounced from his chair. "Objection! That's not relevant here."

"I'm just testing the witness's statements, Colonel," Jones said, turning to the Legal Advisor. "The Respondent testified last night that he wasn't a 'practicing homosexual.' I'm trying to probe what he meant by that term."

***

"So you're some sort of 'Evangelo-sexual,' Mr. Witherspoon?" the intake counselor for the gay rights group asked, putting a pink pencil eraser to his thick glasses and pushing the rim toward his sweaty forehead.

"No, I'm an Evangelical Christian who happens to be gay."

Darryl had set up the appointment with the advocacy group at their D.C. office. They'd defended a dozen other military members pro bono in the past three years, two of whom had been retained at their discharge boards despite being gay. Captain Miles had provided the contact information and had even sent an e-mail in advance, asking them to take the case.

"So you're gay, but you don't support gay rights?" the counselor persisted.

"I support the rights of gay people just like everyone else. I just happen to be Christian."

"And as a Christian you don't believe in sex outside the bonds of marriage."

"Right."

"But you don't believe in gay marriage, either."

"Right. That would go against my faith."

The counselor scratched his head. "So you don't believe in sex then?"

***

Lieutenant Colonel Harrison raised an eyebrow. "I know exactly what you're trying to probe here, Captain Jones, and I'm not going to allow it. Objection sustained."

"Thank you, sir." Jones stepped back to the podium and peered at his file. "Okay, then. As you know, Major, one of the reasons we have DADT is to preserve morale and good order and discipline in our units. Now that you've told everyone you're gay —"

Darryl raised a hand. "Wait. I wouldn't have told anyone anything if my commander hadn't brought these allegations against me at this board."

"But now that everyone knows you're gay, isn't this going to pose a problem in your unit?" The spectators crowded onto the benches began to stir and whisper.

"I don't think so."

"But didn't Congress think so?" Jones grabbed hold of a paper off his podium. "Didn't Congress make specific findings on this issue after extensive hearings?"

"Politicians may say that, but I don't see why anyone in

my unit cares. I'm not a practicing homosexual, so how's this any different than putting married men and women in the same unit? They're not supposed to have sex with each other, either."

Jones had been frowning the entire time Darryl spoke. "Please just answer the question asked, Major. This is already a long process. A simple yes or no will do."

"Then yes."

"Your example isn't on point anyway, is it? I mean, you do get deployed, right?"

Darryl looked down at the Purple Heart he'd received for the wound he suffered while exhibiting courage under fire. "I've been to Iraq."

Jones flushed. "Right, and thank you for your sacrifice. But let me ask you this: in deployed locations, aren't you in close quarters with other men, where intimacy is forced and privacy non-existent? Sometimes even having to take group showers?"

"Sometimes."

"But men and women don't shower together in your unit, right? So isn't it fair to say that being gay will pose a problem with how you interact with other military men?"

***

"How you feeling, sir? I come bearing gifts." Sergeant Hunt lingered at his hospital bedside, two Tom Clancy novels sandwiched between his thumb and slender fingers.

Darryl smiled. "Jeffrey. That's nice of you."

"I know it's only been a few days since you got here, but these will help if you get bored. Read them already?"

He shook his head. "Clancy's my favorite. Just haven't had time to keep up."

"Me neither."

Jeffrey perched next to his bedside, and they chatted about Hollywood's failed attempts to translate the brilliance of Clancy to the big screen. An hour passed in seconds.

"Looks like I'll be joining you back in the States, sir," Jeffrey said, when visiting hours were ending. "I hear you're shipping out to Walter Reed for recovery in the next few days."

"You going there, too?"

"Yes, sir. It's my back — a prior injury, not from the other day."

"Sorry to hear that."

"It's what we signed up for, sir, but you gotta look at the bright side on these things, right? I'd like to think of it as an opportunity to get to know a new friend better."

***

"Can you repeat the question?" Darryl said.

"I asked if your unit will be disrupted now that the men know you're gay?"

Miles had coached Darryl on this question. He'd advised him not to blurt out his gut feeling—that the only reason his unit was treating him differently now was that the Air Force had made such a big deal of all this. That answer apparently wouldn't play well with the Members, so he needed to attempt something a bit more nuanced.

"Captain, the men in my unit know my integrity. When I say I'm not going to ever violate the policy, they believe it. Some of those guys even deployed with me."

"But they didn't know you were gay back then, did they?"

Didn't they? Hadn't some of them figured it out by the

absence of girlfriends and the nonexistence of girlie magazines in his locker, not to mention his silence when all the others were telling conquest stories? Hadn't he caught their odd glances at the pubs, when they'd all flirt with the women while he sat alone sipping his pint of Guinness?

"No one asked, but I think some knew. It doesn't matter to those who know me."

"Because of your integrity and honesty with them?"

***

Darryl's mother extended her arms and hurried across the kitchen to him, dropping her apron to the floor. "I always knew. In my heart I knew."

He had just received word from Captain Miles that General Fernandez intended to go forward with the DADT board of inquiry. There would be no stopping the process now. The press would likely get a hold of the story in a matter of days. How would his parents feel if they discovered that their son was gay by watching the nightly news?

"It doesn't change a thing, sweetie." His mother squeezed his cheeks between her open palms and kissed his forehead like he was five. "I'm as proud of you as ever."

His father lingered at the table. He hadn't spoken a word since Darryl broke the news.

"Dad?"

"Can't you try to fight it, Darryl?"

"Fight what — the discharge?"

"The gay thing." His father's voice quivered. "Just because you feel a certain way doesn't mean you can't change it."

How to respond to that without lashing out or crying?

"I tried when I was younger, Dad. It just seems to be the way I tick, for whatever reason."

A tear meandered to the man's lip. "Was it something I did, son? Was I a bad father?"

Darryl lifted him from the chair and held him tight. "You were always the father I needed, Dad. I just think God has a different plan for me."

***

Darryl stared ahead voicelessly, pattering a finger on the corner of the witness stand. Captain Jones was still waiting to hear all about his integrity and honesty.

"No, Captain. The policy doesn't let me be honest about everything. The men in my unit couldn't ask, but I couldn't tell, either."

"Okay, well, let's go back to your claim that you never engaged in homosexual acts. And let's just stick to your time in the Air Force. You're asking these Members to believe that you've never violated the DADT policy? Not even one time?"

"That's correct."

"And you also haven't had any girlfriends during all that time, either?" The Legal Advisor rolled his eyes at the Recorder's question.

"Right," Darryl said. "That's what being gay means."

"So no sex in all these years. You're celibate? Like a priest?"

"Not like a priest."

***

"Best Bond film yet," Jeffrey said as they exited the theater into the half-empty parking lot.

"Agreed." He'd parked next to Jeffrey's cherry red 1968 Mustang.

"Hey, you wanna grab a nightcap, sir?"

Darryl looked at his watch—10:30 pm. Time for bed, especially since this was his first week home after a month at Walter Reed Medical Center. Plus, he hadn't been on a date in a decade. Not that this would be a date — just two guys sharing a brew.

"Sure. What the hell."

They wound up in Georgetown at a tiny pub frequented mostly by locals. Three beers later they were snickering at every silly reference, even Darryl's corny joke about Attila the Pun.

"I haven't had this much fun in forever," Jeffrey said. He set down his glass, his hand dipping to the table and finding its resting place against Darryl's arm. "You're a blast, sir."

Darryl jerked up his arm to check the time—after midnight. "Oy! I've gotta get to bed."

Jeffrey grinned for a passing moment. "Right. Hey, sir, maybe we can do this again. I've got all the Clancy films on DVD. You should come by the apartment for some movie nights."

***

Jones paraded back to the podium and shuffled his papers. "So, Major — you say you never violated the policy, but let's talk about that for a second. Even though you claim you didn't have sex, doesn't the policy also apply to the words you say?"

"What do you mean?"

"I'm talking about 'Don't Tell.' If you tell someone that you're gay, then Congress says that's grounds for discharge, right?"

"That's because Congress thinks merely telling someone you're gay means you're going to have sex. That's not the case for me because of my faith."

"But you did tell someone you were gay, right? Isn't that why your commander initiated this board — because you ignored the policy and made a statement that you were a homosexual?" Jones flapped a document in the air as he spoke, to let the Members know he held damning evidence and to dare Darryl to deny the truth.

"It wasn't like that," he said.

"You told Senior Airman Stephen Turquotte that you were gay, didn't you?"

***

He'd met Steve at a bar—not even a gay bar. Maybe he should have figured out that the kid was military, but Steve wore his hair longer than standards allowed. Anyway, it wasn't a pickup: the kid was barely twenty-one, more than ten years Darryl's junior.

It was one of those nights where loneliness had ferreted him from his apartment on a quest for companionship—not for a sexual interaction but for a genuine human connection. God hadn't made man to be alone, but Darryl had felt quite alone since the Air Force had moved Jeffrey to Seattle two months earlier. Darryl hadn't found anyone to fill that hole in his heart. Not that he'd searched; heart-filling could be a perilous activity in more ways than one.

As they hung out all evening, something about Steve seemed off. Of course, he was gay; Darryl could spot that a mile away, so that wasn't it. But the kid was melancholy, despondent. While they emptied their bottles, Steve dropped clues—not just about his orientation but about his mental state. He repeated certain words and phrases too often: "alone;" "no way out;" "misunderstood;" "unbearable life." And he wouldn't hold eye contact when it mattered.

64

They'd finished their drinks and headed to their cars. If this had been any other night, that would have ended it. Darryl had flirted with these types of conversations over the years, and he knew how to terminate them gracefully. Not that night.

"I want to show you something," Steve said.

"I don't know. It's getting late."

"Just come here." Steve went around to the passenger side of his rusted green Honda and opened the door, stretching his body through the opening for a moment. He emerged with a .38 caliber revolver in his hands.

"What the hell are you doing?"

"Did you ever play Russian Roulette?" Steve spun the silver cylinder.

"Not funny. You got a permit for that?"

Steve shrugged and put the barrel to his head.

"Whoa! You need to put that down right now." Darryl jutted a hand toward him.

"It's okay, I do this all the time. If it's meant to be —"

"No, it's not okay. Give that to me. Now. I'm not kidding."

Steve smiled just barely and then pulled the trigger.

***

Darryl glared at Captain Jones. He wasn't supposed to hate; Jesus had taught that with the strongest possible example when he suffered and died on the cross for sinners. But Jones was playing with people's lives now, and all to score points in a twisted game.

"It wasn't like that, I just told you." Darryl's tone crossed the line. The warning glare from Captain Miles signaled that his client needed to stand down immediately. Even the *Times* reporter had stopped writing and was studying his scowl.

"On December 12 of last year you made a statement of your homosexuality to Stephen Turquotte. Yes or no?" Jones raised the document higher.

Darryl bit his lip and gave a bitter nod. "Yes, like I said last night."

"Right. You testified that Airman Turquotte seemed 'down and out' and that you thought it might make him 'feel better' to know he wasn't the only person hurting."

"I didn't know he was in the military at the time."

"And does the DADT policy have an exception for making statements about your homosexuality in order to cheer someone up?"

Steve had been busted for multiple homosexual acts. Like many stupid kids, he apparently thought that naming names to his commander would save his career. So he'd named Darryl's name as someone who'd self-reported as gay, but he'd left out all the most important facts, hadn't he? And facts mattered.

Fact: Darryl had guided Steve through that night alive. Fact: he'd convinced Steve to begin counseling. Fact: he'd probably saved Steve's life in the long run. Fact: he'd promised God that he would never throw Steve under the bus by digging up the skeletons in his graveyard. Who knew how Steve would react if all his secrets got out?

Darryl put his hands in his lap to hide his clenching fists. "No. Not any exception like that, Captain."

"And under the policy — unless and until Congress repeals it — telling someone you're gay can indicate a propensity to engage in homosexual acts, right?" Jones asked.

"Not for me."

"Because you're different than everyone else. Is that it?"

***

"What makes you think you're different than us?" the advocacy group's intake counselor asked.

"I didn't say I was different, just that I was Christian. It's a moral issue for me."

The counselor pointed to the wall behind him, where a poster hung with the symbol of the Purple Hand. "We've been fighting anti-gay discrimination for decades, but you think you're better than us because of your so-called morality?"

"Not at all." Darryl stood. "Listen, I don't want to waste our time here. I take it from your questions that your group won't be representing me at the board of inquiry?"

The counselor glanced across the room at his supervisor and gave a nod. "That's correct, Mr. Witherspoon. Unfortunately, we don't have the resources to defend every potential client. We look for certain other" — he paused — "personal qualities, which you seem to lack."

***

Captain Jones didn't wait for Darryl to answer the question before he asked another. "Do you know Technical Sergeant Jeffrey Hunt?"

Miles shot to his feet. "Objection, Colonel. What's the relevance? This isn't someone on the witness list or in any report that I've seen."

Jones smirked. "Sir, if you'd just give me a little latitude here, the extreme relevance of this line of questioning will become apparent in just a moment."

Harrison rocked back in his chair and pondered. "I'll allow it for now, Captain Jones. But you better get to the relevant part ASAP."

"Yes, sir."

When Miles returned to his seat, his eyes locked with

Darryl's as if to inquire why he'd never mentioned a "Sergeant Hunt" to his defense lawyer before.

"Answer the question please," Jones said.

"Yes, I know Sergeant Hunt."

"Where did you meet him?"

Darryl pointed to his Purple Heart. "In Iraq. The day I got this medal."

This time Jones ignored the reference to Darryl's combat wounds. "And did you later carry on a personal relationship with the sergeant?"

"He saved my life. He took an interest in my well-being."

"When you were transferred to D.C., did you go to the movies together?"

"Yes."

"And to bars?"

"Yes."

"Did you spend time alone in each other's apartments?"

Miles raised his hand and addressed Harrison. "Sir, if this is what counts as homosexual conduct, then we should all be discharged for being gay."

The Legal Advisor frowned. "Is that some sort of objection?"

"May we approach the bench?" Miles asked.

Harrison nodded and the lawyers conferred in a whisper that Darryl could overhear, since he sat just two feet away in the witness chair.

"My client isn't being brought up on allegations of officer-enlisted fraternization, sir. Now, unless there's something sinister here, this is unfairly prejudicial for Captain Jones to continue this line of questioning. This isn't a fraternization case."

Jones gripped the edge of the judge's bench. "This is a valid line of questioning, Colonel. If the members find there are grounds for discharge under DADT, they'll next have to consider the issue of whether the Respondent should be discharged from the military. His fraternization could be relevant to that second question."

"That's true, isn't it?" Harrison asked Miles.

The defense counsel stared at the floor. "Maybe."

Jones continued. "And there is something sinister here, as we'll soon see. So again, sir, I'd ask for a bit of latitude."

Harrison leaned back. "I agree. Objection overruled."

The pow-wow broke up, and Jones strutted back to the podium. "Now where were we? Right — you and Sergeant Hunt at each other's apartments."

***

Jeffrey pressed off the power button on the remote and sighed. "I love Sean Connery. He's got to be the sexiest man alive, I don't care how old he is."

Darryl chuckled. "To each his own. He's kinda wrinkly next to a young Alec Baldwin."

They'd watched every Clancy flick together, ending with "The Hunt for Red October."

"Even Alec's not as cute as you, though," Jeffrey said, winking.

Darryl stood up suddenly. "I've got to take a whiz."

"How long are we going to keep doing this, sir?" Jeffrey tossed the remote on the sofa.

"Well, that was the final Clancy movie," Darryl said, taking several steps away. "So I guess we won't be doing it much longer."

"You know what I'm talking about. This thing between me and you. How long are we going to keep dragging this out? I know what you are, and you know what I am."

Darryl leaned against the door jamb for support.

"Sir, come on over here to the sofa. I've got something to give you."

***

"Sergeant Hunt and I did watch movies at his apartment a few times," Darryl said, avoiding eye contact with the Recorder.

"And isn't it true that you engaged in sexual relations with Sergeant Hunt?"

Darryl kept his voice as level as possible. "No, that is not true."

"You never had sex with him?"

"Never."

"Not even a kiss?"

"No."

"You didn't shower together? You didn't spend the weekend together in bed?"

"No and no."

"You didn't —"

Miles shouted out his objection before he could get to his feet. "Asked and answered, sir. Major Witherspoon has made it very clear that he didn't have a sexual relationship with the sergeant. The Recorder is just harassing him at this point."

"Sustained. Captain, you got your denial, if that's what you were looking for."

Jones smiled. "Thank you, sir. No further questions then."

Darryl scoured his memories while Harrison polled the four board members to see if any of them had questions for the witness. They did not. Nor, apparently, did Captain

Miles wish to spend time on re-direct examination, prolonging the agony of his client on the stand. "The witness may step down. We're in recess for ten minutes."

Back at the counsel table, Miles had ripped a sheet of paper to shreds. "Let's talk," he said, leading Darryl across the hall to a room set aside for the Defense. "What the hell's going on, Major? You never mentioned this sergeant to me. Why? Strike that — I don't want to know. What I do need to know is why Jones asked you all those questions. Chances are, your friend Hunt is going to take the stand next."

"Impossible. That'll never happen."

"We'll see."

"This whole process is outrageous," Darryl said. "President Clinton said we'd be able to serve with distinction if we didn't have sex. I've kept my part of the bargain."

"Clinton said lots of stuff, Major. Don't forget, the President also lied about having sex with Monica."

Minutes later they headed back into the courtroom, where Miles told the Legal Advisor that the Respondent had no other evidence to present. "We rest our case."

"Captain Jones, any rebuttal evidence?" Harrison asked.

"Absolutely, sir. The Government calls Tech Sergeant Jeffrey Hunt to the stand."

Miles hadn't even bothered to sit down. "We object. This witness wasn't on any witness list, nor did the Recorder disclose his existence. It's unfair to let him testify."

"This is a rebuttal witness," Jones said. "We had no intention of presenting his testimony until the Respondent took the stand and started spouting off about his courage and faith, and how he's never had sex with anyone in the military."

"Why didn't you disclose this witness?" asked Harrison.

"The witness has no exculpatory evidence, sir. And like I said, we had no intention of calling him until the Respondent just testified the way he did."

Harrison turned to Miles. "He's a rebuttal witness. I'll allow it."

A minute later, Darryl jerked his head and grew pale when Jeffrey filed down the aisle of the courtroom in his service dress and stood in front of the witness stand, swearing to God that he'd tell the whole truth. When Jeffrey spun to take his seat, he turned his intense gray eyes on Darryl like a weapon.

"State your name for the record," Captain Jones told the witness.

Jeffrey recited his personal information and answered a series of preliminary questions, giving the board members a basic understanding of his background and how he came to know Darryl. Jeffrey had recently retired from the Air Force with a medical discharge due to his chronic back injury.

"Sergeant, how would you describe your relationship with the Respondent?"

"Well, sir,"— his voice held no emotion—"Darryl and I were lovers."

***

He took a step from the doorway toward the sofa, but then restrained himself. "Jeffrey —"

"Come on, sir," Jeffrey said, his mischievous dimples in bloom. "You can do it."

"No. I can't. This is wrong."

"It feels right to me. Listen, if it's the officer-enlisted thing, I can promise not to call you 'sir' ever again—unless you ask me 'pretty please.'"

Darryl inched toward the sofa. "You know I'm Christian."

"So am I. What's the problem?"

"I'm the kind of Christian who believes sodomy is immoral."

"You're kidding, sir, right? After all this foreplay, you tell me that our feelings are a sin."

"No. It's what we do with our feelings that matters."

"You're serious about this?" Jeffrey's voice hardened. "Why do you think God made us this way? Or are you one of those geniuses who thinks this is some lifestyle we chose?"

"Believe me, I've wanted to be rid of this curse my entire life."

"That's crap, sir. You need to accept who you are, the way God made you."

Darryl nodded. "But what if God's reason for letting us be like this is different than you think? What if this is our call to holiness?"

"So being gay means we get the special privilege to never have sex; never marry; never have kids? Thanks, but no thanks."

"Who doesn't suffer?" Darryl said. "How is this suffering any different than if I'd been born with a disease or to a poor family in Haiti? It's what we do with our suffering that counts."

"You're starting to piss me off, sir."

"I had a friend once who made a new life with a woman and a family."

Jeffrey grunted. "You mean he lived a lie."

"It worked for him somehow, but not for me. So as a Christian, I've been trying to figure out why God is calling me to a life of celibacy."

Jeffrey told Darryl what he could go do to himself. "And then you can go be a freaking priest if you want." He swore again. "After all the messed-up history in my life that I've shared with you, I can't believe you're pulling this crap on me now."

"I've been trying to find the courage to talk to you."

"You know, sir, if you didn't like me, then why did you get into this thing with me?"

Darryl held out his hands. "I do like you."

"No! I saved your life, and this is what you do? You get some sort of deranged thrill out of leading people on and then pulling this religious crap on them? You're sick, sir."

"I'm just trying to do the right thing."

Jeffrey raised two clenched fists toward Darryl's face. "Just get the hell out."

"Jeffrey —"

"No. You're going to regret what you're doing here, sir. You can take your lonely, suffering ass and get out of my house. Now!"

"I'm not rejecting you, Jeffrey. Listen, this is my fault. I shouldn't have gotten this close."

"Damn straight, Darryl. It's your fault."

***

Captain Jones paced over near the four board members for added effect. "Lovers, Sergeant? You mean you engaged in homosexual acts together?"

Jeffrey laughed. "If that's how you want to say it, sir."

"Well, how would you say it?"

"How graphic would you like me to be, sir?"

"Not very, please."

Jeffrey spent the next ten minutes explaining how he and Darryl had evolved from friends to lovers over the course of a few months. Movies and pubs progressed to DVDs and apartments. Then they'd taken their relationship to the "next level." He described all nature of sodomy and other intimate interactions between them, lasting several weeks until the Air Force reassigned Jeffrey to a base in Seattle.

"And all of this activity took place while the Respondent was an active duty officer in the Air Force?" Jones asked.

"Of course."

Jones gathered his papers. "Thank you, Sergeant. No further questions."

Darryl could feel the unsettled eyes of the four board members resting on him while Captain Jones ambled over to his seat.

"Respondent, you may cross-examine the witness," Harrison said.

Captain Miles stood. "Can we have five minutes, sir?"

When Harrison recessed the board, Miles pulled Darryl back into their private room. "You have something to tell me, Major?"

"He's lying."

"Okay. Then we burn him. What dirt do you have on this guy?"

Darryl said nothing.

"Major, you're in deep kimchi. I need to know if he confided anything in you that we can use against him: lies, immoral behavior, anything to hurt his credibility."

He shook his head. "I'm not betraying his trust."

"This is no time to be a hero, sir. This guy is not your friend."

Darryl closed his eyes. "No, I won't hurt him. I love him." He hid his face in his hands. "Lord, help me." He suddenly grabbed a nearby trash can and vomited.

Miles handed him a tissue. "All right, Major. It's okay." He paused for a moment of silence while Darryl worked out the pain. "Listen, sir. I've got a few questions I can go with, but is there anything you can tell me to show that he's making all this up?"

A paralegal poked her head in to inform them the board was ready to reconvene.

"Major?"

Darryl blew his nose and then pulled Miles close to whisper an idea in his ear.

"No. Too risky. Never ask a question if you don't know the answer."

"Just do it," Darryl said. "It's my career, not yours."

As they hurried back to the courtroom, they passed the *Times* reporter, watching from down the hall. Darryl avoided eye contact with her and found his chair again. Jeffrey still perched at the witness stand, arms folded.

After Harrison reconvened the board, Miles approached the podium without even a single sheet of paper in his hand. "Sergeant Hunt, isn't it convenient that you waited until you were medically retired and had nothing to lose before you came forward with this outrageous story?"

"Just 'trying to do the right thing,' sir." When he said these words he rested his gaze on Darryl, his eyes glowering.

"So you flagrantly broke the DADT policy for years—with lots of men, right?"

Jeffrey studied his cuticles. "Well. It's not a fair policy."

"So you ignored it, because you wanted to do what made you feel good."

"I wanted to do what was natural."

Miles shook his head. "So you'll do whatever you want regardless of the rules, won't you? You'll even lie to this board today if it suits you."

"No. I'm telling the truth."

Miles shot a glance at Darryl, who gave a wink to confirm his decision. "Now, Sergeant, according to your testimony, you were in quite a torrid affair with Major Witherspoon—showers, weekends in bed, quite a lot of it, too."

"What can I say, sir?" Jeffrey smiled. "We got up close and personal."

Miles sauntered to the area near the Board Members. "Well then, with all that up-close time together, you'd have no trouble telling us if the Major is circumcised."

Jeffrey's face drained, and his gray eyes grew darker. He started to fidget with the top insignia button of his service coat, causing it to lilt like a sinking ship. "Well. I — what are you asking exactly?"

"I think you know what I'm asking. You are aware of the difference in appearance, aren't you?"

"I'm not stupid."

"Well then, this should be an easy question, what with all the 'interaction' you described." Captain Miles nodded knowingly to the four Members while they waited for Jeffrey to make up his mind on the question.

"Well. I guess I never thought about it. And, okay. Sure he was circumcised."

"Are you certain?"

Jeffrey paused. "He might not have been. Wait." He looked up at the ceiling and seemed to be making some calculation in his mind. "Yeah. He must be."

"Thank you, Sergeant. No further questions."

Neither Jones nor the members had additional questions for the witness. Jeffrey stepped down and exited the courtroom, his eyes glued to Darryl's for the entire time he strode up the aisle. Then the Recorder announced that the Government had no other witnesses to call, but he wanted a brief recess to confer with his opposing counsel.

"Well?" Jones said, after Harrison recessed the board. "You asked the question; he gave the answer. Either you plan on pulling down your client's pants in open court, or we're going to do it in that back room. I don't see that we have another choice."

Miles sighed in frustration. "No. We'll stipulate to the fact that he's circumcised."

"So your client is circumcised? Excellent."

Miles took Jones by the elbow. "Brad, you saw your witness: he didn't have a clue; he's a liar. Let's have Harrison instruct the members to disregard his testimony."

"Nice try, Miles. Not happening."

When the board reconvened, Harrison informed the Members that the parties had stipulated for the record that Darryl was, indeed, circumcised. They then proceeded to closing arguments, where Jones did his duty and argued with gusto that Darryl had violated the DADT policy by disclosing his sexual orientation to Steve, and that Jeffrey's testimony proved Darryl had lied about never having sex while in the military.

For his part, Miles made an impassioned plea, discrediting Jeffrey as a liar and a "lucky guesser." He especially dwelled on the earlier testimony of Darryl's pastor, the Reverend Horace Tate, who had verified Darryl's sincerity as a born-again Christian who opposed sodomy and had for years lived in purity and chastity. Harrison then gave the board members final instructions and sent them off to deliberate.

After several more minutes of formalities outside the presence of the members, Darryl waited for the verdict with Captain Miles in their room across the hall.

"Is Hunt still on base?" Darryl asked after a while. "I'd like to talk to him."

"Let him go, Major. Anyway, I saw a paralegal load him up for the airport run."

The wait dragged on another hour before Darryl's cell phone rang — his father. Darryl gave him the update. "Thanks for calling, Dad."

"I love you, son. I'm proud of you, whatever happens."

***

"God loves you just the way you are, son," Pastor Tate said, as Darryl wiped his tears into his sleeve. "He sees your heart. He's proud of who you are, despite your struggles."

"Thanks, Pastor. I'll try to remember that when those bastards put me on trial."

"Never forget that God is calling each of His children to a special task, based on who we are. There are no coincidences. Being gay is part of what makes you exceptional, Darryl. Your struggles have made you uniquely qualified for the mission that God intends for you."

"Whatever that is," Darryl said.

***

Two hours later, Harrison reconvened the board and polled the Board President, Colonel Smith: "Has the board reached its decision, Mr. President?"

"Yes." Smith read from the paper in hand. "This board, after considering all the evidence in this case, has, in closed session, by secret written ballot, a majority of the voting members concurring, made the following findings and recommendations."

Was Darryl asleep? It felt like one of those groggy dreams that one prays isn't true so that reality can begin again. As the President read the findings—that Darryl had indeed violated the DADT policy and that he should be immediately separated from the Air Force with an honorable discharge — the courtroom fell into stunned silence.

"The board is adjourned," Harrison said, rising.

Darryl stood paralyzed in the face of the condolences and hugs that bombarded him the next several minutes. "We knew that last question was a risk," Miles told him. "God bless you, sir," a paralegal said. "Sorry for you, Major," said a member of his unit. Then Miles swooped him off to the back room and shoved the post-board paperwork in front of his face. Darryl had little idea of its actual content as he scrawled his signature.

"So what happens next?" he asked.

"We'll ask General Fernandez to disregard the board's recommendations, but he won't agree, Major. You'll be out of the Air Force in a few weeks — a few months, tops."

Darryl sighed, no tears left in his eyes. Had Jeffrey's plane landed yet in Seattle, or wherever he'd retired? Did he realize that Darryl had forgiven him already?

When the halls had quieted, Captain Miles said goodbye to his client, and Darryl dared to attempt an exit.

He stepped out the door of the Legal Office into a nearly empty parking lot. There, the reporter from the *Times* paced in front of his car, the neat bun on her head starting to unravel.

Darryl breathed deeply and marched out with an air of dignity.

"Got time for that interview now, Major?"

"Probably not." He unlocked his car door and waited for her to step aside.

"Tough day," she said, eyeing his Purple Heart. "But what you said and did in there this week — it could give people like me a lot to think about. If you're for real."

He retrieved the Bible verse from his shirt pocket and handed it over.

She read it aloud: "'Blessed are ye, when men shall hate you, and when they shall separate you from their company, and shall reproach you, and cast out your name as evil, for the Son of Man's sake.'"

She folded the scrap of paper and rested it in his palm. Then she took out a pen.

"Major, you don't strike me as a man who believes in coincidences. I think you were meant to give me this interview here today."

The screaming wakes me up again.

I groan and pull a pillow over my head. The sweat of too many rough nights has combined with the memory foam to give it a sick, cloying smell. I could just make out the stale fruity undertone of the wine I'd spilled before finally nodding off. The pillow stinks, and pressing it against my ears won't help, but I do it, anyway. The pressure is comforting, if nothing else.

I keep repeating "They're not real" until I fall asleep.

Throughout the night, I heard their screams of pain.

***

Late to work, I have to pass through the protestors. I see the Lifers got there first, stationed the requisite 100 feet from the clinic entrance while the Choicers have to make do with the other side of the street. After the last round of arrests, everyone is quiet: Lifers praying on their beads or in muttering groups while the Choicers pace with their signs. Think I liked it better when they yelled. Would they start yelling again if I promise to stay out of it this time?

I pass a Down Syndrome child, smiling, wearing a T-shirt: *Would you have killed me?* Probably doesn't even understand what that means. On top of everything else, she's being used for her mother's cause. What kind of life is that?

I hurry past before we make eye contact and nearly crash into a woman who has stepped into my path. She takes my hand in both of hers and presses a paper into it.

"God bless you!" she says.

Was she for real? "Excuse me?"

"I pray God blesses you with ears to hear. I pray every night that you'll listen."

I laugh. "To whom, lady?"

She glances at her group, then the group across the street, then back to me. "Not us. No, there's nothing any of us can tell you now. But there are others. You know who I mean. I pray you'll listen to the cries of the innocents."

Her gaze unnerves me and I feel a spike of adrenaline, but I refuse to engage. Instead, I roll my eyes and go inside, tossing the pamphlet in the trash can by the door. Pictures, no doubt; like I didn't see such things every day.

I pass through the reception area, barely taking in the plush couches and flowery prints on the wall. Today's canned music is '90s pop. I barely give it a glance. Usually, I'll stop to say a kind word to anyone waiting, but no one's there but the bored receptionist putting our stickers on the latest shipment of informational pamphlets.

As I scrub to the elbows, Nancy reads me the file. "LaCresha. 22. About three, four months. Blood work's clean. She's been counseled — it's not her first time."

I feel the tension leave me as I enter my domain. Our on-site counselor, Carol, insisted on making the front room as comforting as possible, but for me, the comfort is in the cool surgery. Scrubbed Formica floors, white tiles, modern equipment. There's a reassuring hint of cleaner under the vanilla air freshener, and a Bach prelude plays quietly over the speakers. It's not a very big surgery, but I like the compact feeling. Everything clean and having a purpose. The order calms me. Here, I can get outside myself and think only about the patient and the procedure.

LaCresha may have been clean at the moment, but I

could tell it wouldn't be for long. I'd seen too many like her: addicts, drunks, shacking up with an abusive boyfriend or selling her body for the next hit. Outside, those protestors didn't know the number of crack babies I prevented, the number of children who would not have to be abused. I kept lives of misery from happening.

I wonder about LaCresha's story, but that was the counselor's job. I already have sterile gloves on, so I resist the urge to set my hand on her tangled dreadlocks and smile reassuringly instead. "It was good you came this early. This'll be a simple procedure."

"Just get rid of it." She turns her dead gaze back to the ceiling. No tears, no sighs. Just...resignation.

Anger flares through me, burning my compassion like paper to the match. I was freeing her of a burden. She could walk out of this clinic, independent and able to make changes to her life to get out of whatever trap kept bringing her back here. "Sell everything and hop a bus," I want to tell her, "Start a new life in some podunk town waiting tables like in a movie." It's got to be better than whatever she's going back to.

Did our counselor ever say things like that? Did Carol ever want to grab them by the shoulders and yell, "We're helping you, goddammit. Help yourself!"

I could see it, just like a movie. Podunk town with two stoplights and one diner. LaCresha in a blue dress and apron, clean of the drugs, smacking gum and laughing at some old guy's jokes, her dead eyes full of life again. Going home to a tiny little house with a picket fence. Cornfields all around. At night the crickets drown out the screams.

"Doctor?" Nancy's brows are furrowed with concern.

I shake myself and get to work. "Okay, you're going to feel —"

"Don't care. Just shut up and do it."

I make a note to tell Nancy to let LaCresha out by the back, away from the protestors. She does not need any more guilt.

***

A few die-hards are still there when I head home. I try not to look at them.

"Do they cry?" the Down's girl asks as I pass.

"What?" Despite myself, I stop.

"When you kill the little babies in the mommas. Do the babies cry?"

I wonder if they'd primed her to ask that. I kneel down where she is sitting. Her sweet brown eyes under the mongoloid lids are so innocent, so uncomprehending. Her parents should be reading her children's stories like *Snow White*, and instead, they shove her into the forefront of their own personal battle and tell her to fight the Evil Witch.

Well, I'm not a witch, and I won't play one to satisfy their own fairytales.

"It's not a real baby," I say, daring the others to interrupt. "It doesn't cry or laugh or think, like you and I do. You are lucky. Your mommy loves you. The pregnant ladies that come here won't love their babies if they are born. I help keep babies from having to cry." I smile as I stop, but inside, I know I didn't make sense. How can I when she probably can't understand the difference between a fetus and a child?

"But do the babies cry when you kill them?" she repeated.

This is pointless. "They aren't babies. They cannot cry," I tell her as I stand.

They look at me, some with hate, some with pity. I know when I leave they'll tell her I was lying, and she'll believe them. She probably didn't understand what I'd said, anyway. I have half a mind to call Social Services. Maybe if I notice her again, I will. She shouldn't be here.

What was I doing, anyway? I should know better than to talk to these people. I should have kept my head down, walked by, avoided eye contact. When has anything good come to my life from engaging with them? Too late now. At least I tried.

On the drive home, I think about LaCresha's dead eyes. My mother had the same look. Sitting at that cheap plastic table, drink in her hand, staring dead-eyed at nothing while I took care of my little brother. She didn't want us.

You did all right, a voice whispers to me. *Studied hard, went to med school...*

And now I can save other children from the life I had. I wipe my eyes as I wait for a light to turn green.

After dinner, I take a shower. I scrub to the elbows again and again. I take a brush to my fingernails. Despite the washing and the gloves and all the precautions at work, I have to wash like this when I get home. I just do, or I don't feel clean. I stop when my skin begins to burn and slather myself in lotion.

As I walk to the bedroom, I run my hand over the shadowbox with my brother's picture and Medal of Honor. SSgt. Barry Hillfield, killed in battle, but he saved five of his buddies that day. I still get letters from them now and then. Barry was all about saving lives, changing the world. I wish he'd have seen I felt the same way, too. I wish we hadn't argued that day in front of the clinic.

Why did I look at the protestors? If only I hadn't, I wouldn't have seen him with his "All lives matter, including the unborn" sign. We wouldn't have had that argument that ended up going viral. I wouldn't have had to deal with a riot in front of my clinic, and he wouldn't have gone to war with a black eye and a Letter of Reprimand on his record. Instead, we'd have had a nice, friendly dinner together, and he'd have deployed knowing I loved him.

Suddenly, I'm so tired I can barely stand. My hand feels hot and heavy as my fingers trail down the shadowbox, leaving lotion streaks on the glass. They look reddish in the light. My eyes are playing tricks on me. I am tired.

Once I lay in bed, however, I cannot sleep. I wish I knew why. I've talked to Carol about it. She says it's just stress, maybe some guilt over Barry. "That's why you hear the screams," she says, but I don't know. They're so much higher than a man's. Higher, younger.

I can't think about that before bed. I debate taking a sleeping pill, decide on a glass of merlot and a sweet romance novel. By nine, I am ready to turn out the lights.

***

Throughout the night, I hear their screams of pain.

VICTORIOUS
Katy Huth Jones

This monstrous cancer now a part of me
That steals my life and rapes my joy in you
Seems certain to destroy our harmony.
The poison that will kill it harms me, too.

We pray for healthy days to come again
And loving nights be more than memory.
As bald and scarred and bloated as I've been,
All thoughts of pleasure die inside of me.

At last the monster lives in me no more;
My ravaged body can begin to heal.
We turn to one another and explore
All ways to rediscover how to feel.

Though fearful of your gaze upon my flesh
I see true love reflected in your eyes.
And as our awkward bodies once more mesh
We understand the bond that herein lies.

This battle showed our hearts still beat as one.
More tender moments are the spoils we've won.

MOVEMENTS
Michelle Buckman

Gert rocked back on her heels and pushed herself to a stand. She wiggled her bare feet in the sandy South Carolina soil on the surface until she reached the cooler dirt that fed the garden roots. Her whole body ached. She caressed the mound of her belly and rubbed the small of her back to alleviate the ache from hours bent over rows of beans. Things were settling enough now that maybe she could quit looking to the past and relax into the future.

She patted her tummy a few times to make the baby move. Sure enough, its thin legs kicked. One foot protruded with its tiny narrow shape distinctive beneath her skin, a bony foot that would someday need shoes. She felt a flutter. Flailing arms, she thought, and then it quieted again. She imagined fingers finding the mouth and the slurping, sucking of a thumb as it settled back to sleep. Sleep, not death. Mamma had died, but this baby was fine, safe, floating in its protective watery sac.

She gazed back at the weeds she'd heaped in the furrows as she'd gone along picking beans for supper and then turned to her younger sister perched in a peach tree at the edge of the garden.

"Dottie," she hollered at her, "come gather up these weeds, honey. I can't bear to stoop so many times."

Dottie continued to gaze at the dud egg in a robin's nest for a full minute before she dropped to the ground and picked up her basket. Gert bit back a reprimand; Mama had always said she had Daddy's temper, but she aimed to prove her wrong.

She wondered if Dottie would recollect much about Mama in years to come. Daddy had diminished to nothing more than the black and white portrait that hung in the musty front room. Mama would likely fade away as well. Gert knew she may as well claim to be mother to both Dottie and the new baby, because that's how life had laid things out.

Dottie's stiff, braided pigtails, tawny gold like the withering cornstalks, bounced as she skipped through the garden and swung around every time she turned back to reflect on the nest. Gert sighed. No doubt Dottie was dreaming of hiding the abandoned egg under her pillow to see if it would hatch, as she had done at that age, always fighting to save the less fortunate: a dog, an injured bird, a baby rabbit unearthed by Daddy's tractor.

Dottie tramped through the brambles and snagged her school dress on a briar. Before Gert could stop her, she tugged it free, leaving a tear in the material. Gert gritted her teeth, but said nothing. *Patience.* The old gingham hand-me-down hung on her like a rag, anyway, halfway to worn out before it was even given to her.

Gert went back to picking beans, ignoring the weeds now. She snatched a clump of four, dropped them into her bucket, and moved to the next bush. Hunger ate at her so steadily nowadays she could taste the beans already, boiled soft, seasoned with salt and glazed with butter, tasting like the new green of spring even now in late October. That was the good thing about beans; they produced until the first frost, and they'd had a great crop this year. Romper, the wild cat Dottie had started feeding last winter, had been a good idea. Romper had kept the rabbits at bay all summer. Gert hadn't thought it through like that when the cat first showed up. It'd only been good fortune. She'd let the cat stay because she hadn't had the heart to carry it off to the shelter with Dottie needing something loving to hold while Mamma slowly passed on.

The thought turned her head back Dottie's way again just in time to see the little girl stop midway across the garden, distracted from picking up weeds by something that caught her eye under a cabbage. She squatted and peered closely, then backed off and searched the ground till she found a stick. Returning, she stood as far away as possible and reached out with the tip of the twig to fold back the leaves of the cabbage.

"What is it?" Gert asked.

Dottie gasped. "Come see! Quick!"

"Aw, Dottie, you know I'm beyond hurrying anywhere. What is it, honey? I need them weeds picked up, and you're dallying as usual."

"It's a kitten."

Gert sighed. Romper had been a blessing, but they didn't need more animals to feed or sick ones to worry over. They were doing well to keep afloat as it was with the pittance Johnny brought home from Bud's shop every week. Not that she'd complain. At least Johnny was earning something.

Mamma had insisted Johnny was no good. "He'll never amount to nothing," she had said, hacking away between words. "Gert, you ain't nothing but a worry to me, and that worthless Johnny hanging around just doubles my fretting."

Mamma had been too far gone at that point for Gert to argue against. Instead, she had done her daughterly duty, trying to appease her mamma like Preacher told her to, keeping things easy and lighthearted. "He loves me, Mamma. You're just jealous 'cause you ain't young and in love no more."

"I ain't jealous of nothing. I got no desire to go back through all the foolhardiness of being your age. I'm just trying to settle some sense on ya from what I learned coming along. The boy's a dreamer. He's looking for the easy road, and there ain't such a thing. You need to settle on a solid fella like Clem who'll provide for you." The discourse didn't come out so smoothly, though, with pauses for clearing the sputum out of her throat and spitting phlegm into the bucket at her bedside. Six months earlier, when Mamma was still walking around, not so helpless, Gert would've ignored the speech and stormed out the door, but she had a bit of loyalty to her. After all, she and Mamma had survived a lot of hard times. Daddy had passed on when Dottie was still a toddler, and Mamma had gone to work in the local factory leaving much of the homemaking and childcare to Gert. Going out with Johnny may have started out as a way to rebel, an escape from the drudgery of helping with the housekeeping and raising of Dottie, but he'd become her crutch when Mamma started ailing.

Nevertheless, lectures on Johnny had worn thin. Johnny was pure romance, sitting on the porch on fine evenings, strumming his guitar and singing ballads to her. He could look at her with a love in his eyes that even the best cameraman couldn't capture for a cinema shot. But Mamma wouldn't be convinced of his sincerity. Her dying breath in that stark white hospital bed had been the end of another lecture about Gert shedding herself of Johnny and finding a good man.

Mamma had been wrong, all wrong. Johnny had come through for her. She'd gotten pregnant in Mamma's very own bed soon after the funeral, a night when weeping and sorrow had found comfort in hands and kisses and vows of love. Two months later, when she'd told Johnny that he was going to be a daddy, he'd moved into the house with her and Dottie. He'd set down his guitar and gotten a job at Bud's car shop. He hadn't married her yet, but they'd get to that later on, after the baby was born, after things had a sense of normalcy to them.

Gert didn't want anything interfering with their progress now. The baby would come before Christmas. By next summer they'd be a proper family, her back to her job at the grocery, and Johnny taking over full time at the shop. The owner, Bud, had hinted at it last week. He'd walked up to them in Rosie's diner and slapped Johnny on the back. "You're coming along real swell, son," he'd said. "Gives me comfort to know there's a good mechanic waiting to take on my shop, especially with you settling down to a family and all." He'd latched his thumbs into the straps of his greasy overalls. "No, sir, this old body can't keep up the pace like it used to. I might have to see to giving you more hours and set myself up fishing down to the stream."

Gert had beamed gratefully at Bud, thankful for giving Johnny, high school dropout that he was, the chance to earn a respectable living. Bud's declaration had struck Johnny dumb. He hadn't had anything to say the rest of the meal. Gert figured he'd been contemplating how they looked, turning into a real family living in Mamma's house with a baby on the way.

Gert turned back to the beans. "Dottie, leave that creature be and come get these weeds before the sun's gone."

"But the kitten; it's sick. We have to save it."

Gert shook her head. Dottie had a soft heart that even Mamma's dying hadn't hardened, while Gert's heart was tied in knots, nowadays, with all kinds of notions and emotions seeping out of it. She'd never imagined looking forward to being a mother herself, or crying at the thought of seeing her baby's face.

Reluctantly, she plodded down the furrow and stepped over the withering row of cantaloupe and around the hose that lay drizzling water into the roots of the pumpkin patch. Over another row and twenty feet further along, she reached Dottie's side and flopped down, the thud of her bottom sending up a cloud of sandy soil. "Let me see," she said, taking the stick. She pushed the cabbage back and poked at the kitten. It didn't move. She leaned forward and grasped the misshapen cabbage and pulled it out, tossing it to the side to retrieve later. The kitten still didn't move. Flies and yellow jackets buzzed around it, hovering around the glazed, unflinching eyes and the raw flesh of the tail end where the anus should have been.

"There's no hope for it," Gert whispered.

Dottie's face screwed up, fighting back all the emotions kept so carefully at bay.

Gert stared at the maggots wriggling in the matted fur and thought of Mamma's body stuck in the ground with worms. She wondered if death really was something peaceful like Preacher talked about, because life sure wasn't. Life meant agony dulled by medicine that hadn't taken the pain out of Mamma's face.

"Please, Gert, we have to do something."

The thought of what had to be done pounded in Gert's head and clutched at her throat. "Bring me a plastic bag out of the kitchen."

Dottie's face paled with suspicion. "For what?"

"Just go get one."

"You can't kill it."

"I can't save it, Dottie."

"We'll take it to the vet."

Money, Gert thought, but pushed the miserly notion away. Even if they had money, it wouldn't help this kitten. "Doc Hardy is thirty miles away, and Johnny's still got the car at work." She gazed at the orange glow of the horizon. "Anyhow, it's after five, easy. Doc Hardy's office is closed, and he ain't gunna rouse hisself from the TV to save a half-dead kitten."

"But that's what a vet is supposed to do."

Gert figured Doc Hardy may have thought along that theory when he was young, but over the years he'd lost fervor for anything other than injections and simple spaying cases. "He'd tell us there's a time to live and a time to die, and this kitten is stuck betwixt the two."

"That's what Preacher said about Mamma at the end, but he didn't kill her. He made her wait."

"People is different. God has to see to them. But he put us here to see to the animals 'cause they can't see to themselves. Now get me a bag."

Dottie opened her mouth to speak, but Gert kept a stern look focused on her till she changed her mind and headed toward the house. She moved like the kitten should have, her bare feet padding silently through the garden, a light, swaying movement across the lawn and easy leaps up the wooden porch steps.

Gert waited for the screen door to slap shut before she bent her cumbersome body forward and picked the kitten up by its tail. Yellow jackets rose with it, irritated at being disturbed. Blood oozed from the raw orifice beneath the tail. Gert let the thin body flop back down, ashamed that her fear of germs overrode empathy.

The kitten, as if privy to Gert's intentions, raised its head just slightly. Gert poked it. "Are you going to move?

Are you going to live?" She didn't want it to respond. She didn't want a reason to help it, to force-feed it, to seek medicine and tend to it around the clock. It was a kitten sitting in death's door. She only wanted to push it through.

The kitten lifted its head again, tried to pull itself to a stand, but only managed to roll onto its front feet. Its hind end remained resting on the ground. It wobbled in its half squat and fell flatly back to the earth, its eyes still glazed, its mouth cocked open, stiff-jawed.

Gert jerked at the bang of the screen door. Dottie plodded back across the yard, ever slower, until she reached Gert's side. The kitten was still again, looking comatose again, no evidence of the momentary spark of life.

"Give it here," Gert said, reaching for the bag.

Dottie clutched it in her right hand, her attention going fully to the kitten. She crouched down and buried the bag in her tiny lap. "No. Make it live."

Gert grabbed the edge of the bag and pulled it from Dottie's grip. "Now get on back to the house. You got homework to do. You go on and get them worksheets done that Miss Judy sent home."

"What are ya gunna do, Gert? Please don't kill it. God brought it right here to us. We're obliged to help it."

"Yup, we're obliged to help it, which is what I'm fixing to do. I'm gunna put it out of its misery."

"No, Gert, no!"

"Get on to the house, now."

"I can't let you do it."

"You don't want to see this, Dottie. Get on." She quit thinking about Dottie and started to think about how to do the deed. She tried to imagine wrapping it in the plastic bag and waiting for it to suffocate, but she was afraid it would take too long to run out of air. It would squirm and she'd rip the bag open to rescue it. She thought of breaking its neck, but she had no idea how to do that, and imagined how wrong it may go, damaging the poor thing, creating more pain and not ending its life at all.

She pushed herself to a stand, and bumped into Dottie. "What are you doing here, still? Get!"

Tears streamed down Dottie's face.

Gert knew what she was thinking. They'd rescued animals all their lives. But today Gert maintained her stone face with her lips thin and unsmiling.

Dottie turned from her and ran to the house, leaving a cloud of dust in her wake.

There is only one way to do it, Gert thought. She squatted, bag in hand, and picked up the kitten with the plastic, afraid to touch it, afraid to feel the fur, afraid to feel movement in its limbs, afraid of germs. It was light, but heavy enough with life for her to know it was in her grasp, not stiff, not limp with death, but giving in to gravity, bending in the middle like the helpless thing it was. She twisted it into the bag, held the looped handles in either hand, and stared at the body. It didn't twitch like she expected, but arched. She waited till it relaxed again, wishing the breaths would subside and quit, but its stomach rose and fell rhythmically.

Clasping the bag in one hand, she moved between the plants to the hose. She knelt, one hand holding the bag up, the other grasping the hose nozzle.

When the water hit the kitten, it woke from its comatose sleep, lifting its head and turning its eyes toward her. In equal time, the icy water from deep in the well had soaked it, plastered down its fur until it was dark, almost black. It's eyes, still stony, seemed to glare at her. She hesitated, unsure, wishing it all away. To save it now, chilled besides whatever else ailed it, would be practically impossible. It flopped back again. The water continued to fill the bag. One inch, two inches. The kitten struggled feebly, lifting its head, reaching for air, then fell still again. Three inches. Its feet scrabbled in the water for a moment, making no progress.

Gert's stomach twisted. How could she go forward? How could she go back?

She dropped the hose into the row of dead tomato plants and breathed deeply as she shut her eyes seeking some inner strength. With determination, she looked into the bag again. The kitten's head was floating at water level, gasping in half water, half air. With her free hand, she pushed against the plastic to force the kitten's head under. Legs flailed as it gulped water into its lungs. Gert held her breath, willing the kitten to die, begging it silently to give up. It went still, and she released the pressure on its head. Seconds later, a spasm racked its body and it breathed again. Gert cried silently and pushed the head under again. One, two, three... she counted up to sixty with her eyes squeezed shut, trying to ignore the twitching beneath her hand, ignoring the life ebbing away under her fingertips. Seconds lasted an eternity.

The breaths stilled. The mouth gaped. The fur wafted in the water.

Gert let out the breath she held, a long sigh, not of relief as she'd expected, but of despair.

She tilted the bag, letting the water seep into the ground, leaving the limp, wet body cradled in plastic. She knotted the handles, cinching the bag shut. With long strides, her body swaying under the weight of her baby, she reached the pile of brush beyond the garden. She set the bag into the center and backed away, shaking. Tomorrow was Saturday. She'd tell Johnny to set fire to the pile then.

Gert ambled across the rows and picked up the bucket of beans. The sun had diminished to an orange ball behind the tree line. Collecting the weeds would have to wait till morning light. Across the field, she saw Dottie crouched at the screen door, crying, her body shaking as she swiped at the blotches of tears on her cheeks.

It was probably best that Johnny wasn't home yet. He'd probably stopped off at Rocky's Bar and Grill to sing for a beer or two, which would time things about right. Dottie needed to sit quietly a spell to calm down, and the beans would take a good hour to stew, anyhow.

In town, Johnny emerged from the lit interior of the shop to the evening dusk. He glanced at his paycheck, folded it, and stuck it in his wallet as he approached the worn out Oldsmobile. He reached to the backseat to stroke his guitar before settling behind the wheel. A guy only had one chance in life. He revved the aged Oldsmobile and headed out Highway 74, toward Nashville.

As Gert ambled across the yard, she kneaded her belly. "Move, baby. Move."

"I think you should do it, Tatum." Finley reached overhead and made a twisting motion with his hand. The flat image on the wall-sized screen showed his character grabbing a lever on a window in the 3D game. The view through his personal entertainment headset would've made it appear realistic. Now he raised both hands, lifting the virtual window.

"Sorry, Finley, I'm not doing it." Sitting curled up on the couch, I moved my index finger over the flexi-phone on my wrist, and my heart skipped a beat. An icon of two overlapping rings indicated that another ceremony had begun.

I tapped the control to reach the site, and an image projected from my flexi-phone. Finley paid no attention, but I kept the image small, no higher than a hand-length. A girl and boy both about my age — twenty-something — stood face-to-face, holding hands and exchanging vows.

"I promise to be true to you in good times and in bad, in sickness and in health. I will love you and honor you all the days of my life."

The sweet words warmed me inside. Would they really keep those promises? Just because the new governor thought this was the way to go, the way to a stable society? Our nannies and teachers had always discouraged exclusive, long-term relationships, though some people still had them. Finley and I had been together since shortly after I transitioned from Secondary, so, like, five years. Would he ever consider getting married?

I soaked in every detail of the girl's dress, a flowing white gown similar to what the last girl had worn. Maybe even the girl before her. Might've been the same dress. Who would know? Only the brides. I doubted these couples wasted credits on wedding clothes. They'd wear it once and then what? The governor wanted people to get married — let him pay for it.

"What're you playing over here?" Finley plopped down beside me on the couch and stripped off his shirt. His hair, longish in front and typically worn swept off to one side, stuck to his forehead.

I tapped a control on my phone, bringing up the image of a hairstyle I'd saved earlier today. A cute style with tufts replaced the image of the couple.

"Hey, looks like cat ears." Finley grinned, glancing from me to the image. "It'd look great with the way you do your eyes."

I shrugged, pretending not to care, though I totally agreed. I outlined my eyes with thick black lines that almost reached my shaped brows. It brought out the greenish-gold of my irises. Sometimes I wore ridiculously thick, fluffy lashes, too. Other times, I drew black and gold cat eyes on my lids.

"Come on, Tatum," Finley whined, jumping back up and un-pausing his game. He gave me a forlorn glance over his shoulder, his lips pouty. "I know three girls at work that are doing it."

His puppy-dog eyes tempted me to cave in. I flipped to the next hairstyle, a cropped thing that wouldn't look good with my narrow chin. "Don't you get what would happen? It would totally change our lives?"

"I don't know. Would it?" Fist clenched, the game showing he held a rolled-up document, he bent at the waist and lifted one leg, then the other. As he climbed through a virtual window, the gaming sound effects changed, adding chirps of birds and crickets to the peppy music.

"It's not like you'd get pregnant right away," he said, "if at all. Isn't that what they said? But we'd have a new 3D game and a heap of other bonuses." Feet pounding the worn carpet and chest glistening with sweat, Finley jogged in place. At least his game obsession kept him fit.

"You're only thinking about the bonuses you'd get if I did this. You're not thinking about what would happen to me." His selfishness irritated me. Everything was about him. How had I ever fallen in love with such a selfish man?

"Nothing bad is gonna happen. Things might even stay the same."

"I'd have to undergo surgery."

"It's an outpatient surgery. Plus you get two weeks off work with pay." Finley stopped jogging and flashed his winning smile at me, creases and dimples flanking it. "You can stay home and play the new game while I'm at work."

"I don't know. Maybe I'll do it next year."

He frowned. "Next year? This offer won't stand forever. Won't take them too long to see the adverse effects of all this."

"What do you mean?"

"They go reversing sterilizations for every girl who wants it? This is gonna send population numbers climbing out of control. This new governor is cracked. You know that, right? But *we* might as well take advantage of it."

The new governor announced the program last month, and several women already stepped forward. Not me. I'd seen too many of the Breeders come into the commissary where I worked, them with their round bellies, some with babies or toddlers. We weren't supposed to call them

Breeders anymore, not since the Breeder Facility had been converted to ordinary apartments, and all the geneticists had been dismissed.

It didn't seem right, this new way. We all grew up learning about the benefits of genetic engineering, how scientists had rid the world of so many diseases and how each generation was healthier than the previous one. *Now* that didn't matter.

They said the earth could only sustain a specific number of people, so they allowed a precise number of births each year. *That* no longer mattered. Or actually, now they said the opposite. The suicide rates have climbed so high and too many people failed to contribute to society, so we needed even more people to sustain civilization. The earth had once held over seven billion people, the governor's people claimed. We'd always been taught three to four hundred million was the max. Who knew what to believe?

I never saw this coming though, the takeover of the government by this radical group. Their ideas contradicted everything we'd grown up believing. Our previous government belonged to the world government, so I had a sliver of hope that someone would come to our rescue before the radicals destroyed us completely.

I tapped my flexi-phone to shut off my internet connection and stood to stretch. Voices traveled through the open window, a man shouting. The off-white sheet draped over the window billowed with the breeze, giving a glimpse of the blue sky outside.

Wrapping a fleece blanket around my shoulders, I shuffled to the window. A gust of wind blew the sheet up higher, and I slipped in between it and the open window. I sucked a deep breath of fresh air into my lungs, realizing how stale the air in my apartment had become. If not for the chaos outside, this would be a beautiful day for a walk.

A group had gathered on the sidewalk across the street, thirty or so young adults. Their voices carried to my second-floor apartment. The bearded man in the straw hat stood in the midst of them. The vagabond priest. Right below my apartment! A childish urge to run outside nearly overcame me.

I had seen him several times on my way to work, the mall, or to clubs at night. Rumor had it, he'd spent a considerable amount of time in the Re-education Facility. A lot of good that did. He walked all over Aldonia spreading his message.

He presented ideologies that our government once deemed a threat to our security. He talked about invisible things that he could never prove, things entire civilizations once believed way back before science and logic made their beliefs seem childish. People still flocked to him. Some challenged him, a growing group ridiculed him, but most hung on his words. He had charisma, and his message stirred me deep inside. What did he talk about today?

"What's up?" Finley came up behind me, pushing the sheet out of the way. He slid his hands under the blanket and wrapped his sweaty arms around my waist.

"Want to go outside?" He kissed my neck, overwhelming me with his manly scent. "Or you wanna go to bed?"

My skin prickled at his kisses. "You know we wouldn't be able to do that whenever we wanted if I had the reversal."

"Sure we would." His hands roved all over me now. "Doesn't take any time to heal from the surgery."

"Right, but what about after I get pregnant? Have you

seen how big girls get?" Not interested in sleeping with him at the moment, I grabbed his hands and peeled them off me. Then I faced him, sat up on the windowsill, and wrapped the blanket around myself.

With a playful glint in his eyes, Finley wrestled the blanket open and pushed my knees apart with his hip. Then he pressed his body against mine to show me how much he wanted me.

I didn't understand how we could be so physically close and intimate and yet, at times, I felt so alone with him. He saw me, but he didn't. He saw me the way I saw the 3D game on the screen behind him. Without the 3D headset, the flat images showed people and places, but they lacked depth and realism.

I wanted more from him, but what more could a man give?

Someone outside hollered, his voice angry and hard. Cruel laughter followed.

I shoved Finley back and scooted off the windowsill. We both peered outside.

Three people threw things at the priest, probably garbage they'd found on the ground. Two other guys waved their arms and shouted in the priest's defense, but the priest simply turned and walked away. Half the group followed him.

"Why does he bother?" Finley said. "He should go back to wherever he came from. You know he's not from around here?"

I'd heard he came from somewhere outside the Boundary Fence, from a community that once lived without our government knowing about them. His people did not share the ideologies of the world governments. They believed in the invisible things, so I imagined they were very primitive. The new governor planned to take the Boundary Fence down in a few years and allow everyone into the Fully-Protected Nature Preserves, where we would eventually come across these little colonies. I didn't understand the logic of this. Wouldn't we destroy everything? The way people had in the past?

The man who had shouted the loudest bolted after the priest and threw something else at him, hitting him in the back, but not breaking the priest's stride.

Sickened, I turned away and looked at Finley. "Why can't people just leave him alone?" I felt sorry for him. He didn't stand to gain anything by talking to people, so he must've felt he had something important to share.

"He says crazy things, you know, like there's a God who made us, and this God looks like us." Finley laughed and stepped away from me. He pulled the sheet back into place.

"Who cares what he says?" I pushed through the sheet, enjoying the smooth feel as it glided over my face and head. "The new government doesn't care what you believe. People should be happy with that freedom." We grew up watching what we said, living in fear of re-education. Few people risked talking against the government or against their ideologies...or about anything of consequence. Now, it didn't matter.

Finley shut off the game and gathered empty plates and cups from the floor.

I tossed my blanket onto the couch. "So you want me to get the reversal. Does that mean you want to marry me?" I had to force the question out. A part of me desperately wanted him to say *yes*.

The plates he carried clanked as if something had slipped from his hand. "Isn't that the language of the priest? Marriage? Husbands? Wives?"

"The governor says it, too. He recommends that a girl be in a permanent relationship before she volunteers for the procedure. Haven't you watched the ceremonies?" The new governor wanted to broadcast the exchange of vows of every couple who decided to marry. I'd probably watched over thirty of them in the past few weeks.

"Not really," Finley said. "I may have seen one, that first one."

I gathered dirty clothes from the floor and tossed them into the basket outside my bedroom — our bedroom, really. Finley had been staying with me ever since the change in government, and my government-assigned roommate hadn't been back since. She probably lived with her girlfriend now. I doubted she'd go for the procedure. She wasn't interested in men, so what would she care about her inside parts?

"Tatum, you and I, we've been together since you transitioned from Secondary, just about. That's not going to change. We don't need some ceremony to prove we're going to stick by each other, to prove we love each other. In fact..." He grinned, his dimples coming out. "...I'm going to show you how much I love you as soon as I'm done cleaning up."

I gave him a dismissive wave of my hand. "You can shower when you're done cleaning up."

He clanked dishes in the sink and blasted the water. Odorless bubbles rose up, making me miss scented dishwashing detergent. They stopped making it, claiming the unscented soap was better on the environment.

Dirty dishes covered the countertop on both sides of the stove. I stacked bowls and plates, trying to make room for the dish drainer. "You expect me to get this reversal with no guarantee that you're going to stick around?"

"You're blowing it out of proportion. You might not even get pregnant." Finley brought the old, stained dish drainer out from under the sink.

"But I might. That's the point of it. You know, they're really asking us to have two vocations. We'll still have to do our regular work, but then we'll have to do what the girls in the Breeder Facility always did, taking care of a baby."

"Well, you'd get one whole year off. I'd get a month. We'd figure it out, don't you think?" He scrubbed a plate then ran his hand over it under the water.

"It's not like we can send the child to live in Primary when it turns five."

"Really?" His squinting eyes said he hadn't known this, but the people with the new way had been very clear. Maybe now he'd understand.

"They're hoping the creation of families will make the government-run residences unnecessary." I took the rinsed plate from his hand and set it in the drainer. "It's the whole reason they want a man and woman to commit to a permanent relationship. They'll be bringing a baby into the world and would have to care for it until it became an adult."

"Oh." He scrubbed the next plate with a thoughtful expression on his face.

I took the plate and rinsed it. I did not want to get pregnant. First, I would have to carry the baby inside me for nine months while going to work for as long as possible. Given my petite frame, I imagined this would be very uncomfortable. Second, our relationship wasn't strong enough to introduce a third person. Finley worked all day and played games all evening, barely giving me attention in between. With a baby, we would have to share our apartment, attention, and credits. Third, I didn't want the extra responsibility of another person. The government said it would no longer tell us what to do, so we had to come up with our own plans. I didn't like having to plan for myself. How could I make plans for someone else?

"Did you know," I said, "we'll have to attend parenting classes once a week?"

"No, you don't." He made an exaggerated expression of annoyance, pulling his lips back and shaking his head. "They encourage it, but we can read up on stuff. And the classes don't even begin until two or three weeks after."

"Because I'll be healing from the surgery." I flung my hands into the air. "Don't you get it? Aren't you thinking about me at all? You're being selfish."

"Hey, hey, stop." Finley grabbed my arms with soapy hands and pulled me close, grinning and gazing into my eyes. "I love you, girl. Let's do this. You and me. It'll be an adventure."

I threw my head back and groaned, knowing he'd keep at me until he got his way. "I'm not promising anything, but I'll think about it."

The hint of a grin came to his lips, a triumphant gleam to his eyes. He scooped me up in his arms and carried me to the bedroom.

***

"Light burned out in aisle five," Keever said, resting an arm on the tunnel scanner at my register. He hated working and tried to make me do everything extra. I hated working, too, so we had developed a competition to see who could get away with doing the least work.

"So change it." I glanced up from the game on my flexi-phone. "I've done enough today." I arrived to work, the local commissary, ten minutes late and spent the first hour watching the delivery boy unload and scan canned goods and boxed products. Keever hadn't come in yet, so I had to shelve everything myself.

"Oh yeah? You've done enough? I've had to reboot the computer in produce three times. Couldn't get the info to show up on the smart screens."

"No one looks at those, anyway," I said. "Your flexi-phones tell you everything you should be getting." Mine always told me to buy more protein, but I hated the tofu and beans it suggested.

"All that's going to change." Keever peeked around the bulky tunnel scanner and looked at the game on my phone. "Soon as these come out." He tapped his palm, indicating the RFID implant we all had since birth.

The governor hated them, hated the way the old government spied on and tracked people. He cut his implant from his hand years ago, risking death and having to go off the grid. If a person tried to remove the implant, an anti-tamper feature released poison into the bloodstream. Our crazy governor got around that by having his entire hand chopped off. Now he wanted everyone to give them up, saying they were too invasive. He claimed to have a device that would remove the implant, leaving little more than a cut on your palm.

Living without ID implants seemed impossible to me. We earned credits for fulfilling our vocation. And we spent credits by having our implants scanned. We could check our credits, payments, and purchases with our flexi-phones which read our implants. Nice and tidy. No big deal. He wanted some messy system that involved carrying plastic cards everywhere we went. Guaranteed, I would lose mine within the week.

The glass doors slid open. A blond woman in her twenties, maybe younger than me, pulled a toddler in a wagon into the commissary. The boy had hair so blond it seemed to glow. The woman parked her wagon out of the way and grabbed a shopping cart. Before the new government took over, I had only seen customers shop with baskets. We never had enough credits to fill a cart. But ever since the Breeder Facility officially closed and the Breeders had reentered society, the carts had started getting some use.

"No! Me do it." The toddler twisted away from the Breeder — *I mean, the woman, or ... I guess, his mother* — and stuffed his fingers into the honeycomb holes in a plastic shopping cart. He stepped onto the tray under the basket and reached his hands higher.

The woman grabbed the boy under the arms and lifted him into the cart. "Settle down, Cedar, and I'll let you run around outside, okay?"

Cedar stamped his feet, rattling the cart, and chanted, "Run, run, run..."

"Yes, run," the woman said, shaking her head while she pulled up the Shopping Helper on her flexi-phone. Her gaze caught mine, and she rolled her eyes.

I smiled to show sympathy, then went back to my game. It was a stupid, but addictive, game where I fed colorful food to various cartoony, endangered species. I hoped to make the next level before the third-shift workers arrived.

Twenty minutes later, the blonde pushed a full cart to the register. Her boy sat surrounded by groceries, rocking back and forth in the cart and singing a silly song that I remembered from Primary.

I tapped my flexi-phone to pause the game. "Got any bags?" I asked the woman.

"Oh, I forgot." She thrust her hand into her hair, short blond waves that she obviously hadn't spent much time on.

I wouldn't have left the house looking like her. But maybe motherhood would change my mind. What was Finley trying to do to me?

I grabbed an eco-tote and waited for her to load her groceries onto the conveyer belt. Check-out usually took two minutes, less if I was on my game.

She had only placed two items into the tunnel scanner when the little boy threw a plastic box to the floor. He may have been trying to help, but the woman groaned as she stooped for it. "Don't touch anything," she snapped. "Be good and you'll get to run."

"Run, run, run…" he chanted, banging the side of the cart.

Feeling sorry for her, I stepped around to help. "You were one of the Breeders, huh?"

She glanced then nodded. "I know. Everyone's shocked to see us out and about. It's weird for us, too." After loading cans onto the belt, she pried the boy's fingers from a box. "Life sure isn't what they promised before we went in. It never was, though. They built it up to make everyone think it was the most awesome vocation. It was always a lot of work."

I grabbed two gallons of milk from the tray under the basket and set them on the belt. I had always envied those girls whose perfect biological makeups merited the vocation of Breeder. We all knew the benefits they would have in the Breeder Facility: the food, entertainment, pampering, and the comfortable living areas.

"Where do you live now?" I scooted around to the other end of the register to bag her items.

"Same place, only little Cedar stays with me, and I'll have my new one with me, too." She rubbed her belly, which had the slightest roundness to it.

"Do you work — I mean, now that things are different?" I tried to keep resentment from my tone. If I got the reversal and had a baby, I would have the chore of carrying, then caring for, a baby — on top of the struggles of daily life — but without the comforts of the Breeder Facility. How could they expect us to have two vocations just so they could get the population numbers up?

"Yes, I work. I wanted to stay close to Cedar, so they let me clean the place. He's with me all the time." She smiled at him and smoothed his shiny blond hair. He continued chanting and pounding on the cart. "We all do other things now. Every Breeder has two vocations."

"Doesn't seem fair." Wanting to talk with her more, I stuffed her groceries into a bag at a slower-than-usual pace.

"A few girls have gotten married." She smiled as if finding the idea humorous. Then her smile faded. "I'd get married if I could, if I found someone who would love Cedar as much as I do. We could be a family."

Family, marriage, husband, wife, mother, father... Using these words to refer to human relationships was new to us. We used the word *family* in school when categorizing organisms. The words *mother* and *father* we used when referring to social habits of animals like lions, buffalo, or elephants. It felt strange, even uncomfortable, to use them for human relationships.

I loaded the bags into her cart and tapped the credit total button on my register. The total would flash on her flexi-phone. Come to think of it, it would be electronically stored, too, so that doctors or anyone official could access it. I bet the governor would want to change that one day.

"Do you ever wish the old government were back," I said, "that things were the same as before?"

"No way. After delivery, they never wanted a girl to bond with her baby. They always gave it to a different Breeder. Didn't even want us to know which baby we carried. They tried to implant embryos in at least two girls on the same day so they'd be born around the same time. But this little boy..." Her sky-blue eyes became two glittery pools overflowing with love. "I've always known. He came from my body, from my egg. I nurse him at my breast, rock him to sleep, comfort him when he wakes at night. I wouldn't want things to go back to the way they were. I wouldn't trade this for the world."

Something inside me stirred, making me physically shudder. I watched as she loaded the little boy and her groceries into the wagon that she had left behind the carts. I watched as she pulled the wagon through the sliding glass doors, as the sunlight made their hair glow, and as they disappeared around a corner.

***

Finley smiled when he communicated, whether on his flexi-phone or in person, whether talking business or pleasure, whether speaking with a friend or stranger. Deep creases and dimples sprung out every time, making him look sincere even when his eyes held different emotions. I always thought he'd make a good infomercial model, smiling cheerfully as he promoted shoes made of recycled materials or energy-efficient curtains, his image in every mall and store. But those vocations went to people on the West coast. How did those cities, the Regimen-controlled ones, feel about our city now? Did they still do business with us?

In a chair nearby, Finley sat with one leg draped over the side and one hand tapping his flex-phone. He hadn't stopped playing games since we'd arrived at Aldonia's hospital.

I lay in one of ten hospital beds in the pre-op ward, gazing at the gray curtains that separated patients. A nurse had come an hour ago to insert an IV in my hand and to check my vitals. She left the blood pressure cuff on my arm and a little glowing thingy on my finger.

Closing my eyes and letting my mind wander, indistinct voices, hums, and beeping machines lulled me. Then my empty stomach growled.

Part of me couldn't believe I was doing this. Was I making a mistake?

Random thoughts swirled in my mind, overwhelming me with a dizzying effect. I had only been thirteen, on the verge of blossoming into a woman, when they'd brought me to this same hospital. Every girl, except for the Breeders, had to get the procedure done. They'd made it seem like a rite of passage to adulthood.

A chill hung in the air. I rubbed my arm.

When I was thirteen, I'd worn a thin gown like the one I now wore. Alone and afraid, I had lain trembling, waiting my turn. When they'd finally come for me, they put something in my IV and rolled my bed down a cold hallway. Then it was all over. I awoke a new person. A doctor had tied off and snipped parts inside me, making me sterile.

Goosebumps came out on my arms. Now, within a couple of hours, my body would be put back together. "The way God intended," the vagabond priest would say. My body would be capable of doing what only a woman's body could do: conceive and carry life.

Was I ready for this? That Breeder I'd spoken with at work — *not a Breeder, a mother* — that look in her eyes... she really loved her baby. She said she wouldn't trade her life now for anything. She seemed to have found what I wanted. Personal fulfillment.

Would I find that in having a baby?

We'd been raised to see sex as a form of entertainment. But now, with my parts back in place, it would be so much more. We'd never know. Each time we made love, we could be making a baby.

A baby! What was I doing? Had I lost my mind?

I took a deep breath and let it out slowly. Finley wanted this. Was it just because he wanted the bonuses? Maybe he felt something that he couldn't express. Maybe he instinctively longed for a something bigger, for a love that would create. The vagabond priest spoke of God as Creator. We would share in that creation through our love-making. Maybe this would draw us together.

"Taking a long time, huh?" Finley said, shifting in the chair.

I opened my eyes as he shuffled to the gap in the curtain that hung around my hospital bed. He peeked out, then glanced at me over his shoulder and flashed a smile.

I smiled, too, but only on the inside. "You're sure you want me to do this, right?"

He shook his head but said, "Yeah." Uncertainty flickered across his face until his smile took over. He sat beside me on the bed and took my hand. "Yeah, we want to do this. It'll be fine."

***

Lying alone in bed, I stared at a sliver of blue light on the ceiling. A triangle of light used to shine there, stealing in through a tear in the sheet that once hung over the bedroom window, before Finley had picked up actual curtains. Ever since my operation, Finley spent a lot of time shopping, at least two hours every day after his job. In addition to groceries, he'd gotten us a new dish drainer, bedsheets, pillows, curtains for the living and bedrooms, matching mugs, and a 3D game — this on top of the free one they'd given us the day of the surgery. I'd told him the extra credits were supposed to be spent on preparing for a baby. So today he came home with a soft, little blanket and put it in the second bedroom.

Finley hollered from the living room, probably excited about racking up points in one of the new games. It didn't sound like he meant to quit soon, though he had told me an hour ago he was coming to bed.

Tired of waiting, I sighed, threw the covers back, and creaked open the bedroom door.

Colorful, flashing light streamed from the wall screen in an otherwise dark room, illuminating the edges of the couch and chair and giving Finley a big shadow. Finley sat cross-legged on the floor, his arms moving all over. Apparently, he'd turned off the full-action mode. Probably because he was getting tired.

"Finley," I shouted, leaning against the doorframe.

He paused the game, turned, and looked me over, his gaze stopping mid-way down my body.

Wanting to entice him, I had changed into a sleeveless nightshirt that barely covered my panties. "I thought you were coming to bed."

His gaze lifted to my face. "I am. Just finishing a level."

I rolled my eyes. "You've been playing the game every night since we got it, so like, for three weeks."

"No, this is the other one." He faced the game again. "Want me to turn it down?"

I moaned, stomped into the living room, and flung myself onto the couch. "Why won't you sleep with me?" I stretched out on the couch and rolled onto my back, my shirt hiking up past my navel.

"What are you talking about?" He laughed, throwing

glances at me. A few seconds later the game went off, and the screen turned blue. "I sleep with you every night." He pushed me over on the couch, sat beside me, and rubbed my leg from calf to thigh.

"You come to bed late, after I've fallen asleep," I said, sounding pouty. "And you haven't touched me since the surgery."

He leaned over me and planted several kisses on my neck. "I want to make sure you're healed, that's all."

"They said we didn't have to wait. We could do it whenever we're ready." I shifted my hips, scooting over more, wanting him to lie beside me. "It scares me, too, Finley, knowing that when we make love something might be happening inside me, but this is what you wanted."

Emotion overwhelmed me, making me hot, making my heart race. I knew without a doubt; this experience would deepen our love. I draped my arms over his shoulders and brushed my lips along his cheek until I found his mouth.

He hesitated, then kissed me back, but his kiss lacked desire. He touched me, his hands moving along my skin, but without the caresses I had come to expect from him.

Kissing him deeper and losing myself in his embrace, I traced my fingers down his chest and tugged his shirt up. I didn't want him to worry about me. I was fine. I was ready.

He pulled back and sucked in a breath. The blue light from the screen shone on the whites of his eyes and highlighted his thick lashes. "Tatum, let's not do that yet. Let's do other things tonight. I can make you happy other ways."

"Why?" I propped myself up on my elbows, not sure if I should be hurt or if I needed to reassure him.

He slid off the couch and onto his knees, then he dropped his face into his hands for a moment.

I swung my legs off the couch and sat before him. "You don't have to worry about hurting me. I barely felt anything the day of my surgery, and now I'm completely fine." I lifted the hem of my shirt and peeled my panties down a bit to show him the tiny scar.

He glanced then grabbed my hands and turned his puppy-dog eyes to me. No smile this time. "I want you, Tatum, like I always have, maybe more. But I can't do this." Shaking his head, squeezing my hands, I'd never seen him so intense. "When I was shopping for baby things, seeing all that stuff in the mall...stuff that never used to be in the mall..."

"Well, before, it all went to the Breeder Facility."

"I know. And they didn't have to pay for it. You know how much it's going to cost caring for a third person? The baby's not going to earn any credits. And the time we'll have to spend watching it, caring for it. It would mess up our lives, make them too complicated —"

"Are you kidding me?" Anger tensing me, I wriggled my hands from his grip. "I can't believe you're talking like this."

Finley cast himself onto my lap, burying his face and gripping my hips. "I love you, Tatum, but I can't do this. I don't want you to get pregnant. I'm not ready for that responsibility. Everything will change. It's too complicated."

Tears of frustration bubbled up and spilled out. "But you said..." I pushed his sweaty head, wanting him off me, but couldn't get him to move. "I did this for you."

"I know and I'm sorry, I'm sorry. I was selfish. But we can still do things, just not like we used to. We can still have fun, make each other feel good."

Exerting more strength than I realized I had, I shoved

him off my lap and pushed his chest with my foot. "No."

He fell back and landed on his butt, gazing at me through eyes that began to see me. All of me. I was not a girl he could simply mess around with.

"Is that what it's been about all this time?" I said. "Feeling good? Don't you want more than that? Shouldn't it be deeper? Doesn't it make sense that our love — that true love — should make something and change the world?"

"I don't want to change the world. I don't want to work on the population of Aldonia. Others can do that. That's why we had Breeders." He grimaced, smile creases forming but his eyes showing a rigid heart. "This governor is screwed up, and he won't stay in power for long. He'll be overthrown, and things will go back to the way they were." He heaved a sigh, his body going limp. Then he gave me a real smile, one that always had the power to make me do whatever he wanted. Leaning forward, he reached a hand to me. "Tatum, honey, I just want it to be you and me. Forever."

Eyes on his outstretched hand, I stood, and realization came over me. "Finley, it's not a game. It's not just for fun. If you don't want all of me, then you get nothing from me."

I stomped to my bedroom, slammed the door, and stood trembling in the darkness. Tears threatened but did not come. Was it anger that held them back? Or had I changed? Whichever it was, I'd made my choice. I would not belong to anyone who did not want all of me. I wanted love: real, total, and messy love.

***

A gust of wind blew, making sunbeams blink through the leaves of the tree I stood under and making my eyes tear up. I stood in the outer edges of the crowd that gathered around the vagabond priest. On my way home from the commissary, I had heard him speaking, and my feet had taken me here. No protestors had come today, just those who wanted to hear his words.

"God does not want us to be alone," the priest said. He sat on a cement retaining wall, one hand to his straw hat whenever the wind kicked up.

I was alone. I hadn't seen Finley in over a month, ever since I'd told him to leave. Had he found someone else? He would want someone committed to the old ways, a girl who hadn't decided to get the reversal. A girl he could use.

I took a breath and exhaled slowly. As much as I missed him, I felt satisfied being alone. My heart rested in a new song, a message that I barely grasped. I was made for love, for a total giving of myself to another who would give himself completely to me. Our love would have the potential to make something, to blossom into life.

The vagabond priest had said that somehow human love reflected the love of God. God made it this way, because he wanted us to know Him. Everything in creation pointed to God, but most especially we did, in our bodies and in our capacity to love.

Trying to understand this, I felt like I grasped at sunbeams. But I understood it in my heart. I understood that married love, to be real, must be complete, holding nothing back.

A stronger gust of wind rustled the leaves, making them dance with the sunlight. I closed my eyes, enjoying the strobe light effect it created on my eyelids.

The priest's words stirred a longing in my heart. He taught something old and yet new. There was more to life than what we could see and feel and experience, but the physical things gave us a glimpse of it. Our teachers said people and entire civilizations once clung to belief in God and invisible realities. With our superior knowledge and developments, we no longer needed those childish beliefs. But the things we learned in Primary and Secondary now seemed as sterile as they had made our bodies.

The priest had stopped talking and someone else spoke, asking a question I couldn't hear from where I stood.

"It is important that marriage and family are restored to our culture," the priest said, his voice carrying. "The union of man and woman, of husband and wife, foreshadows something eternal. God is a Trinity of Persons in an eternal giving and receiving of life-giving love. This same God, the God who created you, invites you to live with Him in this love."

"Tatum."

I gasped at the sound of Finley's voice coming from so close behind me. It hadn't been easy telling him to go. Was I ready to see him again, to look into his eyes and not melt from his smile?

Bracing myself, I turned to face him.

He wore his work clothes, a dark green uniform with the Environmental Stewardship logo on the chest, a tree, and a shovel with the letters ESU. The breeze ruffled his hair. He strode toward me with his head down and one hand in his pocket. Then he reached me and lifted his head. His eyes shimmered in the sunlight. As our gazes connected, a smile stretched across his face...dimples and creases, youthful charm.

I sucked in a breath and held it. I could resist.

"Couldn't find you at the commissary. When I saw the crowd, I thought maybe I'd find you here."

"Yeah, I..." I waved my hand, sort of pointing over my shoulder, meaning to indicate that I'd come to hear the vagabond priest, but not finding the words.

"Yeah, that's what I figured." He pressed his lips together and blinked. "I got a pay raise this week."

"A raise?"

"Yeah, it's the new way. If you work hard and prove yourself on the job, you get more credits."

"Oh." This was unheard of. To avoid discrimination, we had always received a fixed amount regardless of effort or outcome. If the amount increased, it increased for everyone. "That's great. You deserve it. You work harder than anyone I know."

"Thanks." He continued staring, not glancing away. Did he even blink? "I...I miss you. And I've been thinking."

"I miss you, too, Finley, but nothing's changed for me." I forced the words out as quickly as I could, struggling to hold his gaze but finding inner strength. I could do this. Despite the way my heart flopped about in my chest, I was not going to cave in.

"I wondered if maybe you'd give me another chance."

"Finley..." I shook my head, my eyes blinking rapidly. My resolve flickered.

He slid his hand from his pocket and opened it. There in his palm lay two golden rings, glittering in the sunlight. "These are wedding rings. The married couples wear them. It's an old custom from generations past."

"Oh." I reached but drew back, uncertain of his intention.

"I want to marry you, Tatum. I was wrong to walk away. I was scared. But I'm not scared anymore." He looked past me, probably at the priest, and smoothed his hair over his forehead. "Maybe I should be. Have you heard what's coming? Have you heard about the upheaval in the world?"

I stood stunned, staring at him, unable to close my mouth or even blink. He wanted to marry me? Had he changed the subject already, before getting my answer? "What upheaval? What do you mean?"

His gaze returned to mine, no smile on his face, his jaw twitching before he spoke. "If we want this — marriage, family, the right to choose how to live — we may have to fight for it."

I shook my head, trying to understand. "I don't want to fight. Why can't everyone just get along, live how they see best?"

"Because that's not the way of the world. But if you want me, if you want this, we'll be in it together. You and me and whatever family we create."

Tears welling in my eyes, joy bursting the seams of my heart, I nodded and flung my arms around his neck. "You and me. And our family."

IN THE DEATH OF WINTER
Arthur Powers

"Who in that land of darkness and blind eyes
Thy long-expected healing wings could see..."

H Vaughn (1621-1695)

In the death of winter
when ice cracked the long coast of Michigan
and night held the city sixty days —

a blind technician groping in the dark —
as the thin hand reached the scalpel
and pale fluorescence gave off dark rays

the child screamed dead. Later,
walking home through first large snowflakes
touching her face, gentle, swirling

under streetlights, she heard
a fierce sudden
flapping of wings.

GUESS WHO'S COMING TO SUNDAY BRUNCH
Erin McCole Cupp

The view of the city from Dottie's penthouse was breathtaking on this perfect autumn Sunday. The sky was blue and cloudless with the Manhattan skyline zig-zagging beneath it. Small, crumby plates littered the rooftop deck table. Atop an embroidered linen tablecloth, a bowl of fresh fruit sat next to a platter of picked-over pastries. Sunlight beamed through a crystal pitcher, now empty but for a residue of freshly-squeezed orange juice and quality champagne.

Piano notes flowed softly from the music room, its French doors open to let in the late morning air. The music sweetened the dimmed chaos of the city traffic below.

Thea touched her perfectly manicured fingers to Dottie's arm. "You know, I just can't get over this feeling that I know you from somewhere."

Dottie patted Thea's hand. "Same here! I've been trying to place your face since you and Parker arrived!"

"Well," Thea sighed. "Even if we never figure it out, I must say, your Skyleigh is the most lovely girl. I am so happy she's becoming part of our little family."

Moved, Dottie pressed her own manicure over her heart. "Really, Thea — may I call you Thea?"

Thea gave a deferential smile. "Of course! We're practically sisters now!"

Dottie nodded. "Or will be next October!"

Both mothers laughed.

Dottie brushed a joyous tear from her cheek with a knuckle. "But really, Thea, I couldn't be more delighted with Parker. He's everything I could have wished for in a son-in-law: talented, good-looking, well-spoken, and completely in love with my daughter."

Thea nodded, her eyes filling once more with delighted tears. It had been such a wonderful morning! They laughed again at their own sentimentality, then sipped some more of their mimosas.

Dottie sighed. "I love how, even though they both play strings in the orchestra now, they still go back to piano, given the chance. Skyleigh said Parker started on piano just like she did, right?"

Thea nodded. "He did. His father was a professional musician — well, his biological father."

"Really! So was Skyleigh's. I'm so sorry you're not together anymore. Must you brace yourself for seeing him at the wedding?"

Thea laughed an outrageous laugh. "Oh, no. I don't even know him, to be honest. I've always been a single mom. When the time was right, I selected a sperm donor."

"Huh. That's pretty much my story, as well. My career was going so well, but it left no time for dating."

Thea pursed her lips in understanding. "And it's not like there was internet dating twenty-five years ago!"

"Nope. Back then it was —"

"Personal ads!" They finished together in a deluge of embarrassed giggles. Comrades-in-arms, they clinked their glasses together in a toast to their shared state.

The music stopped for a moment while the bride- and groom-to-be shared a laugh over something as beautiful as they. Both mothers smiled, sipped their mimosas, then grew thoughtful.

"Dottie — may I call you Dottie?"

"Oh, please do."

"Have you always lived in the city?"

"No, not always. I moved here when I got my first job at the firm."

"So you've been living in New York for...?"

"Not quite thirty years. Once I had Skyleigh, I thought about moving to the suburbs, but nothing beats the cultural opportunities available to enrich a child here. Knowing she had the genetic background to become a musician, I couldn't bring myself to deprive her of that. It wasn't always easy, but you see, it seems to have paid off!"

Dottie's voice ended brightly, but a puzzled shadow passed over Thea's face.

"Thea? Are you all right, sweetie?"

Thea put her mimosa glass down on the small table next to her chair. "Well, I used to live here, too, you know, but I made the decision to move Parker to the fresh air of Montana."

"Oh, I didn't mean to imply —"

"There were plenty of opportunities for him to develop his gift."

"As I can see! We just made different choices is all. I apologize if I sounded —"

Thea took a deep breath. "Thank you. It is good to be back in the city, though. I did miss the bustle of it all. I don't come back here nearly enough to see Parker play now that he's living his destiny here."

"Well, you're always welcome to stay here whenever you like. Or do you still have family here?"

Thea smirked. "None I'd have, if you know what I mean."

Dottie nodded. "I do. We have so much in common already. We're both strong and independent career women —"

"— with unbearable families of origin."

Dottie had to nod again. "Neither of us let a lack of available men impede our dreams of motherhood…"

Thea grinned. "It's like we've just met, and we practically *are* sisters."

Dottie pointed at Thea. "I bet *that's* why we feel like we know each other already."

Thea squinted. "No. I'm sure I've seen your face somewhere before…"

"And you did say that you used to live in the city."

"I did. Brooklyn. You?"

"Upper East Side."

"And you moved here for work, so we wouldn't have gone to the same schools."

"College?"

They compared notes while the kids began a fresh duet in the music room. They went to different graduate schools, frequented different bars, could determine no common friends, and otherwise traveled in completely different circles.

"Oh, well," Thea said at last. "Maybe we were just fraternal twins separated at birth or something."

Dottie nearly snorted mimosa out her nose. "Don't say that. The kids would be devastated if they found out they were first cousins!"

Both mothers laughed uproariously until a demanding crescendo of piano music pushed down their laughter.

"That could never happen."

"Of course not! Statistically impossible!"

The city and the music wove together over the next few moments of silence.

"Thea, if you don't mind my asking, where did you receive your IVF?"

"Borough Park—"

"—Reproductive Endocrinology Associates?"

Thea's face blanched. "And your donor—"

"—was a professional musician?"

"I remember your face from the waiting r—"

Now Dottie blanched. She and Thea both lifted their glasses for a swig, only to find them empty. Both mothers' hands were shaking just the slightest amount.

The piano drifted down into something soft, flowy, and undeniably pretty. Horns on the streets below blasted at each other. Dottie blinked. Thea blinked.

"Suddenly, I'm so thirsty. Aren't you thirsty?"

"Yes! Totally! So thirsty!"

Dottie reached for the empty crystal pitcher. "Why don't you follow me into the kitchen, Thea, darling? You can help me make another batch."

"I do make a mean mimosa."

"Do you? Maybe you can make them for the reception, then!"

Thea laughed more loudly than she had all morning. "A dinner-into-brunch wedding reception?"

"Why not?" Dottie asked. "Rules were made to be broken!"

"I agree. That sounds perfect. Just perfect."

NICE
Gerard D. Webster

I had to admit that I was very proud as I stood next to Bart, my husband of eleven months, and surveyed the results of a week's worth of hard work. Not just for me, but for the whole McGonnigle clan.

The "old barn"— as they called it — was beautifully decorated with Chinese lanterns, balloons, streamers, folding tables covered in white linen tablecloths, and even a "band-stand" under the hayloft. Whenever there was a family gathering, for whatever reason, the whole family — aunts, uncles, cousins, brothers and sisters — pitched in and transformed the "old barn" into a magnificently large and warm reception hall. The cattle and horses were housed in the "newer" barn and stables on the other side of the big stone farmhouse. Today was a reception for Kim's wedding. Six months ago it served as a gathering place for an honest-to-goodness Irish wake after Bart's grandfather passed away. Be it a sad occasion or a joyous one, the McGonnigle clan knew how to throw a party. And whenever they did, the whole extended family would descend on our farm like a flock of geese migrating to their ancestral home.

As my eyes scanned the wedding guests, I focused on a tall, handsome, muscular man as he swaggered toward the wet bar.

"Who invited him?" I asked.

"Who are you talking about, Stacie?" My husband's gaze searched the wedding guests.

"Him," I nodded towards the self-serve wet bar where the man was pouring himself a double scotch.

"You mean Dean Stoddard?"

"Who else?"

"He's Dora's date. So I guess she invited him."

"Dora?"

Just then a beautiful young woman in a full-length pink gown sidled up beside Dean and looped her arm through his, staking her claim early on her prize.

"Yeah," Bart pointed. "Dora — Kimmie's bridesmaid."

Kimmie is Bart's cousin. We'd all just come from her wedding at St. Joseph's Church in Howell, Michigan — a mere eight country-road miles from our farm.

"God only knows what she sees in him."

"Oh, I don't know," Bart said, "maybe that he's rich, good-looking, and tremendously famous?" It was as close as he'd ever come to a rebuke.

I shook my head and remembered when both Dean Stoddard and I attended Michigan State together. I almost felt sorry for Dora.

She doesn't know...not yet; but she will. Dean can't keep up the act forever. Poor girl. Dean is about my age — but already married and divorced twice. No surprise there. Fidelity was never one of his strong points. I ought to know.

Dean and I were engaged towards the end of our junior year—that is, until he asked for something he was not yet entitled to, at least not until after the wedding. But Dean Stoddard felt entitled to anything he wanted. So, when he couldn't get what he wanted from me, he got it from an MSU cheerleader — while we were still engaged. That ended as soon as I found out. He was not a keeper. I would not marry a man who couldn't — or wouldn't — be faithful.

"Sometimes, Bart, you are just too nice," I said.

Just then a herd of young nephews rushed into the barn. Tommy, the oldest, was holding the pigskin they'd been tossing around when he noticed the pro-football star.

"Hey, it's Dean Stoddard!" he yelled.

As one, the boys swarmed around Stoddard. Tommy proffered the ball for an autograph. Dean pulled an ever-present Sharpie permanent marker from his suit-coat pocket, signed the football with a flourish, and then pointed Tommy towards the open barn door. Tommy ran a pattern through the guests. Dean floated a perfectly spiraling pass above the throng, straight into Tommy's outstretched hands. The crowd broke out into applause. Tommy raised the football in victory; Dean flashed his TV-ad smile; and Dora basked in his reflected glory.

I still admired the athletic grace of the man. He was like our Red — the fine stallion we rent out for breeding every spring. Thoroughbreds. Both of them.

And to think I could have been Mrs. Dean Stoddard.

For an instant, I felt a fleeting tinge of regret. But only for an instant.

"I just hope he doesn't cause trouble," I said.

Before Bart could respond, I turned and walked away — in the opposite direction from Dean Stoddard, but I couldn't help a backward glance to see if Bart followed. He didn't. Instead, he weaved his way through the guests to shake hands with Dean and welcome him.

That's my Bart.

Nice.

At first that's what I loved about Bart: that he was "nice"— the exact opposite of Dean. It wasn't that Dean didn't care about people. It was more like he wasn't aware other people existed. He just tooled through life grabbing for whatever he wanted...and usually getting it.

For an instant, I had to admit, the allure of being in the media spotlight on the arm of a rich and famous professional athlete appealed to me. Instead, I'm the media-anonymous wife of a struggling farmer and horse-breeder. The contrast couldn't be more stark.

The feeling of regret returned uninvited. I shook it off, regretting that I felt regret.

Bart was Dean's polar opposite. It wasn't until a few months into our marriage that I realized Bart could be overly concerned about other people. About their feelings and what they thought of him. Whereas Dean thrived on confrontation, Bart would do almost anything to avoid it...like when the repairman presented us with a bill for fixing the furnace. I was certain the man was overcharging us; but instead of haggling, Bart just paid him, even invited him in for a beer while he wrote the check. Too nice. You'd think he'd have more spine, having been a Marine and all. I've seen him handle Hulk, our bull, when he would get too frisky during mating season. Or grab Red by the ears to keep him from biting whoever was trying to saddle him. With people, however, Bart was different. He'd just smile, nod his head, and pay the bill...or let them fish in our stream, or hunt pheasant in our cornfield...whatever they wanted. Nice. Sometimes maybe too nice.

My thoughts were interrupted when the DJ introduced the bride and groom as they swept into the barn through a lattice tunnel festooned with flowers and silk. When he announced their first dance, I melted into the crowd — as far away from Dean Stoddard as possible.

That's when I noticed Grandma McGonnigle sitting in her rocking chair towards the back of the barn. That gave me as good an excuse as any. I made my way to her. She was smiling and rocking back and forth, tapping her hickory cane to the music. Eighty-six years old and as feisty as ever.

"You doing okay, Mawmaw?" I called her by the name her great-grandchildren attached to her as soon as they could talk.

"Wonderfully so. I just love weddings, don't you?"

"Yes," I admitted. "I do." And I remembered our own reception held in this very barn last year. It seemed like yesterday.

"Kimmie and Donald make such a cute couple — so much in love."

I glanced over at the wedding couple.

I remember that starry-eyed look. If only we could keep that magic alive forever.

"Every wedding I attend reminds me of my own," she said. Instead of being sad at her loss, she seemed happy for her memories.

She kept it alive, I mused. How does she do it?

"Can I get you anything, Mawmaw? A drink?"

"I'd love a glass of wine. Maybe some of that elderberry wine that Tom used to make." She smacked her lips in anticipation.

"You got it," I said.

They didn't have the homemade elderberry wine at the wet bar, but I knew where it was in the cellar of the old farmhouse. Grandpa McGonnigle made his own special brand every summer. It had been over six months since his death. Even the most recent batch would be good and fermented by now. Besides, going to the cellar would keep me away from the dance floor — and Dean Stoddard — or so I thought.

I was wrong.

As soon as I turned around, I almost bumped into him. Dora was holding onto his arm—as if to keep him from getting away, and Bart was standing right next to him.

Smiling.

Nice.

Always nice.

But right then I wanted to kill him.

How can he not know I'm trying to avoid Dean?

"Grandma," Bart said. "I want to introduce you to Dean Stoddard, the football player."

"Nice to meet you, Mr. Stoddard," she said.

"So you're Mew's grandma," Dean said as he took her hand.

"Mew?"

"Yeah," he said. "You know. As in Bartholo-mew." He laughed at his own joke.

Bart was the only other one to laugh...just to be nice.

"That was our pet name for him in college," Dean said. Laughter again. "We called him 'Mew' because he was such a pussycat." Now he was slapping his knee and laughing so hard that he spilled his drink. Dean was already well into his cups. What little restraint he might have had was long gone — probably about four drinks ago.

"Actually," I said, "Bart's more of a tiger than a pussycat."

Why am I defending him? He should be sticking up for himself.

Dean looked up at me as if just discovering there was another person in the room. It had only been four years since I'd seen him, but the befuddled stare betrayed that he was trying to place who I was.

Dora tugged on his sleeve.

"Dean, let's dance," she said.

"Just a minute, Babe," he said.

Babe. I winced. Every girl is "Babe" to him. Guess that way he doesn't have to remember our names.

"I believe you already know my wife," Bart said, as if on cue.

Dean smiled, recognition registering on his face for the first time.

"Yeah," he said. "We go back a long way." He directed his comment to Bart, just to remind him. Then he turned to me. "How're you doing, Babe? It's been a long time."

"Not long enough for me," I said. "And it's Stacie. My name is Stacie," I added, just to remind him.

"Of course. Stacie." He turned to Bart as if he needed an explanation. "Knew her from the good ol' college days." He turned back to me. "You remember the good ol' college days, don't you, Babe?"

"I'd rather not. And, once again, my name is Stacie, but you can call me Mrs. McGonnigle."

For a split second, Dean's look went blank. Then turned dark.

Uh oh, I thought when I saw the old anger return. *I've done it now.*

Music started again in the background, which seemed to distract him for a moment. The DJ announced that the dance floor was now open. Dean seized the opportunity.

"Well, then, Mrs. McGonnigle, may I have this dance?" He extended his hand and smiled that TV-ad smile of his.

I'm not buying whatever you're selling. Not this time, Mister.

I looked to Bart.

Rescue me, my eyes pleaded.

He either didn't understand my mental message or ignored it. Instead, he turned to Dora and extended his hand.

"Dora, would you like to dance?"

Dora flushed, shot Dean a withering look, and took Bart's hand. Together they drifted towards the dance floor.

If I don't dance with him, he'll either leave me standing here alone...or make a scene.

I was still debating what to do when Dean reached over, gripped my wrist, and pulled me like a reluctant dog on a leash to the dance floor.

"I never said 'yes,'" I protested.

"Yeah? Well, you didn't exactly say 'no' either."

With that he grabbed me around the waist and brought me to him. Over his shoulder, I saw Bart dancing with Dora — a respectable space between their bodies — while Dean pulled me close.

Well, at least Dean knows what he wants — and is not afraid to take it, I involuntarily thought. And Bart lets him do it. I have half a mind to play along — to make Bart jealous. Except that Bart doesn't get jealous. He's just too nice for that.

Dean loosened his octopus grip just enough so he could face me and try to look into my eyes. I looked away, towards Bart, who was oblivious to my predicament as he tried to dance and make conversation with Dora at the same time.

"You know," Dean said into my ear, "you're the only woman who ever turned me down."

"I doubt that."

"No, really. You have a mind of your own. It's one of the qualities that makes you so desirable."

I didn't answer. Instead I noted that he said "makes" me desirable — instead of "made" me desirable.

"Do you miss me?" he asked.

Typical. Everything is always about him.

"No, and I doubt I ever will."

"You sure 'bout that?" I could smell the liquor on his breath.

"Absolutely positive. I never miss. Bart taught me how to shoot too well."

It took a second, but the meaning finally registered. He threw his head back and laughed.

"So 'Mew' can shoot. I didn't think he had it in him."

"There's a lot you don't know about him," I said. "And don't call him 'Mew' in my presence. He's my husband."

There I go — defending Bart again — when he should be coming to my rescue.

The music stopped, but Dean pretended not to notice. He kept his arm around my waist and leaned close.

"I think I know how to make you miss me," he said.

I averted my face. His breath was strong enough to make me drunk if he actually kissed me.

"I have to go," I said and tried pushing myself away. I didn't think he'd let go until Bart walked up and tapped him on the shoulder.

Dean turned to face him. He seemed surprised that Bart would actually cut in to dance with his own wife.

"I have to go," I repeated.

"Where?" Dean asked.

Before I could answer, Bart took his arm and turned him just enough to distract him.

"Dean," he said, "how about I show you Red."

"Red?" Dean's muddled mind derailed for a moment, but long enough for me to back away — out of his reach.

"You know. Red," Bart said. "The Stallion. About using him for breeding." He turned to me and explained. "Dean's starting to breed horses for his ranch — riding trails and all — up near Big Bear Lake."

Big Bear Lake, I quickly calculated. About three or four hours north. Thank God it's not any closer.

"We were just discussing stud fees," Bart said.

"Right!" Dean brightened and turned to me. "You know all 'bout studs, don't you, Babe? Remember the good ol' days?"

"Excuse me," I said. "I promised Grandma a drink."

I have to get out of here before I grab a pitchfork and skewer him to the wall.

"Wanna' hear 'bout the good ol' days with Stacie?" Dean turned to Dora.

"No, I don't," I heard Dora whisper.

At least you found out what he's like before you got too far into it. *Lucky for you, Dora. Get out while you can.*

"Come on," Bart said. I could sense him steering Dean away while I made my way to the back door. "You can tell me all about it while we check out Red. After all, you want to make sure you're getting your money's worth, don't you?"

I'll skewer both of them to the wall!

My tears ran hot as I burst through the back door and ran to the house. Rather than going to the cellar, I went straight to the kitchen and splashed cold water onto my face at the sink.

Bart, the man I married, isn't a man at all! He's not "nice" — he's a blasted "pussycat" — just like Dean said. I cried bitterly in the discovery that my husband — the man I vowed to spend the rest of my life with, to love — is a coward.

My vision cleared as white-hot anger took over.

I looked up from the sink and out the back window. There they were. Bart holding Dean by the elbow — guiding him to the new stable where we kept Red.

Like they're best buddies.

Volcanic blood flushed my cheeks just thinking about it.

Well, even if "Mew" doesn't have the stuffing to defend me, I can still defend myself. I don't know what I'll say or do, but it would at least be something. Nobody is going to treat me like that in my own house.

I watched them disappear into the stable before I left the kitchen. Then I went out the back screen door, and headed down the path to confront both of them at the same time.

Good thing I don't have a pitchfork. They'd charge me with double murder, but I wouldn't get convicted if there were any women on the jury. They'd all agree it was justifiable homicide.

As I approached the stable, I heard Dean's raise his voice.

"You're telling me to leave?"

"I'm asking you politely to leave," Bart corrected in a soft, controlled tone.

Nice.

I slowed my pace and listened.

"And if I don't, what are you going to do 'bout it?"

"I don't want to fight," Bart said quietly. "But I'm asking you to leave. Quietly. To avoid any further embarrassment."

There was a long pause.

"I remember now...in college...you used to say that you never learned to fight."

"That's right," Bart said.

"Well, then, Mew," Dean said, "it's about time you had your first lesson..."

The words hadn't fully escaped Dean's mouth when I heard a sound — like a "whoosh" — then a thud and someone gasping, choking.

He's killing him. Dean is killing Bart, I thought.

Fear anchored me in place. My feet couldn't move. Then I heard Bart's soft voice again.

"You're going to be okay. Just breathe. In and out. That's it. Would you like some water?"

Footsteps. Something sloshing in Red's water bucket. More footsteps.

"Here. Drink this. Easy now."

Deep, sucking breaths.

"Better? Now let me help you up. You okay?"

I backed towards the house quietly.

"It hurts," Dean said. Voice raspy. "You said...you never...learned to fight..."

"That's right," Bart said.

"What...the hell...was...that?" Dean could barely choke the words out.

"The Marines never taught me how to fight. They only taught me how to maim or kill. Got it?"

For a long moment there was no answer. Finally, a voice that I almost didn't recognize — higher pitched than I'd heard it before — faint, almost weepy in its pleading.

"Don't...hurt...me..."

"I won't. As long as you do what I said. You're going to leave...quietly."

"Yes...sir..."

I hurried back into the house through the rear screen door before they left the stable. Then I remembered Grandma's wine. I retreated to the cellar and took my time picking out a good strong vintage of Grandpa McGonnigle's special elderberry brew. By the time I got back to the old barn, neither Bart nor Dean Stoddard were anywhere in sight. Dora was dancing with one of the groomsmen — and seemed to be enjoying herself.

I grabbed a glass from one of the tables. Glass in one hand and bottle in the other, I made my way across the dance floor to where Grandma was rocking away merrily.

I handed her the glass and was struggling with the cork when Bart walked up — as nonchalantly as you please.

"Need help with that?"

I handed him the bottle. He whipped out his Swiss Army knife, flipped up the corkscrew attachment, and deftly opened the bottle of wine.

"Where's Dean?" I asked.

"Oh, he had to leave."

"So suddenly?" I feigned ignorance.

"Yeah. Slipped on one of Red's giant road apples and fell," he said.

"Did he get hurt?"

"Naw...more embarrassed than anything. Fell right into it. Got horseshit all over his suit."

I took the wine bottle from his hand and began to pour it as I glanced at the dance floor.

"What about Dora? He left her without a ride."

Bart looked up and noticed Dora slow dancing with the handsome groomsman.

"She'll be fine," he said. That ever-so-slight twisted smile flashed in the corner of his mouth.

I turned my back so Bart wouldn't see; but Grandma caught the glint of a tear when I offered her the glass.

"Why, honey, what's wrong?" she asked.

"Nothing," I said. "I guess the elderberry wine made me think of Grandpa Tom's passing — and how much you must miss him."

It really wasn't what I was thinking; but I had to come up with something to say.

"Aw, honey. Don't feel bad. Don't you know? That's how every good marriage ends."

All I could do was nod.

So true. That's how every good marriage should end.

Bart took my hand.

"Dance?" he asked.

"I'd love to."

He pulled me towards him and I felt his strong arm about my waist, my hand resting on his solid shoulder.

Nice.

They say at the end of every rainbow, there is a pot of gold
And so I began my eager search many, long years ago.

It started on a sun-filled morning in the Springtime month of
May
When all of nature bloomed and the newborn rabbits played.
By afternoon the storm clouds gathered
Dark, foreboding and bold
I knew that now I'd have my chance to find my pot of gold.

On a hot and humid day in the middle Summertime,
I strolled along a woodland path under the pungent pine
And stopped awhile to rest and dream beside a murmuring
stream.
When I awoke the storm clouds gathered
Dark, foreboding and bold
I knew that now I'd have my chance to find my pot of gold.

When the golden days of Autumn came and the vivid leaves
blew down,
With scents of wood-burned smoke and apple cider all round,
I watched while storm clouds gathered
Dark, foreboding and bold
I knew that now I'd have my chance to find my pot of gold.

It is now bleak mid-Winter when snowflakes fill the air.
I sit beside the crackling fire and nestle in my chair
Reminiscing of days gone by, of true and faithful friends,
Of a loving family, and a husband's devotion that never ends.

My "rainbow" is filled with grateful love, as much as it can
hold.
Because I searched within my heart, I found my pot of gold.

CLAUDIO
Arthur Powers

There were three men in the jeep, and he wasn't even the handsomest. They stopped to drink water. The other two went back to the jeep, but he stayed for a few moments in the cool front room of the thatched roofed adobe farmhouse, drinking more water dipped in an aluminum cup from the clay pot. He had dark hair, light skin, clean fingernails; his eyes and face looked sensitive, and suddenly Maria das Dores felt embarrassed, aware of her dusty bare feet and the small bulge of the child in her belly beneath her faded blue dress.

"I didn't know anyone would be stopping," she said, "or I wouldn't look so messy." Her hand went up and pushed back a wisp of light brown hair from her temple. His eyes alighted on her, and he smiled.

"You shouldn't worry about that," he said. "You're very pretty."

It was a light compliment, she knew, the kind men from the city make easily. Yet he'd said it, and his eyes looked as if he'd meant it.

"Claudio," one of the other men shouted from the jeep. "Let's go!"

***

The brown palm-straw broom set aside; dust still rising from where she'd swept the dirt floor, hazing the afternoon sunlight. Carefully, she set the small chipped mirror on the wooden table and looked into it. Hazel eyes, smooth browned skin, small nose, square chin. Pretty — they'd all said she was pretty when she was seventeen, but that was

153

five years and three children ago, and who ever said she was pretty now? Except this afternoon...

***

João sat silently on the stool, eating his supper, one huge hand cradling the tin plate, the other clutching the spoon as it dug into the rice and beans and shoveled them into his mouth. Click of the spoon on the plate, whish of lifting, chewing; click of the spoon on the plate, whish of lifting, chewing.

***

She lay awake in the hammock, sleepless in the black night. Claudio. They'd called out his name, Claudio. He would be standing in the front room. He would reach out and gently touch her cheek.

***

The small statue of Our Lady of Aparecida stood on the tiny wooden shelf against the bare adobe brick wall, her black face looking sightlessly at Maria das Dores, her black hands held palms forward, her blue robe decked with glass jewels.

"Mother of God," Maria das Dores whispered. "Mother of God..."

II

Pretty, they said she was, the day at Colher she'd been a bride: Maria das Dores, the prettiest of the brides. There had been seven couples getting married in the clearing under the giant mango tree; the priest came through on his yearly visit, and everyone for miles around was there. Seventeen years old, and João standing beside her, twenty-five, independent with his five *alqueires* of land, large and strong and quiet, handsome.

***

Sometimes Claudio would come in the day time — whether it was morning or early afternoon, she could never decide — driving over the hill in the jeep, alone. He would step out of the jeep and close its door behind him, looking up the little slope to the farmhouse, and she would be standing in the front door. She would be wearing her best dress — the white one with pink flowers — and would have just bathed — but how could that be if it were still only early afternoon? — but maybe she was going out somewhere special. She wasn't heavy — was the baby born already? — but that would be months away. Maybe she was heavy still, but he didn't mind; he thought she was pretty, anyway — and he would walk hesitatingly up the slope, looking at her with sensitive, kind eyes, and a few feet away he would stop, and they would look at each other and he would softly say, "das Dores" — but how could he say that? He didn't know her name. He would have asked. At some other farmhouse he and his friends would have stopped, and he would have mentioned that they'd passed by a little farm on a hill, and the people would say, "that must be João and das Dores," then would go on, the way country people do, to talk about them. Claudio would listen. "She was one of the prettiest girls around." "She had the best marks in her class the year she graduated," — but that would only be fourth grade, maybe he wouldn't like that — "She's a good wife and a fine mother..." He would listen, outwardly calm but fascinated inside. So he'd know her name, and he'd reach out and touch her cheek...

***

"The rice will be ready to harvest next week," João said. "I'll be trading work days with Zé Farias and Sebastião. I'll have to take food."

***

Sometimes João had died. It would be all right then.

155

He'd died — maybe just died, of a heart attack. He'd go to heaven because he was a good man. She was a widow. It was the seventh day, and she was at the cemetery with everyone there. They were all thinking, "Poor das Dores, what is she going to do, alone with two children and another on the way?" Or maybe "with three children" — yes, the baby would be born and in her arms and she wouldn't be heavy. They'd hear the jeep drive up, and the others would look because cars weren't very common here — they wouldn't recognize the young man getting out of the jeep. Das Dores wouldn't look; she'd be praying, but she'd know who it was. She'd turn away from the grave and he'd be standing there, hesitantly, not knowing if she felt what he felt. And his eyes would look into her eyes...

***

"I'm going to chain one of the dogs down in the lower field," João said. "The wild pigs are getting at the mandioc crop."

***

"Das Dores," he would say, and he'd reach out and touch her cheek — but how could he do that there at the cemetery with all those people around? No, it would be later when she was back at the house, her mother and sister helping inside, and she would have stepped out the front door as she saw him walking up toward the house. He'd touch her cheek and say, "das Dores," looking at her with those caring eyes — yet with passion in his eyes, passion held in, controlled because he loved her. She'd look down at the ground and say softly, "Claudio," and he'd know she'd been thinking of him, and the words would come tumbling out of his mouth — how he'd thought of her since that day he'd stopped for water, how he'd stayed away because he knew she was married, but then he'd heard just yesterday and he'd come as quickly as he could

— he loved her, he wanted to take care of her and the children, he wanted…. "Claudio, not now," she would say. She was just newly a widow; she needed time. He would wait for her, he would say — could she only give him a promise? And she would look into his eyes and whisper, "Yes."

***

"Pedro and I are going this morning to slaughter his steer."

***

The slow silence of empty hours alone in the house.

***

"Mother of God…" It's not real, Maria das Dores. "Mother of God, I know it's not real. But what else do I have?"

III

He would almost always be in the house now, and her life rotated around him. She cleaned the four rooms with extra spirit, sweeping the dirt floor, dusting the few pieces of rough wooden furniture, decorating the house with flowers and green branches, with pictures from a magazine her mother had once brought back from Goiania, singing to herself happily, showing him what a good wife she could be: taking care of the babies with joy, conscious of his eyes on her. She wouldn't let him know, of course, that she was thinking of him; she made special meals for João and got herself pretty for him when he came home, greeting him warmly — after all, he would be watching. Let him envy João a little, thinking how lucky João was to have such a wife. Let him want her for his wife. Some day, some how, it would happen. But for now, let him be a little envious.

***

She lay awake in the hammock. Claudio would have wanted to kiss her that afternoon; she'd turned her face away, but he'd held her strong and close in his arms, and she would have stayed there a moment before she pushed him away.

Now she felt him near. His face was close to hers, and his finger reached out and stroked her cheek. "Maria das Dores, I love you," he said. She reached up and held his hand in hers, then felt his other hand gently touching her shoulder, her breast, her side, her thigh.

"Mother of God, help me," she whispered. She shifted in her hammock and stared into the black empty darkness of the room.

IV

After supper she talked to João, loving — laughing and alive — flushed with joy — weaving little incidents of the day into a bright tapestry of words, because she knew — although João couldn't — that he would be there watching them.

João's dark eyes followed her as she moved around the kitchen, sparking, reflecting her liveliness.

"So I picked the baby up, and there he was with yellow flowers clutched in his hand..."

"Das Dores." João was looking at her.

She went over and sat on a stool near him, looking at him, attentive. He would want a wife like that, to listen to him when he came home.

João reached out and took her hand in his big, callused hand. He looked down, tracing the toe of his sandal along the dirt floor.

"This afternoon..." His lips were searching for words; he was always slow to talk. "Right almost at nightfall... the sunlight...it was on the rice. It made it look all gold. I thought..."

He stopped talking, and his eyes came up to her eyes.

"Do you ever feel a kind of... heaviness?"

For an instant she was startled, thinking of the baby bulging in her belly.

V

"Did you see how pretty das Dores is," she overheard Dona Lucia say to Tia Ana outside the kitchen as the wedding dancers whirled by. And later, old Chico Pardo, half drunk, had lifted up his arms and shouted, "She's the prettiest of the brides." And Maria das Dores had been embarrassed because she knew it was true.

***

When was it that she stopped wanting João to touch her? Not at first. At first she *queria ele bem* — as people said — wanted him a lot. They spent days together, laughing, working, playing, making love. But then came the bad harvest, and the babies, and the long hot days. She noticed how sweaty and dirty he was, how hard his hands were. He talked of fields and corn and pigs. When he wanted her, he wanted her hard, dropping right off to sleep in the hammock. When she was pregnant, though, she could get him mostly to leave her alone.

***

She was restless in the hammock, half hoping, half afraid Claudio would come. He would touch her cheek and whisper, "Maria das Dores, I love you." His hand would gently touch her breast, pass over her stomach, touch her thigh...

She felt a hand touch her in the dark — a big hard hand — João, driven — she knew — by his need for her — and

159

her body alive and ready and waiting. She reached up and pulled him toward her.

***

João looked at her, standing in the kitchen doorway in the morning light. Something in his eyes, something new, or maybe something from a long time ago.

He said, "Maria das Dores..."

"What is it?"

Silence. Chickens clucking; breeze rustling palm leaves.

"Nothing."

He turned and walked down toward the fields.

***

Sometimes Claudio would arrive silently in the afternoon when she was all alone. She would somehow know he was coming — and what he would want — but still.....

***

"Mother of God, help me."

Look out the window, Maria das Dores.

She rose and went to the window and looked down the gentle slope to where the fields lay. She saw João struggling up the path, stooped under the weight of a full sack of rice — saw him startlingly clearly, as if all the air between them were crystal glass: his bare feet, his torn trousers, his home spun shirt. And for the first time she saw an old man within the young one: hands hard with labor, face lined with worry, body crooked with heavy loads.

"Mother of God," she whispered. "Forgive me."

VI

Still, it took four days to do what she had to do.

160

It was a moonlit night, and she went out into the back yard to a place at the split rail fence. She knew he would be on the other side, where the pasture sloped down gently, open and free.

She stopped by the fence and listened, listened to the night sounds of the land, the insects singing, the distant *chee* of a monkey.

She spoke out loud.

"Goodbye, Claudio."

He would understand. He would always understand.

"Goodbye," she said again, and she saw him turn and go walking down the hill. She stood for a moment more, then started back to the farmhouse where her husband lay in his hammock, snoring, fast asleep.

Sylvie was sixteen. She and her best friend, Mariah, had just come from the clinic. Each girl had told her parents she was spending the day at the other's house, so no one would question their whereabouts.

Sylvie had driven Mariah's car all the way down to Kansas City, Kansas — the farthest she'd ever driven. The girls had headed up to the forest preserve after the procedure. Mariah was too quiet on the ride up, and Sylvie sensed her friend needed some alone time. A walk in the woods would help clear her head.

She glanced over at her friend as she eased the car into a parking space. Mariah didn't look well. Her face was flushed, and her body was trembling.

"Are you cold?"

Mariah shook her head.

"Car sick. Need fresh air."

Sylvie raced around to the passenger side of the car and helped her friend out. She could feel her burning up through her sweater.

"I think we should get you to the ER."

"No! They'll know! They'll tell!"

Just then, Mariah doubled over and vomited.

"Stay," she spit bile onto the ground. "Stay with me...please."

Sylvie looked around. There was no one around, nowhere to call for help.

"Come on, let's go back to the car."

"No," Mariah rasped. "The bench…"

About fifty feet ahead sat a wooden bench, so Sylvie wrapped her friend's arm around her neck, supported her waist, and managed to get her the distance.

"I'm worried," Sylvie said. "You look really sick. What are we going to do?"

"Nothing," the flushed girl responded. "Stay here. I just…need…rest."

Sylvie lifted Mariah's legs up onto the bench, then folded her own jacket like a pillow under the girl's head.

The metallic odor of blood reached her nose before she saw the stain spreading out from between her friend's legs, darkening her jeans to a rust red color.

She tried to keep her voice even.

"I've got to go. I need to get you help."

Mariah gripped Sylvie's wrist.

"Stay," she whispered weakly, "I'm afraid."

What were just minutes seemed like hours to Sylvie as she pondered what to do to help her friend. She couldn't leave her, but Mariah needed help — much more help than Sylvie could give. The blood scared her. Could she be dying? Or was it just routine bleeding from the procedure? She didn't want to ask. She didn't want to scare her friend.

She reached out and held Mariah's hand. It was freezing cold. Her face was pale, and her body trembled. The blood had trickled down through the slats of the bench and pooled on the packed dirt in a shape that reminded her of a broken heart.

"I have to get you some help. You're really sick."

Mariah was too weak to protest. Impulsively, Sylvie leaned over and kissed her friend's forehead.

"I promise. I promise I'll be right back."

The words of the promise were the last words her friend was to hear on this earth.

***

It had been years since Sylvie had puked involuntarily. Yet, here she stood, doubled over, the meager contents of last night's dinner traveling the wrong way up her slender gullet. She spit bile into the sink and groped for her toothbrush.

I can't get sick now. I have a shoot in a few days.

She straightened up and checked the mirror. Black circles shadowed her distinctively violet eyes; her olive skin looked ashy, and her ebony hair was dull and lifeless. She thrust a costly jar of rich moisturizer in the microwave and let it warm for a few seconds. Dabbing minty foam from the corners of her mouth, Sylvie then splashed cool water on her face and blotted it dry with a luxurious Egyptian cotton hand towel. She slathered her face and throat with the cream and then let her bathrobe fall to the floor. The image facing her was...satisfactory, at least from the neck down.

"This is my body. This is my livelihood. I need to *not* be sick," she insisted.

Her phone chortled.

Remington.

Rem was not only her agent, but a mentor. In the cutthroat world of modeling, he was a refreshing anomaly. He was an astute businessman, but he had a soft side. She knew he had helped a number of the girls' families out of difficult situations, and he was kind, especially to the younger models. Everyone knew they could depend on Remington Scott.

She let the call go to voice mail. Half a dozen weeks ago he'd brought over her new contract — which made her the highest paid model in the agency — and the celebration had turned physical. It was a fun night. He was a skilled lover. But he seemed a little too connected now whenever they spoke. She didn't want strings. Her aspirations certainly didn't involve an ongoing relationship. Relationships could be messy. And her life plans were nestled safely in an impenetrable box and all tied up with a pretty pink ribbon.

***

Sylvie was bored. The shoot had gone well. However, the occasional vomiting had continued. She picked up her phone to call Remington to see if there was a doctor he could recommend, and she realized that he hadn't phoned recently. Reluctantly, she admitted to herself that she missed him.

"Hey, stranger."

She heard Rem sigh. "Sylvie, I... now isn't a good time."

This wasn't like Rem. He always had time for everyone.

"Is everything okay?"

"My brother," his voice broke, "my brother died. We just got back from the funeral."

Rem's brother? She didn't even know he *had* a brother. What do you say to someone who's lost a sibling?

"Okay, well, I'm sorry. Uh, sending warm thoughts to you and your family."

"Sylvie, we could use prayers more than anything. He has a family. We have a lot of decisions to make here."

She slammed her body back into the couch and tossed her phone on the nearest cushion. Pray? A kaleidoscope of images swirled through her mind: stained glass windows, a chalice, her family kneeling in prayer.

When had she *stopped* praying?

Generic music played and cutlery tinkled in the background as the waiter led Sylvie and Rem to their table.

Their dinner was sprinkled with awkward small talk. Sylvie didn't want to bring up the death of Rem's brother. She had kept things on the surface the past couple of weeks. It seemed too intimate to be talking about his family, his sorrow. She avoided pain religiously.

In the cab on the way back to Sylvie's apartment, Rem put his arm around her.

"I wanted you to be the first to know: I'm selling my condo."

She couldn't conceal the shock on her face. "No! You're kidding me!"

Rem's two bedroom apartment was located on West 52nd Street and was wrapped in glass windows, affording it spectacular views. She secretly coveted his place.

Emotions played over his chiseled features, and his eyes moistened.

"I've been reflecting a lot about my life since my brother's death, and I've decided to get out of the business. I'm leaving the agency."

So many thoughts ran through Sylvie's head, the biggest being that she was losing the one person she'd counted on for so long. There weren't many trustworthy people in the modeling business, but Rem had always done right by her.

"Chandler was my twin. We were so close as kids but, life just got away from us...from *me*. He was a great guy. Talented carpenter. He has...*had*...a wife...two kids."

Rem ran a hand through his tawny hair.

"I need a change. I need to do something...meaningful

with my life. Living in the city doesn't seem to have any appeal for me anymore."

A lump formed in her throat. She swallowed it. Damn. She had let herself get too attached, and here she was, feeling emotions better left to others. She remembered the orange pills tucked safely in her medicine cabinet and made a note to take two before bed tonight.

"You're upset right now. Why don't you hold off making any decisions until things calm down?"

"No," he was determined. "I've put off my whole life waiting for the money, the power, the prestige. I'm such an idiot! I have more money than I could ever need. Why didn't I see that?"

He sat up straight and took her gently by the shoulders. "My condo is on the market, and I just put in an offer on a home in Huntington Bay. I want to be near my niece and nephew. I want to be a part of their lives. I want that for myself, too: a family."

He peered deeply into her eyes. "Don't you ever think about all of that, Sylvie? About having...more?"

She broke his gaze. "Of course, I do. I'm the highest paid model at the agency. Next stop, highest paid in the states."

"But...but if you achieve your goal, then you'll want to go higher. Do you realize you'll never be satisfied?"

Sylvie's brows came together. She didn't like this conversation. It was an intrusion. "Isn't it good to have goals? To shoot for something?"

"What happens if you reach your goal? Will you be happy then?"

She blinked her eyes as if to flush him — and this discussion — out of her mind.

"I...I don't know. I've never thought about that. I just keep going and don't look back."

"It's good not to look back, but sometimes we need to look *around*. To see the opportunities in front of us."

Sylvie sighed in frustration. "Opportunities for what?"

"To *give*. My whole life has been about the Almighty Me. I never gave anyone a second thought. Now, in the blink of an eye, my brother's gone — *gone* — and his family needs me. And it was like a two-by-four to the side of my head. What the hell have I been doing all this time?"

"That's not true. I know you've helped some of the girls' families."

"Because ultimately it benefitted me. I've never been generous just to be generous. But my brother didn't have a lot of insurance, and he was self-employed. His family really needs me right now. I can't live just for me anymore. That chapter in my life needs to be over. It *is* over."

Sylvie wrinkled her nose. "If you think this will make you happy, then I'm happy for you, Rem."

There. A nice, neat ending. Cue Rem to exit. Permanently.

Except she wasn't sure if that's what she really wanted. In her mind's eye, the future had included him in some way, just without strings — on her terms.

"I'm still here for you, to keep you grounded. To make sure you don't get so close to the sun that you start to burn."

She covered her face with her hands. This was too real, too raw, too much to handle. Skating on the surface of life was infinitely easier than plunging in.

He drew her to him in an attempt to comfort her.

But she didn't want to be comforted. She wanted to be comfortable.

***

Still reeling from Rem's epiphany, Sylvie made it a

point to party. She hung out with everyone who was anyone and took every photo op possible.

But it didn't help. Something deep inside her felt as if it had been shattered. She was angry at Rem. Why did he do this to her — make her a part of his inane come-to-Jesus moment? Why couldn't he have just quietly faded away?

She needed a vacation. She thought of maybe going to the Caribbean, but something stopped her. Instead, Sylvie picked up her phone and dialed her sister.

"Long time no hear," June's warm voice sounded. "How is my jet-setting sister?"

"Eh, I think I need to come home and see Doc Bennett."

"Hey, what's going on? You okay?" June's voice betrayed her concern.

"I think I might have a gluten intolerance. My abdomen has been feeling tight lately, and I've been vomiting a lot."

"So, no fancy New York doctor, just good old, dependable Doc Bennett, huh?"

***

Sylvie flew out the next day, and June met her at the airport in Kansas City. They represented two extremes in their looks. Sylvie's dark, exotic beauty contrasted June's earthy, wholesome looks. The younger woman's strawberry blond curls danced as she sprinted forward, and the women wrapped each other in a tight hug. Sylvie noticed phones flashing as people began to recognize her, but she ignored it, instead focusing on June.

Sylvie's olive complexion was inherited from her biological mother, who had died of a brain aneurysm when her daughter was just eight months old. Lillian and Don Stonebridge, her aunt and uncle, were Sylvie's only surviving family, named in the will as her guardians. June came along several months later, and that made for a small, but happy, family.

"How are Mom and Dad?"

"Excited. They're waiting at the house. Mom has cleaned at least six times since your phone call. She wanted to make those cinnamon rolls you used to love, but I told her to hold off until the after you hear what the doctor has to say."

"Good call, sis."

"So, did you get airsick on the plane? Need a basin?" June's keys jingled as she unlocked her car.

Sylvie grinned at her sister's motherliness. Although June was younger, she was the caretaker of the two.

"No, the vomiting seems to just happen in the morning, and I'm usually fine for the rest of the day."

Brows furrowed, June gave her a sidelong glance.

"You're *sure* it's a gluten intolerance?"

"I think so. I mean, what else could it be?"

***

Doc Bennett was as old as dirt and still going. He had delivered June and just about every other child in Gower, Missouri for decades, it seemed. The doctor had been family physician to Lillian, Don, June, and Sylvie Stonebridge ever since the inception of their family.

"I can do some blood testing to start," he commented, in response to her list of symptoms. "But first we need to do a good, old-fashioned exam. When was your last pap?"

Sylvie squirmed. She didn't like doctors, doctor visits, or anything having to do with the medical profession.

"Um...I don't remember?" Guilt dripped from her voice.

"Now is as good a time as any. Annie!" he called for his nurse. "Come on in here and assist me with this exam, please."

Annie appeared in an instant.

He winked at Sylvie. "Quick and painless."

The ancient doctor slipped from the room as Annie handed her a paper gown.

***

Sylvie sat in the comfy chair opposite Doc Bennett's carved walnut desk.

"When was the last time you had a menstrual cycle?"

"I, um, don't get my period regularly, so I don't really keep track. Maybe a couple months? Three?"

He tented his fingers and leaned back in his chair. He looked as if he were dealing with shoulder angels. Finally, he expelled a drawn out sigh.

"When I did your exam, it was pretty evident that you're, ah, pregnant. My guess would be about nine weeks along, from the size of things."

The room shattered around her like a plate glass window in a tornado. Sylvie's lungs stopped working, and she felt things going black. The world fell away, and all she was left with was a memory — a horrific nightmare of a memory — one that she had blocked out for many years.

She came to with Doc Bennett and her mother peering over her.

"Oh, honey, you gave us such a scare!"

"Feeling better now?" asked the doctor.

She nodded, but tears pooled in her eyes, and she couldn't speak.

Wordlessly, the doctor checked her pupils and took her pulse. Nodding in satisfaction, he walked toward the door of his office.

"I'll give the two of you some privacy then."

Sylvie's heart began to race. What should she do? She was pregnant. *Pregnant!* An abortion was out of the question. Just thinking of it brought the traumatic memories to life again. She blinked hard, as if to purge them from her mind's eye. But she couldn't have the baby, either. It would ruin her body, her livelihood. Fear gripped her heart.

Lillian put her hand on Sylvie's forehead.

"Doc said to come right away, that you had passed out. Honey, what happened?" Her voice echoed love and concern.

"He didn't tell you?"

She sat down in the chair next to her daughter's and took her hand.

"I think whatever this is, it needs to come from you."

Lillian shifted in her chair and tucked her pale, bobbed hair behind her ear.

"Honey, you've been so remote these last few years... actually, it started a long time ago, after...after we lost Mariah. You changed somehow, and I wanted to help you. I still want to help you. But I don't know how."

She cupped her daughter's cheek in her hand.

"Tell me how."

Tears streamed down Sylvie's face, and she shook her head. She couldn't speak, couldn't focus her thoughts. She felt her life — her carefully planned life — spinning out of control. The facade was collapsing. And what was left underneath?

***

There was a soft knock on the door of Sylvie's childhood bedroom; then the door opened, and Lillian walked in carrying a plastic bin.

"Here are some things I thought you might want to go through."

Sylvie peered at her mother through swollen eyes.

"They're some baby clothes, mementos. I've been meaning to share this with you for a long time, but..." her voice trailed. "I'm going to make us some tea, and when I come back we'll see if you're up to it."

Sylvie managed a nod, then fell back on her pillow. She was numb. No thoughts or feelings dwelled within.

Lillian came back in with a tray topped with two mugs of fragrant tea. She set the tray on a desk, then sat down on a stool in front of the bin. Lillian removed a pink, frilly one-piece baby outfit.

"This is what you were wearing the day we brought you home. When we got the phone call, we couldn't get to you fast enough. We didn't want you to be away from family." A sigh escaped her lips. "Your father — my brother — he always prayed for a child. He would have been so happy to know he had a baby girl." A knife cut through Sylvie's heart.

"But he died before he even knew about me. So much death," she whispered.

"Well, it was a war. Operation Desert Storm claimed a number of lives." Lillian's voice was thick. "I miss him. I wish you could have known him. And I'm sorry that you didn't."

War. Death. Blood.

The images came back again, flashing in Sylvie's brain like machine gunfire. She curled up into a fetal position and whimpered. Arms immediately encircled her.

"What is it, Sylvie? What is haunting you and hurting so much?" Lillian's whisper was full of love.

Sylvie sobbed for a long time, but allowed herself to be held.

Through tears she said, "I was there, Mom. It was me. I called the police."

Lillian's eyes became round and her mouth opened, but no words came out.

"Mariah. I...I took her. I was with her. Oh, God! I left her! I left her alone! Mariah died alone because of *me*!"

Her mother was shaking her head from side to side.

"You told us you had a fight and she went out on her own. That she had taken your jacket — that's why it was there." Lillian's freckled face crumpled. "You've been carrying this around for all these years. Have you never told anyone?"

Sylvie shook her head.

"Oh, honey, you've been through so much."

They lie together, arms entwined, heart to heart — mother and daughter, hurting, grieving, healing.

***

A slant of light filtered through the window and fell onto Sylvie's face, softly waking her. She had fallen asleep in her mother's embrace like an infant, and the awakening, though gentle, seemed harsh in the light of day.

A faint knock sounded at the door as it eased open. Lillian appeared with a mug of tea. She approached the bed and laid a hand on her daughter's forehead.

"I'm glad you're up. I was hoping we could have some quiet time together this morning. Are you feeling like company?"

Sylvie's eyes filled with tears as she nodded.

"I'm glad you told me the story of what happened with Mariah. I know you're not a mother yet..."

Sylvie winced.

"But someday you'll learn that every parent wants to share their child's burdens. You're not alone, Sylvie."

"Will you tell Dad and June?"

"That is for you to decide, not me, honey. There is someone, however, that I would like you to speak to if you're ready."

***

The priest's office smelled faintly of old books and incense. It was pleasant enough to relax her a bit, yet she still sat stiffly in the overstuffed chair across from a carved wood desk. A fortyish African American clergyman was settled in its chair.

"So, Lillian said you have some things to work through and might need a bit of help. If you'd like to talk, I'm happy to listen."

Yes. It was time she faced it. It was time to move through the grief and move on from it. She was tired of living a double life. One a charmed life of a successful model, the other full of secrets and self-loathing.

And so the story spilled out: Mariah getting pregnant, her shame, not wanting to tell, her tragic death, and Sylvie's cover up. And all the other ways she had hurt herself and alienated her family. So much pain. It all flowed out of her now, out of her soul, and, it seemed, onto the priest who sat before her, for his face reflected empathy and love.

"Would you like to make a Confession, Sylvie?"

It had been so long since she'd been to the sacrament that at first she hesitated, but then nodded.

He put on his purple stole and looked at her with compassion.

"I'm so sorry for your pain. What happened to Mariah and her child was a tragedy. But you were sixteen. Back then you didn't have the judgment that you would have as an adult. Now that you're more mature, you see that poor choices were made, but you are sorry for them, and now you have confessed them with the assurance that the Lord is merciful and that He forgives."

Tears made trails down her cheeks.

"I talked to your mother at length this week, Sylvie. She loves you, and she's concerned about how you've distanced yourself from your family. She said it's almost like you're trying to prove you don't need them."

Pain knifed though her heart. "No! I, I *do* need them. It's just...I'm not good enough."

"Good enough for your family, or good enough for God?"

"Both."

"And did this way of thinking begin with Mariah's death?"

Sylvie thought a moment. "I guess it did. It just seemed then that my whole world turned dark. I became obsessed with the fact that I was adopted and convinced myself that they couldn't possibly love me just for me. I thought, I *still* think, that if I were rich and beautiful they would have to love me."

Fr. Rodney put his head down for a moment. "I think it's *you* that doesn't love you." His voice was quiet. "I think that you began to think that your abandonment of Mariah was so terrible that it actually made you unlovable."

Sylvie doubled over as if she'd been hit. Her arms hugged her middle, and she sobbed. The priest came out from behind his desk and knelt down next to Sylvie's chair. He stayed with her as her sobs ebbed.

"But that's not true. The Lord gave you loving parents, a devoted sister, and a good home. The truth is you are lovable because God made you that way. He made you *because* He loves you. You don't need to earn His love. You are sorry, and He forgives you. The problem is, you haven't forgiven yourself."

She sniffed. "How can I?"

"Find a good therapist, pray for healing, come and talk to me as often as you'd like. Those will do for a good start."

A tiny spark of hope fluttered in her soul.

"And have a good heart-to-heart with your family. Share your pain. They will want to help you through it."

"Do you really think I can heal from this? But how...how can I make this up to Mariah?"

"For a penance, I was going to have you pray once a day for two weeks for a child who is in danger of being aborted. Pray for the child and the child's mother and father."

Her blood ran cold.

"Father," she whispered, "I have something else to speak with you about."

***

The late March weather was unusually mild, and a gentle breeze picked up some strands of Sylvie's hair as she bent over the grave and placed the ample bouquet of Gerbera daisies on the earth.

She tried to pray, but no words came. Instead, she leaned her head on the gnarled tree next to the burial plot and began to weep. Grief, which had long resided in the depths of her soul, began its exodus.

***

She slipped into the pew beside her mother, who reached out and squeezed her hand.

There was plenty of time before Mass to pray her penance. She prayed for her parents and sister, that her relationship with them might be restored. She prayed for Rem, that he might find peace and joy in his new life.

But she was afraid to pray for the life within her. She was still afraid to have the baby, to lose the perfect body that had always defined her.

Mass began, and the prayers came right back to Sylvie, almost as if she hadn't been absent from church for many years. Her mind wandered during the sermon, dwelling on the changes that were about to happen to her body: the stretch marks, the cellulite, the loss of her livelihood. But the words of the priest broke through her musings, and she snapped to attention.

On the day before He was to suffer,

He took bread in His holy and venerable hands, and with eyes raised to heaven

to you, O God His almighty Father,

giving you thanks, He said the blessing, broke the bread and gave it to His disciples, saying,

Take this, all of you, and eat it,

For This is My Body,

Which will be given up for you.

Images flashed through her mind like lightning.

Her father, giving his life for his country, for his daughter.

Her mother, giving birth to her, nursing her.

Lillian and Don, welcoming her, nurturing her, loving her.

Rem, changing his life for his niece and nephew.

And an image of a child in her womb, needing her, depending on her.

She placed her hand on her abdomen, willing the child to feel her touch.

"This is my body," she whispered, "to be given up for you."

GOOD FOR HER
Erin McCole Cupp

A yellow and black sign on the right warned, "DO NOT PICK UP HITCHHIKERS." Meanwhile, a giant semi surged past her on the left, blasting his horn. Leah swore under her breath.

Under her breath? What for? There was nobody sharing the car space with her. Not anymore.

She was almost at the mountain's peak. There, through thick morning fog, was the blue sign with its white arrow, pointing to a left-hand turn-off: SCI Frackville. She turned left and joined a short line of other cars heading through a tall gate framed by razor wire. Visiting day.

"Well, Gran," she whispered, "here we are."

Leah found a parking space. She hit the lock button on her key fob as she walked away, hoping its noxious "beep" would make it obvious to anyone watching nearby that her car was, indeed, locked. The people getting out of the other cars around her all would have fit under the umbrella "unwashed masses." She clamped her Fendi purse more tightly under her elbow. It was extra heavy. She had a delivery to make.

He was a foster kid, Gran had said, running out of time. *After I'm gone, he'll have nobody.*

Same here, thought Leah, as she progressed through the line into reception.

"Inmate ID number," the officer said.

Leah handed over the little index card on which her grandmother had written a number and the name "Trayce Whitlock" in her looping, Catholic boarding school script.

"Picture ID."

Leah obliged with her driver's license, then surrendered her purse. The guard jabbed inside it with the sort of black wand employed by TSA checkers.

"Excuse me, sir," Leah whispered as the probing continued. "How do I put money on an, um, inmate's, um... account?"

"What?"

Leah repeated herself, more succinctly this time.

At last, the officer actually looked her over — not in her eyes so much as at her merino wool power suit, her tiny gold hoops, and her ringless hands. "You new legal counsel?"

Out of habit, she blurted, "I'm Director of Human Resources."

Shrugging off this visitor's foolish answer and expensive attire, he did not even look her in the eyes. He just thrust his thumb in the direction of a large ATM-style machine that leaned indifferently against the opposite wall. "Chit deposits go in there."

Leah stepped over to the machine. She tried to enter the first deposit toward the total amount Gran had willed for this purpose, but every time she typed in her daily debit maximum of $1000, the green letters on the black screen read "ERROR."

"What in the —?"

"You trying to put in more than a hundred?"

Leah turned to face the person speaking behind her. She shuddered at the thought that someone had been spying over her shoulder and she hadn't noticed. The old woman in the muumuu, however, seemed unfazed by this overdressed, middle-aged white lady shaking in her Manolo Blahnik pumps.

The woman smiled knowingly at Leah through her thick bifocals. "They can't have more than a hundred dollars on at a time, honey."

Leah swallowed the dryness out of her mouth. "Thank you."

She went through the process again, typing in the ID number of her dead Gran's pen pal. Amount to deposit? What if he already had some on there? A man in line behind the muumuu lady was tapping his sandaled foot and muttering something in Russian. Leah punched in $100. The transaction went through. First, she was relieved. Then she realized that a boy who had been in prison for two years already had not had anyone to give him any money. At least, not lately.

And she, Leah Campion, was to blame.

***

Twenty-two years earlier, Leah had been waiting in line at Wendy's, just about to order her salad, her baked potato, her Diet Coke. Her next appointment wasn't for another hour, and Wendy's had a Dollar Menu. Every red cent counted right now, even with her latest salary bump.

She heard loud, familiar voices behind her. Office mates. The girls from the front desk. Leah did not turn around.

"Leah won't be back until tomorrow. She has another appointment this afternoon."

They must not have recognized her from the back, especially since Leah was wearing casualwear, not an office suit.

"IVF? Again?"

Leah felt her neck muscles tighten like a screw.

"Her third, I think. Two miscarriages already, and she still keeps trying."

"Well, good for her! You should never let anything stand in the way of your dreams."

"Even a limited budget? That stuff ain't cheap, you know."

Leah glared at the Dollar Menu. This line was taking forever.

"She just got promoted to director. Nicer salary with that, I bet."

"Yeah, but how old is she?"

Leah stepped forward, shoulders squared. One more person ahead of her. Then it was her turn.

"Forty? Forty-five? Does it matter? You're never too old to go for what you want."

"If you say so. I'm only twenty-eight, and my kid is sucking the life out of me. I'd never get pregnant for the first time if I was her age."

"Well, I say good for her."

"You said that already."

"'Cause I mean it! Good for her!"

It was Leah's turn now. She placed her order to go. She had to wait some more. Desperate to look anywhere but at the coworkers behind her, she couldn't help but lower her eyes down to the clear acrylic donation box sitting in front of the cash register. The donations went to Dave's Kids, a charity that helped foster children find families. Above the box was a picture of a boy. African-American. He wore a striped golf shirt. He had a cautious smile with tiny teeth. The caption in the corner read, "Trayce, Age 4."

Leah paid for her order. Her change sat heavy in her hand. The open slot of the Dave's Kids box invited. Trayce, Age 4, smiled at her cautiously.

You're his mother, a voice inside of her said.

The strange idea startled her. To thaw herself from the shock of it, she looked at her watch. Her appointment was across town in less than an hour. Every red cent. Leah sealed the change back in her wallet. She passed her coworkers, caught their embarrassed expressions ("Do you think she heard us?"), and made excuses for not being able to stay and chat with them. She had an appointment to keep.

Or did she? She thought of Trayce, Age 4, looking for a mother. She, a mother, was looking for a child. Didn't it make sense? Could it make sense?

I could never adopt, Leah thought. *I'm not good enough for that. I'm sorry, but his life will be better without someone like me.*

She dashed out into the spring rain, a light drizzle, and headed towards the fertility clinic. The face of that little boy would haunt her dreams for the next two decades.

***

A guard stepped out from a steel door and hollered inmate numbers. The ID number that Gran had written was called. Leah stood up and followed the next guard. He directed her to put her purse in a locker.

Leah's heart pounded. "Sorry, sir, but can't I keep it with me? I have something to give —"

"You wanna give him something, you're gonna have to buy him something off his chit at the vending machines inside the visiting room. No personal belongings inside."

"Then why did you search —?" She closed her mouth and surrendered her purse. She found herself being herded with the rest of the visitors into a room that looked like half of Kira's grade school cafeteria: round tables, plastic chairs, vending machines along the walls. No windows. Leah swallowed hard.

Leah took a seat at one of the tables and closed her eyes. If she could have closed her nose to the bleach smell in the air, she could have imagined herself back at Butler-Edgers Academy Grade School cafeteria, waiting for Kira to come running out for second grade Mother-Daughter Muffin Morning.

How old had Kira been that day? Seven? Eight? Twelve years later, Leah was a childless mother sitting in a prison visitation room.

I know how hard I am to live with, Mom. I'm sorry, but your life will be better without someone like me.

Not even a year ago Kira had sent that email. A suicide email? Yes. From her own daughter. Leah hadn't even seen it until an hour after she'd had gotten the call from campus security. Kira was gone. Now, Gran was gone. Only Trayce was left, and here she was, about to meet him at last.

A metal door at the other end of the room swung open in a heavy arc. Another guard appeared first. "No touching the inmates in any fashion."

The first inmates came through the doorway. They were greeted with squeals, with sighs, with grudging grunts. Then the inmates and the visitors began to talk.

Talk? What will I say? What can I say to the boy I should have made mine?

***

There was that one Christmas morning when Leah woke even before Kira. Only a horrible dream could have done such a thing, and it had been a horrible dream. In it, Leah saw Tracye, Age 4, now looking more like Age 9 or 10. Kira had just turned seven.

In the dream, the little boy sat on a step and opened a gift bag. Inside were a pair of in-line skates. Scratched, gouged, and with dirty wheels, there was no mistake — the skates were used. The little boy looked around at a room full of other children, none of whom looked like him. There were smiles but not many of them.

Group foster home, something inside of Leah whispered.

"MOMMY!" shrieked a small voice in real life. Leah heard the tearing of wrapping paper.

Leah felt her shoulders ossify. Kira knew she was supposed to wait for Mommy. Leah knew that any reminder of that would cause another meltdown that would ruin another Christmas.

"Low tolerance for frustration," their counselor told Leah after their third play therapy session. "She may meet the diagnostic criteria for bipolar disorder."

Leah sobbed a gasp. "Already?"

The counselor nodded. "Early-onset bipolar, could be, yeah."

More paper ripping. "Choose your battles," another counselor had told Leah in her own sessions.

Leah armed herself with her camera and made her way to the living room. The camera shook in her hands as she centered Kira in the shot: a little white blond girl, alone, surrounded by gifts.

"Mommy, look! MOMMY! LOOK AT ME!"

Leah shook the image of Trayce and his single trash gift out of her head. "Sorry, Kira. I was distracted there for a sec. Okay, honeybunch, smile!"

Thirteen years later, Leah included a print of that shot in the collage displayed at Kira's funeral.

***

Leah looked up into the face she'd seen most recently in

the picture Gran had left. There was no mistake: it was the grown-up version of that foster boy on the acrylic collection box.

"Trayce Whitlock?"

The boy — no, man, Leah reminded herself — nodded. He frowned at her, clearly baffled. "Who are you?"

His voice sounded rough and tired. Suspicious.

"I'm Leah Campion," she replied. "I'm Virginia Reece's granddaughter."

Leah could see the light that came to his eyes at the mention of Gran's name. Gran said she'd sent her prison pen pal pictures. Could he see that Leah had inherited Gran's odd gray eyes? Could he see the slight bump that made Leah's nose as Welsh as Gran's had been?

Could he see the dark selfishness that remained in her heart, that selfishness she was trying to kill by coming here?

Perhaps he could see it. That light in his eyes went out nearly as quickly as it came. He spoke, and his voice was halting and rough. "She said — she said she was coming to see me this spring."

She. Leah voiced his unspoken question. "If she was supposed to be here, then why am I here instead?"

Trayce shrugged. His cuffs clanked. "Well, yeah."

Leah cleared her throat. She was cold, but she pulled the scarf off her neck, anyway. "Did she write you that she was sick?"

His eyes flew wide. His mouth fell. He shook his head like a tree shakes its leaves in a thunderstorm. Finally, he dropped into the plastic seat that waited for him.

Leah again cleared her constricting throat. She'd told so many people already. Why should telling this stranger be this difficult?

"She was diagnosed with leukemia three months ago. She had hoped she'd get better. She fought it for two months, but..."

Trayce Whitlock turned his face from Leah's.

"And I'm here in her place," Leah said, "and in my own. Because twenty years ago, I should have adopted you."

***

There had been another dream, this one on the morning of Kira's graduation from high school. He'd shown up again. This time Trayce was a young adult, sleeping on the floor in what looked like some apartment, but it was hard to tell because there was orange graffiti spray-painted on the walls. The boy jolted awake and sat upright, his back to the corner in which he'd been curled. It was the kind of motion you'd expect a boy to make on waking from his own bad dream, then sighing and closing his eyes again. Trayce, however, kept his eyes open, wide open, scanning whatever it was in front of him. Finally his face hardened, and he got up out of his corner.

Then Leah woke up. She ran for the bathroom to throw cold water on the back of her neck.

Gran had just moved in a few weeks before, after failing the vision screening for her driver's license renewal. She needed someone to stay with, and Leah needed the support with Kira.

Gran appeared in the bathroom doorway. "Leah? You okay, honey?"

"Yeah. Just a bad dream."

Gran patted Leah's shoulder. "You want to talk about it?"

That was Gran, always trying to make things better. "No. We'll wake Kira."

Gran sniffed. "That girl's nearly nineteen. Can't she handle a little sleep disruption?"

"You talk like you've never met her. What are you doing up this early, anyway?"

"Morning prayers."

Leah rolled her eyes.

"And," Gran added, "I was just about to start a new letter to my pen pal."

Smirking, Leah asked, "Has he asked for conjugal visits yet?"

"Oh, hush. Best thing to do if you're lonely is to help another lonely person. Nobody's lonelier than an inmate, I figured."

Leah couldn't help but think of Kira, her own daughter, flesh of her flesh, and the loneliness and depression that child had battled all her eighteen years. Leah had done everything right: the best sperm donor, the best schools, the best counseling, the best medication. Sometimes, on the darkest nights, she wondered if she should never have had Kira, should have spared her the pain of being born. Was it Leah's fault, for wanting her so badly, that Kira lived in such pain?

Of course, Leah's own counselor had said that she mustn't blame herself, that plenty of parents naturally conceived mentally ill children. But Leah had been so careful. She had done everything right. This wasn't supposed to happen to her own child. Now it was a crapshoot as to whether or not Kira would have the spirit to go to her own graduation.

The thought flew into Leah's mind: Had Trayce even had a graduation to go to?

Leah hung her head over her sink and let strangled, baffled tears flow. Silently, Gran rubbed her shoulders some more.

"Sorry," Leah whispered when she'd finally stopped.

She grabbed the nearby toilet paper and dabbed at her eyes. "I just thought this would be easier."

Gran laughed quietly. "Honeybunch, the best stuff never is."

***

So across a cheap table covered in chipped veneer, Leah told Trayce as best she could about how she'd "met" him in Wendy's when she was trying to get pregnant. About how she'd run away from even considering adopting a child not her own. About how she'd dreamed of him over the years in spite of that. About how her own daughter had committed suicide the year before Gran got sick. And then, about the greatest shock of all: the day before Gran slipped into a coma, she told Leah that she wanted to give everything to her prison pen pal, a 26-year-old boy named Trayce who grew up in foster care.

When Leah finally stopped talking, Inmate Trayce Whitlock stared at her blankly for a full fifteen seconds.

"Sorry, miss, but that's some crazy shit you're talking."

Leah couldn't help it. She laughed. Trayce Whitlock did, too. They both laughed harder and harder until they drew stares from the other tables. They wiped their tears with their empty hands, Trayce's cuffs clanking awkwardly.

"I'm so sorry," Leah managed at last. "I know. I sound crazy."

"Nah, that's okay. Gotta tell you that you're the first woman to ever have dreams about me."

Leah leaned in conspiratorially. "That you know of."

He gave a mock-proud smirk. "That's right."

Seeing his sense of humor peek through so quickly like that should have made Leah happy. All it did was make her mourn. She dropped her face into her hands to hide bitter tears.

"Miss, don't cry. I'm sorry. Don't cry. What are you feeling bad for, anyway?"

Leah burst out, "That you're in here! That my daughter slit her wrists! If I had just adopted you when I had the chance, you wouldn't be here and my daughter wouldn't have killed herself!"

More stares from the other tables.

A heavy frown passed over her companion's face. "Look, I don't know you, but I do know one thing. I didn't know it before I got in here, but I know it now. I learned it from Virginia, and I learned it from some counselors in here. Any choice I've made is mine. Any choice your daughter made was hers."

"But my choice made it harder for you to make good choices, didn't it?"

Trayce's eyes widened, and he sat back. "Wow. Nobody's ever said anything like that to me before."

"Anything like —?"

"Like they could've helped me."

"Well, I could have. I think I could have." Leah paused. "Maybe not, since I couldn't help Kira."

Trayce was quiet for a moment then said, "I bet you did. And now you've helped me."

"No, that's Gran. The money on your account here is from her, and she's set up a bank account in your name for when you're released, and I'm supposed to give you her —"

He shook his head. "No, it's not that stuff. It's you. I've had such a hard time learning to apologize, because nobody ever apologized to me before."

Leah felt a swelling in her chest. She couldn't tell if it was more pain or healing. It must have been both.

"They took my purse," she said. "Besides the money,

Gram wanted me to give you her prayer book —"

"The one she said she prayed every morning before she wrote me?"

Leah nodded. "She wanted you to have something that she'd touched."

Slowly, Trayce smiled. "She sent me you."

Visiting time was over. One guard took Leah away, and another took Trayce. Leah gathered her purse, still heavy with Gran's book — Trayce's book. She got back in her car to make her way home. The fog was starting to clear.

PEAR TREES
Dena Hunt

She had that kind of slightly plump whiteness that needed only bare arms or stockingless legs on a new spring day to look suddenly, even startlingly, naked. Her eyes, round, slightly protruding, a pale blue and rather watery, stared into the shop window at the little black dress, so strangely out of place among the bright pastels. The smooth baby-pink edges of her heels made a little sucking sound against the soles of her backless shoes as she went inside. Why did she want this dress? Why did she want to wear this piece of mourning on this bright spring day? It seemed right. Who — or what— had died?

It was a fit. Slinky, clinging, but very modest, really. A high-necked halter style, no cleavage, but bare-shouldered. It looked rather good. The saleswoman seemed impressed. "Oh, your shoulders look fantastic!" It was only eighty dollars. She'd wear it to dinner that night with Patrick. Gorgeous Patrick, so intelligent—a columnist for the *Atlanta Constitution*, known and admired by everybody. He was a defender of women's rights. His column on abortion was still quoted by Jenn, her roommate: "When those men in those red beanie caps and long dresses around the Vatican have to experience the pain, the agony, of any woman in childbirth, they will have the right to speak about abortion..." Something like that, anyway. To be Patrick's partner, his lover, was cause for self-congratulation. It gave her renown, being seen with him, having people know that they slept together, that she was his choice, his woman. *His woman*? What an expression. She surprised herself again.

The little piece of black cowered in the bottom of the hot-pink plastic shopping bag. Yes, it was a mourning dress, even if it was a sexy one, her own response to spring. Spring always depressed her. Bright green budding leaves, tulips shouting their red, rows of singing yellow jonquils— full of exuberance under sprays of pure, blinding-white dogwood, so full of promise, so full of empty promise.

"I don't see anything." Dr. Cooper drew his head back, turning on the light above the examining chair. "I don't know what the problem is. When do you see this cloudiness?"

"All the time."

"Not just in the morning when you wake up — or when your eyes are tired?"

"No. Actually, I see more clearly when I first wake up. It's later that this white fogginess seems to creep in from the sides, toward the center."

"Well, I can see no cause, no clinical cause, anyway. I could prescribe a moisturizer for your eyes, but you'd do just as well with something over the counter. Try that for a while and see if it improves."

That was a week ago. Her vision had not improved; in fact, it was worse. She looked at the Bradford pear trees lining Kay Boulevard as she walked back to her Decatur apartment. *That* was it — the stupid pear trees. They were a hybrid, very popular with landscapers because of their perfectly formed, consistently shaped branches, their white blossoms in spring, and mainly because they bore no messy fruit. They were the problem; with their white clouds of blossoms, they were encroaching on her vision. White cloudiness around the periphery, steadily diminishing her sight, so that she could see only what was directly in front of her, taking away the context for her vision. And every day, on her way to work, shopping, wherever she went, she had to navigate her way through these hybrid white cloud trees.

She twisted her frosted martini glass between her fingers. Patrick was late. He was often late. Was he still angry with her? There wasn't any particular reason she knew of for his being late tonight. Yes, he was probably late because he was still angry. She watched a businessman eating alone at the table in front of her, apparently not so impressed by his dinner as to put aside the folded-up newspaper he was reading. Was he reading Patrick's column? She wondered why she was more curious about what the man was reading than about why Patrick was late. The man shoved his plate aside, removed his glasses and wiped them with a napkin. She could see what he was reading — the stock market pages, not Patrick's column.

Yes, he was angry — still. She tried to muster some anxiety about that and found that she was unable to, that Patrick's anger had been relegated to the side-clouds, ever receding from her view. For the moment anyway, as she watched this unknown businessman in his gray suit, pale blue shirt, and striped tie, she even had some difficulty remembering the scene that had angered Patrick last week.

"I just don't want to."

"But I do it for you."

"Yes, I know —but I don't want you to."

"Why not?"

"I don't like it."

"That's ridiculous — you've always liked it."

"No, I haven't. I just knew that you did.

"But you like it when I do it for you."

"No — no, I don't like that. I just knew *you* did."

Oh, yes, he was angry. Bemused by the striped tie of the businessman, she wondered if Patrick was more angry about the possibility that he'd "read" her wrong than he was about the argument. She guessed it would be irritating to find that after a year of frequent sex, he had not been sending her to the stars after all. Anyway, she tried very hard to bring the subject into her focused thoughts, but it wouldn't go; it stayed on the foggy edges, and the businessman's tie, the frost on the glass, and now the burnt orange cocktail napkin consumed all her attention. Burnt orange with Matisse-style lettering: *Johnny's*. A trendy place, very popular. Lots of noise. It seemed that all "good" restaurants these days were noisy, with waiters yelling at busboys, at cooks — who were, often as not, cooking on an open grill in the dining room — dishes clattering, lots of noisy bustle, customers talking, laughing loudly. She hated eating in a noisy atmosphere. She hated Johnny's, actually. How could that man read in all this noise?

A waiter looked meaningfully at her. They wanted her to order, they wanted this table, they were wondering if her date had stood her up. She ordered another martini and studied the yellow rose in the center of the tiny black lacquered table, dainty and delicate, looking oddly contained in a sleek stainless steel vase. Patrick had sent her a dozen roses last fall from New Orleans when she'd had the abortion. He was there to write a piece on the racism of the Bush administration being responsible for the deaths of thousands of people. He hoped for a Pulitzer on that one, but there were too many others like it, too much competition. There were a dozen deep red roses. Jenn put them in her bedroom on the dresser, but she moved them out to the living room. They looked like blood, a great blood clot. Just a blood clot — a living one, yes, but just a clot. When Patrick called, she told him about the Women's Clinic, how they told her it would be painless, how excruciatingly painful it was, how there were little cell-like rooms all in a line down a long corridor, each one just big enough to contain a treatment table, a stool for the doctor, and a vacuum apparatus. So many, many little rooms, the doctor rushing down the corridor to spend a few minutes in each little room for the procedure, like an assembly-line operator. She thought Patrick might want to write about it—no one ever did, so he wouldn't have the competition he was having with the Katrina disaster and Bush administration. He wasn't interested, though. The steel vase was like a piston chamber, but where there should be a piston, there was a rose.

Three tables away George Paccheo was drinking with two companions, getting drunk by the sound of the raucous laughter. George was a friend of Patrick's — gregarious, one would call him, politely.

Twenty minutes. Very late. Why did Johnny's line the walls with mirrors? Did they think everyone wanted to watch themselves eat? On the wall opposite she could see her milk-white bare shoulders on each side of the black halter dress, her light brown curls dipping into the white neck. Then the clouds closed in; she could only see her black dress, the black table-top, and the rose; all the rest was consumed in fog. The businessman between her and the mirrored wall was smiling, reading the comics. The picture of such a serious-looking man reading comics made her smile, too.

George was very loud. He'd spotted her, waved, and yelled a greeting. She smiled and waved back. She didn't like George. He was a sports writer at the *Constitution*, and she didn't like sports, so she always thought that was the reason she didn't like him. They simply had nothing in

common. She was a copywriter for Houghton-Mifflin —
not an exciting job, she knew, but a job. At 33, she should
have advanced in the publishing business by now, but she
lacked ambition. Her work was adequate, sometimes quite
good, but she was always passed over for promotion; worse
than that, she didn't mind.

She saw Patrick turning the corner from the entrance
alcove. He could see her, but he didn't look her way;
instead, he stopped and chatted with someone, then
moved to George's table, where he stopped and talked for a
while. She began to wonder if he'd seen her. Yes, he had;
he knew where she was, how long she'd been waiting.
Patrick was going to break off with her, she realized
suddenly. For a moment, a little pain hit her heart. He was
gorgeous, fashionably gorgeous. His black hair was
combed behind his ears and met the top of the collar of his
gray tweed jacket. He wore a white tee-shirt underneath
and faded jeans. His perfect white teeth flashed in the
middle of the dark beard stubble. Why were men doing
that now? Why were they not clean-shaven? It was
fashionable to have a day or two's growth on their cheeks.
Patrick was fashionable. The businessman in front of her
was clean-shaven, unfashionably smooth cheeks.

Oh, damn. George was coming to the table with Patrick.
Good Lord, he was staggering, really drunk. Why would
Patrick bring him to the table in that condition? *Damn.*
She focused on Patrick's face as the clouds closed in.

Beard-stubble brushed her upturned cheek, a waiter
darted to the table to take Patrick's martini order, and then
everything stopped.

"My God," Patrick said, "you look fucking gorgeous."

"Hey," said George, "the question is, does she look
gorgeous fucking?"

Patrick grinned and sat down in the chair next to her. George drew up a chair opposite her — then changed his mind. Water filled her lap as the bud vase overturned. George leaned over the table, and his tongue was in her mouth. The table tilted, the martini glass overturned and rolled to the floor. She could no longer see anything at all. She drowned in helpless revulsion. The clouds covered her.

The unexpectedness of violence — not its noise — stilled the air, thinned it, making breathing difficult. Table and chairs were overturned, and George was on the floor with a gray-suited knee on his chest, blood gushing from his nose. Patrick was standing a few feet away, his mouth hanging open in dumb surprise. No one moved. The sudden silence seemed to paralyze the room. She sat as she was, looking down at George, at the gray leg. The waiters stood frozen. There was no movement anywhere until the smooth and ruddy cheek turned to look up at her through wire-framed glasses, where she sat, still and silent, waiting. And long afterward, when she tried, she could never explain or even understand how it was that his eyes banished all the clouds from her own, so that she saw everything at once with laser-like clarity — how she knew in an instant that whoever he was, she was; whatever his name was, it would be her own. She belonged to him.

Sarah inhaled deeply as she stepped out of her car. The smell of old books and old buildings permeated the air. Standing in the college campus, she felt as if she could breathe in the knowledge. It was a reminder of who she used to be, who she still dared to dream she might someday be again. She had needed this time away. Out of sorts all day, she had been unable to think or focus, her mind running like a gerbil on a wheel. Everything her daughters did had been grating on her nerves. In fact, she was quite certain that she had no nerves left. She was thankful her friend Megan had been willing to take them on such short notice, an impromptu play date with her own brood. Megan had seven children. How did she ever manage? Sarah only had two and they were all she could cope with on most days. How many times had she hidden in the bathroom, locked the door, and cried?

She had met Megan at a local homeschool group and discovered that she lived nearby. Megan's six-year-old daughter Rachel had quickly become friends with Sarah's own young ladies, six-year-old Lauren and four-year-old Lily. Megan had been homeschooling for fourteen years; her oldest son was graduating from high school. In addition, she ran a home-based business, found time to knit, and coached her daughter's high school soccer team. She made it all look easy. There was no question Sarah was in awe of her older friend. How did she do it all? Sarah had been officially homeschooling for one month, found time to do nothing, and was wondering if she would ever survive. She had been out of her mind when she decided to homeschool.

It was one of those things she had thought about, on and off, since the girls were very little. She had read everything she could get her hands on about the topic, talked to lots of people, made lists of pros and cons, and spent lots of time on her knees praying. Still, wanting to be normal, she had sent Lauren to kindergarten, only to have her come home crying every single day. She had hoped it might get better with time, that she might adjust, but it didn't happen. While other children went happily into school, Lauren clung to her side, begging not to go. Day by day, she saw the light going out of her daughter's eyes. She had to do something.

She read more, talked to more people, made more lists, prayed more, and then decided to jump off a cliff into the world of homeschooling. All those books and blog posts had made it seem easy, a natural transition from being a stay-at-home mom, not that she had ever actually mastered the whole stay-at-home-mom thing. Why did she find it all so hard? Why was she such a failure? Her older friends said it would get easier once her oldest child was twelve. Six more years. Could she make it that long?

A cool wind whipped through the trees, sending some multihued leaves fluttering to the ground. Sarah pulled her cozy wool sweater tight around her and set off on her walk. She used to love autumn. It meant a return to the books she loved, a chance to learn, to explore, and to be with her friends. Now, it was a painful reminder of what she had lost. It also meant winter was coming and that she would be trapped in the house with the girls bouncing off the walls. The beauty of the fall foliage notwithstanding, she hated this time of year.

A trio of students walked past her. Engaged in an animated conversation, they didn't even acknowledge Sarah. It wasn't that long ago that she was one of them; at least it didn't feel like that long ago. This year would mark her fifteen-year reunion from college. The save-the-date card had already come in the mail and been tossed in the trash. It was hard enough reading of her classmates' success on Facebook; she didn't need to face them in person. She had been second in her graduating class and gone on to get a Ph.D. in Chemistry. People had expected great things from her. She had expected great things from herself. Her classmates worked in labs, doing research, trying to change the world one formula at a time. What was she doing? She had let everyone down. That innocent question, "And what do you do?" filled her with dread.

Yes, she had to confess envy every time she went to Confession. There were times she felt like she could go daily. She didn't want to be jealous. She knew God called people to different lives and that she was where she was supposed to be. Someday, she hoped that she would feel better about that. Maybe one day she wouldn't have to confess the envy. After all, miracles could happen. At least that's what she had heard.

Her cell phone rang, interrupting her thoughts. It was Ben. She ignored the call. He was probably just calling to say he'd be late coming home — again. She had left a note on the counter telling him where she had gone and where the girls were. She wasn't ready to talk to him, not yet. She had taken the test that morning. She had suspected, but kept her symptoms to herself. Ben wasn't that observant. He didn't keep track of the days like she did, marking them on her NFP chart. Her cycles had been a mess lately, and she had said yes on a day when her fertility signs were questionable.

Even on a good day, things between them were tense; she hadn't wanted to make them worse. Plus, she wanted to feel loved, noticed. There was just too much stress. Ben worked long hours. There was never enough money for all the bills. The kids wore her out. They had little time together and no one willing to watch the kids for a few hours so they could have a date. To say the romance had left would be like saying there would be snow in a New England winter. Most days, she felt like he didn't even see her anymore. She could barely remember what they had seen in each other in the first place.

NFP had always been one of those things that grated on Ben, but she had wanted to be faithful to Church teaching and she was thankful that he loved her enough to agree. She understood the reasons behind it; so did he. They wanted to be open to life. That didn't always make it easy to live on a day-in, day-out basis. And now, child number three was on his or her way. She rubbed her abdomen. It wasn't swollen yet, but it would be soon. She wanted to be happy, but motherhood didn't come easy to her. Her friends were so comfortable with motherhood. Sarah loved her girls with all her heart, but she didn't have that natural instinct, the instantaneous bond. She was looking forward to her children getting older, more independent. Lily had just reached the point where she could completely take care of herself in the bathroom. Now Sarah was going to be starting all over with diapers and nursing and sleepless nights. Could she do it all again? The very thought exhausted her.

One day at a time, she reminded herself, taking a deep breath, purposefully crunching the fallen leaves with her boots. She only needed to get through today. That thought had gotten her through many days, days when she didn't think she could possibly make it, when the weight of her particular cross seemed too heavy to bear.

She reached Miller's Lake and stood on the covered bridge that spanned it, looking out over the water. It was so still, so clear. The fall colors were reflected in the pool, glittering in the sunlight. It was peaceful, breathtakingly beautiful. She pulled out her phone and took a photo to capture the memory. She would remember this day. She knew she would, just like she remembered the days she discovered she was pregnant with Lauren and then with Lily. She had wanted children. They had both been planned, yet it still came as a shock to her when the pregnancy test was positive. Especially with Lauren – it all came crushing down on her that her life was changed forever.

Ben had been excited, eager to tell everyone they knew. She had just wanted to hide. She wasn't good with change, and this was the biggest one she had ever experienced. And then the baby came, and she was so tiny and perfect and vulnerable, and Sarah was so scared that she would do the wrong thing, and the darkness of post-partum depression had surrounded her. She barely remembered those days; all she remembered was feeling completely alone. Ben had returned to work a week after the baby was born; her parents lived far away, and there was no one to help. Her friends were busy with their own lives and couldn't understand how much hers had changed or how lost she felt. Overnight, Sarah had gone from being a successful chemist with a promising future to a stay-at-home mom. She never thought of hurting the baby, but there were many days when she herself dreamed of dying. Still, she was determined to prove that she could take care of Lauren, that she could be a good mother, no matter how much the voice in her head told her otherwise.

Meanwhile, Ben's life had continued much the same as it had before. He went to work. He went out with his friends. There were days and nights she hated him for it, especially the nights, when she would be up yet again, beyond tired, rocking and nursing Lauren, while he slept. She spent day after day, with no one to talk to but a baby who couldn't yet talk back, and she was slowly going insane. It was winter so she couldn't even go for walks. She felt like a caged animal, desperate for escape. Somehow both she and Lauren had survived, and she had eventually made friends with some other mothers through a playgroup at church. They would never know how much she had looked forward to their Wednesday morning meetings. Now that their children were school age, their lives were taking different paths, but there was no denying it. Those women had saved her life.

What would Ben say about the new baby? She had no idea. She was scared to even broach the topic. He loved the girls; she knew that, but they had a clear division of labor. The girls were her responsibility. They had been since day one. He was happy to give them hugs and piggyback rides on occasion, but he never wanted to read to them or play dolls with them or take them to the park. When he was home, he just wanted to be left alone to watch sports on television or be on the computer. His idea of parenting was to plop the girls in front of the television. Sarah knew he worked hard — that he was tired, but she was tired, too, now more than ever. She could sleep anywhere, anytime when she was pregnant.

What would the girls be like with a new baby? Would they be jealous, or would they help? Lily loved babies. Whenever she was around the babies in the homeschool group, she would sit next to them and try to play with them. She would pretend to put diapers on her baby dolls and sit them in a high chair and feed them. She said she needed to do this, so that she would know how to care for her new brother or sister. She often asked Sarah when they would have a baby; all of their new friends seemed to have one. Sarah always answered, "When and if God sends one." Now, God had. She knew Lily's prayers had been answered. Maybe things would be different this time with the girls old enough to help a bit. Maybe her new friends would provide the support system she had lacked the first time around. At least she would have them to talk to. Maybe the darkness wouldn't surround her.

She walked to the secluded grotto with the large statue of the Blessed Mother and sat down on the bench in front of it. Even the short walk had worn her out. She needed to rest her legs. Could Mary understand her heartache? Her fear? Mary had faced an unexpected pregnancy. It wasn't quite the same though, was it? Mary was perfect. She had said yes without hesitation and changed the world. Was Mary ever scared? It was hard to imagine. Still, Sarah had to talk to someone. She prayed the Hail Mary softly, slowly. She begged her heavenly mother to help her and to watch over her children, both the two she already knew, and the new one growing inside her. She pleaded for help in being a good mother. She asked for help every day, yet she still wasn't enough. She was never enough. She put her head in her hands and cried, allowing the tears that she been fighting all day to finally come.

***

Thomas walked down Route 23 to the campus, the same way he did every day, the same way he had been doing for the past twelve years, his cane tapping in rhythm on the ground. He had started this daily ritual soon after he had retired. It hadn't been his choice to leave his job of fifty years at the paper plant, but his boss had given him a golden watch and told him it was time to hang up his hat. He had stated the obvious that Thomas didn't want to accept: he could no longer do a younger man's job.

He had gone home in a funk and plunked himself in

front of the idiot box day in and day out, watching old movies he knew by heart, eating food that wasn't on his approved high blood pressure diet.

"You need to get out of the house," Ellen had said, hands on her hips. "You can't just sit here anymore. You're driving me crazy and you're killing yourself, and I'm not going to stand here and watch you do it." Ah yes, the red may have gone out of his bride's hair, but the fire in her personality had never been quenched. She had handed him his hat and his cane and showed him the door. "It's a beautiful day. Go for a walk."

"First, my job. Now, my house. I'm getting kicked out of everywhere," he had complained. "The least you can do is come with me."

She had smiled, that perfect gap-toothed smile that had enchanted him so many years before, and grabbed her hat. "Well, yes, I reckon I can do that."

And so, she had. Every afternoon, major snowstorm and illness notwithstanding, the two of them would have their lunch, then walk the one-and-a-half miles to the campus, make a loop around it, stop to say a prayer in front of the statue of the Blessed Virgin, and then head home. It had begun a new chapter in their lives, after so many years of the same routine. He had begun to look forward to that daily constitutional so much — walking with his lovely wife by his side.

He had thought he knew everything that mattered about Ellen. What else could there be to say, or learn, after a lifetime of shared breakfasts and dinners? They had reached the stage of comfortable silence many years before, but on these walks, they had begun to talk about all sorts of things. He had fallen even more in love with her. Who knew such a thing was even possible at his age? He had felt like a lovesick teenager again, and it felt wonderful.

He knew he had been a blessed man, but he had one great sadness in his life. He and Ellen had never been able to have children. For years, they had tried and hoped, and he had held her as she cried every month. They went to doctor after doctor, endured test after test, but there was nothing anyone could do. None of them had any answers. In time, they had accepted their fate and acknowledged that God had different plans for them. If Thomas were honest, he would say that he didn't always like God's plan. But he wanted to be strong — for Ellen. He didn't want her to hurt more than she already did. He knew she always felt she had let him down, somehow, no matter how many times he'd tell her he loved her — that she was enough, that he still would have married her knowing that they would never have a child. Words can only do so much when the heart is broken.

She had gone back to school and become a seventh grade English teacher. She decided that all her students would be her children, and she had loved them like her own. Some had remembered her long after she had cleaned her last blackboard and corrected her last paper. They would see her in the market and would tell her what a difference she had made in their lives. He was always so proud of his Ellen, happy to have her by his side. She was a good woman. She could always make him laugh and bring a smile to his face. They had a wonderful life together. Even after all these years, he felt incredibly lucky that she had chosen him. Without a doubt, she was indeed his better half.

He had thrown himself into his own work and community projects. He kept busy, and the years flew by. Still, the ache of lost fatherhood had never left him. God had his reasons, right? He wanted to believe that. It wasn't always easy, though. Even now. Especially now. If they had had children, maybe his heart would not be so heavy. Maybe he would have someone who loved him. Maybe there would be grandchildren or even great-grandchildren to brighten his days. No, the pain had never gone away.

Left, right, left, his measured steps hit the pavement. He could make this walk blindfolded. The brown yorkie in the yard outside the blue house on the corner yapped at him, just as he did every day.

"You think you are a big dog trapped in a little body," he said. He bent down and let the dog sniff his hand. "How is my friend today?" He pulled a small biscuit out of his pocket and pushed it through the fence. "Yes, I have a treat for you." The dog eagerly gobbled it down.

Thomas held onto the fence and pulled himself up. He took a deep breath and steadied himself. His bones and muscles protested. When did old age sneak up on him? On both of them?

Time was a cruel thief. On the inside, he still felt twenty. Well, perhaps not twenty — maybe forty, but his body and the mirror told him different. They were constant reminders of the truth. He hated the truth.

It had been three months and two days since Ellen had last walked with him. It was a hot July morning, the humidity already hanging heavy in the air. The sun had streamed in through the window at five-thirty, waking him. He had tried to ignore it, but knew it was no use. Once he was awake, he had to use the bathroom. He had forced himself to sit up, to grab his glasses from the nightstand. Ellen was snoring softly in the bed beside him. He didn't want to wake her. He shuffled to the bathroom, and then made his way to the kitchen to brew some coffee.

He sat and read his morning paper. It was seven o'clock when he headed back to their bedroom. He wanted to get dressed. Ellen was usually up by then. She must have been very tired. He hoped she wasn't sick.

As soon as he walked in, he saw her. He tried to shake her awake, pounded on her chest, pleaded with God. Part of him knew it was no use. The cruel reality of death had already set in. When? How could he not have known? The love of his life had slipped away while he drank coffee. He didn't even have the chance to say goodbye, to tell her he loved her one last time. He held her lifeless body to him and wailed.

He still couldn't bring himself to sleep in their bed, the bed they had shared for every night of their marriage. He doubted he ever would. He dreamed of taking a hammer to it, tearing it apart, piece by piece, and throwing it on the curb for the garbage men to haul away. Sometimes he brought the hammer to their room and just stood there, looking at the empty bed, but he couldn't bring himself to follow through. He would be destroying the good memories with the bad, and there had been good memories, many of them. Still, the image of her dead body was forever etched in his brain. Now, when he did sleep, he took up residence on the couch, wrapping himself in a well-worn quilt that Ellen had made for him, dreaming of the one he had lost. Every night he prayed for God to take him home, to let him see his Ellen again. Every morning he woke up a bit disappointed and forced himself to face the day.

The afternoon she had left him, after the police had come and the funeral home had taken her away, he had taken this path. He hadn't known what else to do. His feet went by rote. The rest of him merely followed. It was what she would want him to do, and so he continued. He would talk to her while he walked, pretending she could hear him, wishing that she would answer. He was supposed to go first. Ellen was the healthy one. He had suffered from decades of heart trouble. It was supposed to be him, not her. The Angel of Death had made a mistake. Why was he still here? What purpose could he possibly still have? No one needed him.

He passed under the wrought-iron entrance and into the campus. The trees were dazzling in the sunlight. Ellen would have loved this day. He wondered if she could see it. She looked forward to fall every year. She would decorate their home and start baking at a fever pitch, singing while she rolled crusts and mixed the ingredients. The house always smelled like apples and pumpkins and cinnamon. She made the best pumpkin pies. He had never tasted better. He missed pumpkin pie. He missed her singing. He even missed her snoring. The house was far too quiet without her.

He crossed the bridge over Miller's Lake and made his way to the grotto. Ellen would bring her rosary beads and pray. He would say one "Hail Mary," then close his eyes as he waited for her. It was peaceful here. He enjoyed the respite.

When he reached the grotto, he stopped short. The bench wasn't empty. In all the years of walking at this time of day, that had never happened. There was a red-headed woman sitting on it, her head in her hands. From that distance, she reminded him of his Ellen. Was she all right? Should he go over? Perhaps she wanted to be alone? There were many other places to sit on the campus. He could find one and continue with his day. That would be the reasonable thing to do, but his feet and his heart didn't seem to want to listen to reason. He was drawn to her, to the memory she represented. He felt like Ellen herself was telling him to approach her.

Thomas walked over and stood before the statue, offering his silent prayer. When he turned, the young woman looked up at him. He could see that her green eyes had been crying. What could be causing her heart to ache? He pulled out a handkerchief and offered it to her. She accepted the gift with a fragile smile.

"Thank you," she whispered. She pushed over on the bench and motioned for him to sit. He eased himself down onto the bench, leaning his cane against the side. He didn't know what to say. If Ellen were here, she would know just the right words to comfort this stranger. That was one of his wife's many gifts. He, on the other hand, often bumbled his way through social situations. Plus, this was a woman. Had he ever understood a woman? No, he had not. Even Ellen had always remained a bit of a mystery. As far as he knew, in the entire history of humanity, a man had never understood a woman.

The young woman blew her nose loudly. "I guess you won't want this handkerchief back," she smiled.

"No, consider it a gift."

She nodded. "Thank you."

"Do you want to talk about it? Something, or perhaps someone, has made you sad? I can't promise any wise advice, but I am a good listener."

"I'm pregnant," she stated, touching her belly.

Thomas drew in a breath — God and his ironic sense of humor. Now he was in even more over his head. If Ellen could see him, she was probably laughing at him. What did he know of such things? Was she single? Alone?

"And the father? What does he say?"

"I haven't told my husband yet."

Thomas exhaled. This was a different situation, but he was confused. "This would be happy news, no?"

She started crying again, holding the handkerchief to her face. He hesitated before he put his hand on her shoulder. "It will be okay."

"I know," she sobbed. "You're right. I should be happy. A baby is a blessing. I know this. I already have two children." She pulled out her phone and showed him a photo of her girls.

"They are beautiful. I see they have your red hair. My wife had red hair, as well, in her younger days."

She put the phone away and wiped away her tears. "How long have you been married?"

"We were married for fifty-three years." Thomas swallowed. "She died this past summer." It still hurt to say the words.

Her face fell. "That's so sad. I'm sorry for your loss."

"Thank you. I admit it has been hard to be without her. I miss her every moment."

"That's a long time to be together. I've only been married for eight. I can't imagine making it to fifty-three." She paused. "I'm not sure I want to make it to fifty-three."

"I imagine there were many days my wife felt the same way. I wasn't always the easiest man to live with," he laughed. "She used to say that God gave me to her to have her earn her place in heaven! I suppose she might have been right. She was my best friend. She and I used to walk here every day and stop here to pray. I'd give almost anything to have any one of those days with her back."

"She sounds like a lovely woman. What was her name?"

"Ellen."

"That's a pretty name."

His face lit up. "Yes, it was a pretty name for a pretty woman."

***

They sat in silence for a few moments. Sarah checked her watch and looked around. She hated to leave. "It's getting late. I need to start heading back to my car."

"Yes, you need to get back to your girls."

"Yes, I do," she said, getting up from her seat. "Thank you again for the handkerchief."

"You're welcome," he said. "I hope your heart feels better and that you have little need for it."

She smiled and took a few steps before turning back around. The older man looked so alone sitting on the bench. "Would you like to walk with me?" she offered. "You could tell me more about Ellen."

He clutched his cane and stood up. "Yes, I would like that very much."

TWO KINDS OF PEOPLE
John McNichol

Dad took off when I was little. A few minutes before he left to get that last pack of cigarettes, he told me the bit about hammers and nails. "Son," he said, staring at the TV, sipping his beer with one hand and tending his cigarette in the other, "there's two kinds of people in this world. Some of us get to be hammers, but most of us are nails. Nothing in between."

I'm not sure who Dad thought he was when he took off to get a pack of smokes and never found his way back. But that day he was a hammer, and he hit me pretty hard without even raising his hand.

Now I'm a grown-up and a cop. They call me a detective, but really I'm a cop with a badge that goes in my wallet instead of on my chest. When my phone went off and I read the address in the text, I closed my eyes and hoped it wasn't a dead kid.

When I called and found out it wasn't a kid, I thought I'd gotten lucky. I was wrong.

"What do we got?" I asked when I got there. Lavin was on the scene first, and he'd put up the yellow tape and blocked off access to the school. He'd done a good job; the school lobby could've been used for a textbook on how to dress a crime scene. Lavin had his quirks, and people said things about him behind his back, but I never got into it. I always had too big a caseload to keep up with gossip in the department. Anyone who saved me time the way Lavin did got a gold star from me.

Now Lavin looked at me from the sidewalk outside the

school, his thin moustache twitching just a little. "Janitor came in at two a.m. and found the guy in the classroom. M.E.'s already inside and upstairs. Where you been?"

"Doin' my job while you were polishing that badge on your chest and eating another round of doughnuts. Anyone else here?"

"You mean besides the Google car driving around? Billy's dusting the scene on the top floor. Don't step in anything up there. It's pretty messy."

After I climbed the stone steps and made it into the classroom, I saw he wasn't kidding. I've seen worse, but never indoors. Usually when someone looked this bad, they were out on a sidewalk in a neighborhood you didn't walk around in after dark. Here, though? In a Catholic school in a working class neighborhood, with kids who came from the Hills and the Valley? Not here. Never here. Murders just didn't, shouldn't, happen here.

I started the routine on the body. You don't want to hear the details. If you do, I've got names for people like you. And most of them aren't fit for polite company.

Mitch showed up about twenty minutes after I did. I knew he was closing the Bricknell theft case, but I'd had a feeling he'd get his paperwork done a lot quicker when this showed up on the blotter. Even a rookie patrolman could see this case had TV written all over it. Soon there'd be news, reporters, maybe even a twenty-something producer from *48 Hours* dropping by in a few days if things got interesting enough. Mitch was good at what he did, but not much else. If he had a chance to look like something off of a show like *Criminal Intent* after eight years of catching purse snatchers and busting pawnshop fences? It'd be more tempting than a young woman to a desert hermit.

"Man," Mitch said, his suit jacket hooked on his finger

and slung over one shoulder just like Chris Noth used to wear his on *C.I.* before it got cancelled last year. "Someone just did not like this guy."

"Yeah, brilliant, Sherlock," I said, going into a crouch, looking at the body with my gloved-up hands. "Double points if you figure out who did it in the next ten seconds."

Mitch looked at me a second. "They bite you know," he said.

"What?"

"Whatever crawled up your arse and made you such a jerk. What's your problem, Jackie? You know this guy or something?"

"Yeah, sort of. He was my kid's teacher."

Mitch got quiet. With cases like this, we'd make inappropriate jokes to get through the night most cops did. But even the best jokes fell flat when someone knew the vic. The teacher, the semi-famous Mister Daniel Anderson, was splayed out on his left side with his knees bent. His eyes were open and glassy. The back of his head had a dark, wrinkled crater behind it, where pieces of his skull had pushed in and mashed a good chunk of his brain. Mashed it enough to stop his heart and the rest of him from working very quickly.

Mitch whistled low. "You okay?" he asked me.

"Fine," I said. Mr. Anderson's eyes stared out at the desks from floor level. No one would be sitting in those desks when the bell rang in a few hours. Not likely tomorrow, either. "Better than him."

"What do you see, Billy?"

"I don't think this was intentional," said Billy Miller, M.E., and still loving it after twenty-three years. He hovered, poked, and prodded the body in his methodical way, like a cross between a guardian angel and an annoying mother correcting her kid's posture. "Someone was mad enough to shove him — hard. Hard enough he got spiked."

"Are we talking a push or a punch?"

"I'll know more when I open him up on the table. But see these discolorations here? Little bit of bruising under the chin? At first glance, it looks like someone was mad, but not enough to haymaker his jaw. This looks more like a push, like they just put their hand on the chin and shoved, hard enough that he smacked into the back of the wall. Unfortunately, he had *that* poking out of the wall behind him when he hit." Billy pointed to a wicked looking hook on the wall. Under normal circumstances, it was the kind of flat piece of metal that would hold up the bottom of a bookshelf. Last night it had slid and crunched its way into Daniel Anderson's head. Now it stood mute with dark, drying blood mixed with bits of what could only be brain matter.

"What else?"

"Whaddya mean, what else?" Mitch said, interrupting. "Jack, he's your kid's teacher. Don't you know anything else about him?"

"Can you even *name* your kid's teacher, Mitch?"

Mitch was quiet.

"Okay," I said, taking and then opening his wallet with hands covered in white surgical gloves.

I didn't even remember putting them on. It'd become that automatic to me. "Mister Daniel Anderson, age twenty-nine. Single, my daughter told me. Member of the..." I started going through the cards; there wasn't much cash. "Knights of Columbus, Triple A, proud owner of four Starbucks cards, and..." I pulled out a picture holder, the kind that could keep a bunch of wallet-sized photos in little transparent plastic packs the size of baseball cards.

There were pictures of Daniel Anderson as a kid with an older man and woman by his side.

Then pictures of him as a teenager with a bunch of other teenagers, all smiling and carrying signs with pictures of babies and slogans on them about life, rights, and God. Pictures of a girl, then the same girl wearing a white dress beside him in a tux.

He'd been married? Janie said he was single. Maybe the picture was from his high school prom or a college formal.

I pulled out my phone and used my code to call for his background check. It'd hit my inbox in minutes, maybe seconds, but my instincts already told me there'd be nothing interesting. Time to wake up the pastor, the principal, and the late Mr. Anderson's colleagues. It was going to be a long night for a lot of people.

***

"I can't believe this," she said, dabbing her eyes with a tissue. The principal had gotten to the place within the hour. And now it wasn't quite six a.m. She was older, maybe pushing sixty. Slim, trim, gray and white hair cut short above her ears. But her hastily applied mascara kept trying to run down her face in little black rivulets as tears squeezed out of the corners of her eyes, dodging even her most diligent Kleenexes.

"Do you know anyone who'd want to hurt Daniel, Mrs. Skein?"

"No. And, please, call me Angie," she said, smiling. I saw her eyes flick down to my hand, then back at my eyes while her eyelids fluttered, and the corners of her mouth turned up just a little.

I didn't need to look at her own hand as she dabbed her eyes for the fortieth or fiftieth time.

Peripheral vision told me she had a ring on her finger. I'd also seen that exact smile on more women than I'd ever want to count, often from married women old enough to be my Mom. Must be my badge.

Maybe the tie. Some people have a desperate need to flirt, and women of a certain age and mindset will even do it when someone near them just went room temp.

"Did he have any conflicts with anyone?" I said, trying to bring her back to the real world.

"Colleagues, parents, or students?"

She stopped dabbing just long enough to look at me, her eyes raccoon-like with gooey, wet mascara dripping around them.

"Detective Capri," she said, "Daniel was a young man in a profession dominated by older women. He was the only man on staff this year in a building full of women. What does that say to you?"

I knew what I was supposed to say. It meant everyone has conflicts with everyone here sooner or later. Men are wired to get things done; women are wired to connect to others. It's why girls can't go to the bathroom together for just two minutes, and boys can't play a video game for just five minutes, unless you pry them off with the Jaws of Life. It's why men tend to break or kill things when you threaten their projects and ambitions, and women destroy your reputations and friendships if you break their connections.

It also means that a man in a building full of women can feel isolated, be isolated like a man on a desert island, or a leper in a room full of the healthy. In extreme cases, he can feel like he's always banging on the door of a clubhouse no one else will even admit exists, wanting to be let in while those inside pretend not to notice.

But I needed to give her room to say that, because then

she might say more. I shrugged my shoulders and kept looking at her.

She kept talking. "Mister Anderson—Danny, he—he had his opinions, but he didn't have a mean bone in his body. Really. Some parents were mad when he brought the kids to a pro-life protest for a field trip, and others when he brought in an ex-gay to Religion class. *That* led to a few choice words with a few people. Several of the parents, even one of the visitors who came by to talk to the kids for Career Day, apparently they all had a long chats with him about it. But he was a good man, Detective Capri."

I jotted that down. She printed out the three angry emails she got from parents who were shocked, *shocked* that their kid would learn what the Catholic Church taught in Catholic Religion class in a Catholic school from a guy with a degree in Catholic theology. Stupid, really. Mom once told me: if you don't want to get your boots dirty, don't work on a farm.

"Anything else?" I said after reading the emails.

"Yes, I was going to bring this up before you left. There was an...well, an unfortunate *situation* with one of the mothers here."

Uh huh.

***

An hour later I was in another meeting room in the school in the middle of another chat, one I wanted to wrap up quick. School had been cancelled for the day, but the news was already going around the gossip channels. Every mom and kid from the school with a Facebook account or a cell phone was burning up the lines, telling everyone who was awake by seven a.m. about the Anderson murder. I wanted to be able to go home today with good news for my daughter. I wanted to tell her we'd caught who did this.

But things weren't going they way they usually did. I'm used to finding out a bunch of dirty little secrets when I go looking into the lives of dead people, especially if they're pillars of the community. But Mr. Anderson's life was going in the opposite direction. This time, our vic was quite the Boy Scout. I'd been through nearly a thousand of Anderson's old emails since breakfast, and nothing gave me a single red flag or viable lead.

When Mrs. Streel sat down, I closed my phone that I'd been reading the late teacher's emails with. Then I looked at her and tried not to gulp.

"Thanks for coming in to talk on such short notice, Mrs. Streel," I said, hoping my eyes hadn't popped too far out of my head.

Caroline Streel was what my Uncle Georgie called a looker. You could tell she turned heads every time she walked into a room. Long blond hair swept into a ponytail, blue eyes set into a high cheek boned face that could've been just as easily on the cover of *Seventeen* as *Cosmo*. And she had a red skirt that ended just above her knees. I'd heard before of legs that just wouldn't quit, but never really understood the term until now. Mrs. Streel made men stare and women seethe, and I could see her ignoring both with equal ease.

Weirdest of all, she didn't have the attitude most women like her had when they talked to me.

She was calm, professional and helpful, working hard and largely succeeding at keeping the tears down. I'd seen women half as attractive act like they were queens granting me an audience instead of a person of interest in a murder.

"It's not a problem, Detective," she said, "I know you're just doing your job, and the sooner we get this done, the sooner you can find the man who did this."

Why do you think it's a man, I thought. *Or, do you*

want me to think *it's a man*? I tucked that away to use later.

"Mrs. Streel, I'm going to get right to the point here. Did you know Mr. Anderson had feelings for you?"

Mrs. Streel's hands fidgeted just a little. If this had been one of the late night, black and white movies my Dad used to watch, she would have taken a long drag on a cigarette, stared off into space, and thought hard before answering.

But she didn't. We were in a twenty-first century American school, which meant no smoking.

Instead she got the big-eyed, staring-off-into-space kind of worried glare that pretty high school girls get when told the school geek has a crush on them.

"Yes," she said, nodding her head while looking at the ground.

"Was anything going on, Mrs. Streel?"

"No," she said, her eyes snapping back up. "Nothing happened, and nothing would. I really enjoyed him as a person. But obviously, I'm very, very married." She looked at me steady, dead on. I tucked that one away, too. After you've broken up about ten thousand domestic disputes, you get to where you can tell the difference between disdain, pity, and love just by hearing the tone of voice and a few words. There wasn't any hatred or disgust in her voice for the teacher who liked her. Maybe a hint of pity, most likely for Anderson. And, if I read her right, there was a lot of love for her husband, too.

"What were your connections to him?"

"He...well, he taught my daughter. My daughter just loved him. He was wonderful with the kids. The activities he did, the stories he told. They just loved being in his room."

I made a show of jotting that down. I already had it

elsewhere, but she needed to know that I did this sort of thing.

"Anything else?"

"Danny Anderson liked to write. I'm a psychologist by training, though I'm not practicing much these days. He asked me for help sometimes, to know how some kinds of pathology worked. My expertise is child psychology, not criminal. But I still found it a little exciting, being just a small part of that world where all the writing and publishing goes on."

"Are you aware if he published anything?"

She kept that steady look. "If you're asking me if he was flattering me, asking for help with stories that never saw the light of day, I'm happy to say I can pick up *that* kind of phony a mile away.

"No, he was published, and more than happy to send me copies of the magazines his stories were published in. It was his way of thanking me and showing his appreciation."

"Okay..." Write a little more, then come back to the point. I'd already seen the stuff he'd written; he kept copies of the magazines that had accepted his work in his desk drawer. He'd written two pieces of heist fiction, a few articles for a teacher's magazine, and a story about an unhappy family. But nothing he wrote was twisted — nothing to make a red flag shoot up in my head. Nothing there or in his emails or his Facebook page gave any indication of an evil, secret side. "You didn't tell me, though, how his feelings made you feel, or what it made you do."

She sighed deeply. "He was such a good man, Detective, and a single one. Rumor is his wife left him years back, though I don't know why and never asked. A number of the moms here batted their eyes at him, and some of us in the school community tried setting him up with people. But he was pickier than some would say he had a right to be. He said once he made one mistake already and didn't want to do that a second time. He told me he was scared of meeting and marrying the wrong one."

I already knew about that. Right after she'd told me about Mrs. Streel, Angie — the principal upstairs — had told me Anderson's wife had left him nearly a half-decade before — and left him for another woman. Strange days. Normal in California, maybe, or on TV. But not here. I knew how something like that could knock you around and change things. A few years after Dad left and I learned how to use the internet, I'd looked him up. He was living in Coso Viejo with his latest roommate, some guy named Devon. Didn't bother talking to him, and I still haven't told Mom. News like that, even nearly two decades later, would send her sprawling. Maybe it explained why Teacher Danny had moved here to begin with and why he still carried her picture in his wallet.

"He wasn't a player, then?" I asked.

"No," she said, shaking her head and making her ponytail wag. "He was a very religious man, and not the Jekyll-and-Hyde kind, either. If you make that kind of mistake in a small community like this, well, everyone knows it soon enough. And they know the most entertaining version of it, too."

She gave a small sigh, looking off to her right. "The worst I can say is that most women can pick up if a man likes her, however he tries to hide it. And Danny wasn't really good at hiding his feelings. Still, he was always a perfect gentleman with me, never even hinted at trying an affair or anything like that.

"But over time I could tell how he felt. His face lit up more and more when he saw me. He got so much more animated when we'd talk, especially after I entered the Church last Easter. People said he looked so down if I passed through the school and he didn't get the chance to talk to me about...well, almost nothing, usually."

"So, he didn't give off any weird vibes?"

"No," she said, shaking her head again. Another pert little ponytail wag. "Not at all. The kids call it being a *creeper* when you do that. Danny just gave off a sense of being...I suppose misguided is the best word for it. He knew it couldn't happen, but he just didn't seem able to really stop. Most folks have been there. I used to get clients all the time who wanted something they just couldn't have. It's hard for them, but so long as you don't do something stupid, those wants usually fade.

"As to how it made me feel..." she continued, her voice trailing off. "Well..." She was asking herself the question now, more than answering it. "It was nice, to be quite honest. When a good person who's not actually bad-looking likes you, I'd say it's nice. Even flattering. But it does become somewhat sad after a while."

She was pretty composed. She'd already known how to detach, to cut off feelings for someone who could harm themselves. "For me" she continued, "at least things were easily solved. He's not the first fellow to feel that way about me when I couldn't return anything. I just made sure I only talked to him in a group setting, and I told my husband right away."

I lowered my pen. "Your husband?"

***

Joshua Streel, age thirty-six, crossed his arms and leaned back in the same chair his wife had sat in not an hour before.

"How do you think I felt?" he said.

"Well, me," I said, "if one of my kid's teachers was hitting on my wife, I'd be pretty mad about it."

"Detective," he said, the fluorescent lights glinting off his glasses, "Guys hit on my wife all the time. I'm very secure in her love for me and our daughter."

"So, how did you react when she told you Danny was one of those guys?"

"Truth?" He leaned forward. "Danny really wasn't one of those guys. He kept his distance. Besides, I wasn't all that surprised. He was loved by just about everyone in this school, but he still had to go home to an empty house at night. My wife is a lovely woman, and she takes her job and her faith very seriously."

"You're both Catholic?"

"She is. I like that she likes it, and Danny was pretty excited when she joined the Church last Easter. But for a variety of reasons, it's not something I can share with her at this time. That was another connection they had. They both loved all that religious stuff. I can see why women would join the Catholics, but a single, healthy man being told he can't play around? There's people in this world I'll just never understand, you know?"

Yeah, I knew. I'd met a lot of messed up folks on this job that I didn't and never would understand. And I liked it that way, thank you very much.

"So, Josh," I said, "can I call you Josh? You were okay with her helping him? With his writing, I mean."

"Helping? Well, more like she made sure he didn't embarrass himself with errors when his characters ran into pathological liars or serial killers. But yes, I was fine with it, so long as nothing happened."

"How do you know nothing happened?"

"Detective, I've known Caroline since we were college kids, and that was over a decade and a half ago. I'd know if something was up. She talked about him a bit, and she liked seeing her name credited in print at the end of his stories, but that was it. Besides, when was the last time you heard of a woman from the Hills cheating on her husband with a schoolteacher? I know it sounds snobby, but it just doesn't happen. I mean, Danny himself was on a first name basis with several janitors here at the school, but that didn't mean he'd feel comfortable going out for a beer or dating them. Even if they were attractive."

I looked at him again. He wasn't huge, but he wasn't scrawny, either. Josh Streel was trim, with dark, close cropped hair and a strong jaw line. He looked like a Marine, but he didn't have the quick, deft movements of a man trained to kill.

But he *was* confident. Wide shoulders, slim waist, probably he was a former college athlete. Not a football player, but maybe a swimmer.

Yeah, confident. I'd been watching him. No sweating, no nervous twitch, no eyes darting around when I asked him about the possibility of his wife having an affair with his kid's teacher.

Either Josh wasn't my guy, or he was a very, very good actor for a Harp Street stockbroker.

He'd mentioned janitors.

Janitor? Hurm.

***

My daughter Janie is a cop's kid, which means any boy who's going to ask my daughter out is either a) such a saint I don't have to worry about him, b) such a thrill seeker he'll think he's faced worse things than me, or c) so stupid he'll have no idea who he's dealing with.

Until I can check him out and prove him otherwise, I'll assume every new boyfriend of Janey's is like a certain kind of young man. The kind of young man I see about once a week in my interview room. The kind of young man like the twitchy young man in my interview room now, the young janitor who found the late Mister Anderson.

When I begin an interrogation, the routine is always the same. I sit down and start pretending to fill out more paperwork. This goes on for at least sixty long seconds.

But, like so many things we do, it's all a trick. I'm not really doing paperwork.

If you're in the hot seat opposite me, what I'm really doing is watching you out of the corner of my eye.

Today, that subject is Jose Mendez. A young male, single and handsome, from the lower middle class. Today, that often means he's likely got a dozen girlfriends and a half-dozen diaper-clad dependents running around in little bare feet, asking their mommies when he's coming home.

He's also got the twitch. It's my name for the little eye-contact-sitting-still problem folks have who're coming off junk. I steal a look at him for a few seconds and decide he's maybe a month clean.

I don't know much else about him, other than what I've got in his folder on my desk. This is his second go around with the cops on this case, but his first with me.

I start with the questions, make him tell his story, then make him tell it again. And again. It's an hour before I start in on for real.

"You're going to have to run that one by me again, Jose. What did you and Danny talk about when you saw each other?"

"Uhhh...geeze, man, well..."

Yeah. Genius. It was early afternoon, and he was tired,

too used to the nightlife. Too used to waking up at around six p.m., eating, playing videogames until about ten at night, then going out wilding with friends or looking for something to steal and sell so he can feed the monster that lived in his veins.

He'd supposedly gotten religion and finished rehab a few weeks back, and the janitor job was his first step back into the world most of the rest of us knew.

"Uhhh..." he said. I could almost hear the long, unused brain cells yelling in frustration as they tried to connect to each other. "TV shows, sometimes. He liked old cartoons, like *Bugs Bunny* n' that.

"Sometimes we'd talk about shows like that one that got cancelled a while back, the one about the superhero? And, uh, religion some, too."

Yeah. He was getting really tired. Taking an early entry ticket to that magic land where people got stupid and thought I was their friend. That's a mistake that usually leads to tripping over their own shoes as they walked down the yellow brick road into an eight-by-ten suite in one of Uncle Sam's finer crossbar hotels.

Time to turn up the heat.

"Did you two talk about laptops, Jose?"

He blinked. "What?"

"Laptops, Jose. We can't find the laptop the school gave him. The one that was worth about a grand. You know what I think?"

"Dude, I..."

"You were in there, Jose. You saw it. You saw a good chunk of change, and you snatched it. Somehow he was in there, and you *shot him in the gut*, Jose!" I was getting in his face now. Keeping him from thinking. Even the stupidest suspect can think up a way to wriggle out of a mess if you give them enough time to think. But Jose hadn't said the L-word, hadn't asked to go, and if I did my job right, he wasn't getting the chance to do any of those things. If all went well, I'd keep hounding him over the next eight or nine hours until he broke.

Of course I was lying. We did have the teacher's laptop. It was sitting in the tech garage, and one of our geeks was going over every website, email, and download of Teacher Danny's with a fine-toothed comb, looking for any clue as to who'd want to shoot a schoolteacher in the gut.

Oh yeah, scratch that last bit. Did you catch it? Teacher Danny hadn't been shot in the gut. I lied about that, too. Did you know we could do that? *Hey, Butch? Sundance next door just gave you up. You better start helping us out, because the window that lets me help you out is closing, closing, closing, and... oh, thanks for signing that confession. By the way, Sundance didn't flip on you. I lied.*

And the Constitution says it's all ok. See you when you get out of Sing Sing in twenty.

Young people instinctively like to correct their elders, and we hadn't released the exact COD to the general public yet. If Jose fell into that trap and corrected me? If Jose said Teacher Danny had died from being head spiked by the bookshelf bracket? You might as well start playing the banjo music now, 'cause now you're Ned Beatty in *Deliverance.*

All I wanted right now was to hear those three, magic words, "I did it," and see whatever passed for his signature on that magic piece of paper, the one that lets me go home because he confessed his guilt.

It was all I wanted. But I wasn't going to get it. Not this time.

Maybe I wasn't fast enough. Maybe Jose had cleaned

out his system enough his brain could still fire a few sparks if you rubbed some neurons together. Maybe Jesus took a break from working at that Evangelical church where Jose had his NA meetings and whispered in Jose's twitching little ear. I don't know. I *do* know I wasn't even close to seeing him break when he said the L-word...

"I want a *lawyer*, man!"

... and I had to stop talking.

Twenty minutes went by while one of our secretaries looked for a court-appointed *lawyer* for Jose. I was praying in my own little way that he'd get the drunk CA who usually worked to get purse snatchers and whores out of night court, rather than the usual two or three sharpies we'd been getting lately. Those CAs were kids in their mid-20s, fresh out of law school, who saw beating the cops and letting junkies free to juice and kill and rape and steal again as part of some bizarre holy crusade.

"Tough night?"

I'd just left the interrogation room when I'd heard the voice. I looked up, and it was Lavin again.

The badge on his patrolman's uniform and his moustache shone in the break room light, like weird little beacons. One of the many rumors that flitted around about him was that he put some kind of gel into his moustache to keep it trim and dashing. No one I knew worth their salt had time to bounce that kind of garbage around in their heads. But I'd seen what happened to folks who criticized others without having the right friends first. And I was too busy doing my job to make the right kinds of friends.

"Yeah, kinda," I said. "Li'l Crackhead over in the interview room lawyer'd up. Now I've got a good hour to kill while they wake someone up, get him down here and he has his interview with Jose."

"You think he's the guy?" Lavin said.

I looked at him for a second. "You knew this guy, didn't you, Lavin? The teacher, I mean."

"Nah, no…well, not really, Jackie," he said. "Remember how you asked for folks to go talk to schools for the Career Day thing they do? I went there last year. He shook my hand for a second or two, but that was it."

I remembered. Community appearances were good for overtime and performance reviews.

Janie had asked me, but I couldn't make it that day, so I'd gone and put up a poster for the guys who wanted to get some hours do-gooding. I'd already seen Lavin's name pop up in a thank-you-themed bulk email the teacher had sent out one of about a hundred, thank-you-themed bulk emails Danny Anderson'd sent out over the last few months.

"Still," I said, "what'dja think of him? You talk to 'im at all?"

Lavin thought for a second, shrugged. "Some. Nice guy. Snapped pictures of everyone. He was always going around with a camera. Some of the moms seemed to look at him a little too long, but that was the worst of it."

Uh huh. I finished the cup of lukewarm coffee as my cell went off again. I started talking and got a pleasant surprise. The CA had gotten into the station house in record time, which meant Jose could be ready to talk in as little as a half hour.

By the time Weasel got done with Jose, I'd talked to a couple of people on the phone, and then clicked around at a few important places online at my desk.

"My client denies any involvement with the tragic death of Mister Anderson," Archie the CA said after I got back into the interrogation room. Most of us just called him Archie the Weasel, but that was more for having a long nose, high nasal voice, and buckteeth than anything to do with his legal work. I could easily imagine him getting his face shoved into some locker when he'd been as old as Teacher Danny's students.

"Furthermore, Detective," Archie continued, "my client demands—"

"Archie," I said, a new printout in my hand, "you can shut up. We're cutting him loose."

Archie was quiet for a second. His eyes lit up. "You mean, we're done?"

Yeah, I thought. You just made a full day of county pay for about an hour of work. You can go home and sleep in tomorrow, you lucky, weaselly little bastard.

"Yeah, we're done. On one condition: Your client has to tell me who he propped the door of the school open for that night. Remember, Jose? About an hour or two before your shift started?"

Jose looked at me, ignoring his lawyer for a second.

"Jose," Archie said. Jose didn't look over.

"Tell your client," I said, holding Jose's gaze and pushing the printout of the satellite photo across the table, "that if he tells me everything, he'll get immunity. I know he's a reformed thief, not the type to willingly be an accessory to murder. At least that's what the preacher at his church and his P.O. said when I talked to them a couple of minutes ago."

The Weasel looked at Jose and nodded his head. Jose was still reluctant to bite. I could tell he'd been burned on a deal before.

"Archie," I said, "I'm busy. I don't have time to bat this around. He's got ten seconds to make up his mind before I walk out that door and take the deal with me."

"Put it in writing first, and I'll talk," Jose said, now looking at me.

I looked at Jose with a little more respect than I had when I came in the room. I expected to find the same twitchy, tired, recovering methhead I'd left in here. Guys like him were usually too jumpy to be in shouting distance of their right mind. I'd met people willing to deny Christ three times if it kept them out of the joint another week.

But Jose — now Jose knew his rights. And he had enough working grey matter between his ears to invoke them. He must be farther along in rehab than I thought.

Yeah, I respected him, but right now I didn't like him. I hadn't slept in nearly twenty-four hours, and he'd just figured out how to make my shift go for an extra sixty minutes or so. Not a way to get on my good side.

"One," I counted, holding up my index finger.

"He wants it in writing, first," Archie said.

"It hurts me deeply that he won't take my word for it. Two."

"Your word isn't what's got me worried, guy," Jose said, looking at me steadily. "I got me a woman and baby at home who need me. And I don' know I'll see 'em without something on paper first."

"You worried I'll back out, buddy? You kill someone else you don't want to talk about? I've got you over a barrel. The alarm company says the door triggers were deactivated. Add to that how any ten-year-old with a laptop can do a Google Earth or any one of a dozen apps like it, and then see what this door on the West side of the school looked like under the streetlamp at midnight," I said, still holding his gaze but tapping the paper with the security company's logo with my pencil, "It was propped open, probably with a rock or a newspaper. Only someone who knows the school would know that's the only door that the security cams can't see. Sad for you that something like the Google car or a satellite that's a couple hundred miles up can see you just fine.

"Plus, Jose, I just got off the phone with your boss. It looks like your shift started after the alarms were shut off. What's the security company gonna say when I ask them whose key was the only key to open the building that time of night, Jose? Oh yeah, Three."

"My client's not worried about you betraying him, Detective," Archie cut in. "We both know that even if the Google car was driving around, it wasn't taking pictures at night. Your bluff won't get you what you want. He just doesn't want a big blue wall to fall on him if he opens his mouth and you don't like what you hear."

I was set to raise my fourth finger, and stopped.

It was Archie's turn to wear the smug expression, and not just because he'd seen right through my Google Earth thing. Archie was looking more puffed up than a pigeon with a belly full of breadcrumbs because he'd just said the last thing any cop wants to hear.

"You got a legal pad?" I asked. I was ready to write down a deal.

"You got a photocopier?" His briefcase was already open.

***

When I was nine, I threw up my Granny's lasagna in front of the whole family at the dinner table. My Granny was there, my Mom was there, my Uncle Georgie was there, and my uncle's girlfriend who I'd had a kiddie crush on was there, too.

I'd left the table feeling two kinds of sick in my gut from throwing up and in my heart for having made everyone else feel sick, too. I felt both kinds of sick now, too.

But when I was nine, I was sick from something I had

done but hadn't done voluntarily.

Now, it was from something I was *going* to do. I would do it of my own free will, but reluctantly as molasses flowing uphill in January.

"How's it going," said a voice behind me. "How's Li'l Crackhead in there, Jackie?"

I looked around. It was Lavin. I looked him in the eyes for a very long minute and he bit his lip.

"Talk," I said.

"Lawyer," he said back.

***

"…You just put the cuffs on *Lavin*?"

"He was guilty, Red," I said. The chief, the commish, they were all different names for the same thing in different precincts. Here, he was just Red.

"You'd better have a case so airtight it can walk on water, Jackie. You know why?"

"I know. I know. No one wants to be accused of homophobia these days. But I've got a witness who just signed the confession: Lavin threatened to tell Jose's P.O. that Jose'd gotten back into his old life. It was a lie, but a cop can slam a guy with Jose's record back in the joint with a phone call, and they both knew it."

"But did Jose know Lavin was gonna kill Anderson?"

"Nope. He thought Lavin was just a dirty cop who was gonna rip off a few laptops from Anderson's classroom. Lavin really wanted something else, though."

Red looked at me and drummed his fingers. "What's Lavin doing now?"

"Spilling his guts to his mouthpiece. He's trying to spin it so's that he tried to talk Anderson into never having an ex-gay into the classroom as a speaker again. Said what

Anderson was doing was wrong. The way Lavin's trying to spin it, he was just trying to talk some sense into Teacher Danny and things got out've hand."

"Fer the love'a Pete, Jackie...you're serious about this? It won't pass the laugh test at the arraignment. A prosecutor'll just ask why he didn't talk to him after school, instead of two a.m."

"Anderson was pretty dedicated, and most folks knew it. Sometimes he'd be in there 'til *four* in the morning on a Friday night, catching up on grading or doing whatever. My guess? Lavin had a crush on this guy and hated him for bringing the ex-gay group into the school. Or post-gay, or whatever they're calling themselves these days. Maybe Lavin thought at first Anderson was like him, but just a tough nut to crack or something, a challenge. Maybe Lavin's the kind that goes after straights. We're still trying to piece that part together."

"You know what the press is gonna do, right?" said Red.

I furrowed my brow. "I'm not following you," I said. "There's a dozen murders a year in the city. They talk about it a little, and then it goes away. Why should this one get more press than any other?"

"Jackie, fer Gawd's sake, where you been the last twenty years? All you guys from the coast have yer head in the sand and yer thumbs up yer asses? It started with Miss California and *Will and Grace*. Now, if you don't jump up and clap and sing 'hallelujah' loud enough when someone says 'gay marriage,' it don't matter if you're a movie star or a CEO. You lose your job, an' the press practically hangs a sign around yer neck with the word 'bigot' on it, then they beam it out on the *Drag Report*."

"*Drudge Report*, Red."

"Whatever. Look, just make sure you keep the gay angle

out of the press, or they'll jackhammer us and try to make this whole thing about something it ain't. You got me?"

I nodded my head. I didn't totally get it, no. But I understood it was what my boss wanted, and that's usually enough around here, or anywhere.

***

Out in the parking lot a couple of hours later. Finally, I'd finished the last of the paperwork and put the case to bed, and now I could look forward to the same for myself. I made a bit of a mistake; instead of walking through the maze of back hallways and traipsing to my car from the back of the lot through a forest of squad cars and the small fleet of SWAT team APCs, I took the short route through the front door of the station house, meaning to go through the front gate where my car had sat waiting for me for over a day now.

As I opened the glass door, I saw the van and the lights. But there was no way I could've known they were there for me. Not until the klieg lights flipped on and pounded my eyes with about two million candlepower.

"Detective Capri? *Detective Capri?*" said a voice as I shielded my eyes.

I recognized the voice instantly, though I wanted to believe I was hearing it in a bad dream. My sister-in-law loved Danny Vine, host of a local celebrity gossip show an hour away in the city.

Whenever she visited, his voice ended up booming throughout the house, and my widescreen TV bashed the living room with his collection of neon-colored suits. He'd tried coming out last year to improve ratings, but the show's struggles were often as much of a story as the latest celeb breakup or DUI arrest.

"Can I help you?" I said, hoping that he was looking for

directions to the cell in the drunk tank we'd put the local kiddie show host in last week.

"Detective Capri," Vine shouted at me while shoving a microphone in my face. He sounded more like a war correspondent in the middle of a firefight rather than a gossip columnist in a near-deserted parking lot at half past five in the morning. "How do you respond to accusations that the department has targeted officer Lavin because of his orientation?"

I looked at Vine. He wasn't the first reporter to try and rattle me. And he wasn't the first guy I'd felt like punching out because he was yelling at me after a long, long day. "No comment at this time," I said while walking to my car.

"Isn't it true that the dead teacher's first wife was gay?"

"The department has no comment on this ongoing investigation."

"Isn't it true he taught homophobic lessons in his classroom?"

"No comment."

"How deep does homophobia run in your department, Detective?"

"No comment."

"How do you respond to accusations that you *yourself* brought bias into this case, because your father left you and your mother for the man he loved?"

I swallowed. Something inside me twisted up and wanted to lash out and die at the same time.

My gut hadn't hurt like that since Tom Greco had given me the biggest beat down of my life back in middle school.

"No comment," I said, hoping my face stayed stoic as I reached my car, wishing mightily I'd taken a few extra minutes earlier to park in the fenced-in lot. As I drove away, Vine was facing his camera again, his voice beating a relentless, rhythmic tattoo as he yammered about 'hate in the holy...' something or other.

Yeah, I thought later, driving home. If they pick it up and run with it, by this time next week Danny Anderson, beloved Catholic schoolteacher, he won't ever have existed. Not in television land, where it really matters today. Whoever and whatever the real Daniel Anderson was will be smashed, melted, and molded into what some TV producer wants. By this time tomorrow night, Daniel Anderson'll probably be reshaped into an evil, hate-filled creature, who brought in the ex-gays as a way of striking back at his ex-wife.

Though the world screams for choice, there are some choices it cannot, will not, allow. And if you choose wrong, the hammers and shapers of the world will first ignore you, then attack you. Not with guns, knives, nets, and lions, but the internet, the newspaper, and a hundred CNN stories.

And, the stories will say, he wasn't trying to give a side you haven't heard before. He only stood for lies. The open-minded will demand your mind be closed. Those who claim to stand for love will demand you hate Anderson and anyone like him. Must hate anyone from the wrong side who dares to hold their head higher than they are allowed to.

More thoughts as I came off the overpass. A week ago this road was impassable, but now it was clear. Just as they changed the road, the image of Danny Anderson could be reshaped until his own mother wouldn't recognize him. The love Danny Anderson had for the students and their families forgotten in a week, his smiling face replaced by the most unflattering photo they can dig up on him.

Every good memory of him replaced by every flaw his

high school girlfriends can remember, and every single comment anyone remembers that could have the least disturbing ring pulled from it.

And Lavin will get a slap on the wrist; maybe even sue the department for arresting him. And he'll win.

For now.

But only for now. I hope only for now.

I pull into my driveway, halfway in a dream from lack of sleep and the surreal process we call justice in our country.

My wife kisses me as I walk in the door. My little Janie sees me five seconds later, looking at me with big, blue, twelve-year-old eyes, asking me if I found who killed Mr. Anderson.

Yes, we got him, honey, I say, the need for sleep making my voice and thoughts thick as peanut butter. "But do me a favor first, would you? Before you go on Facebook, would you do something for me, honey?"

"What?" she asks.

"Go upstairs, and write out every good thing Mr. Anderson ever did for you and everyone else.

"Tell me why he was your favorite teacher, why the students loved him, why the parents loved him, and put it in a safe place where no one can ever take it from you. When you've done that, come see me. I'll still be awake."

After she leaves, I keep thinking.

Please come see me, Janie, and help me know that those who hate in the name of love can't eclipse a good man. Help me know a good man's memory can last when everyone wants to rewrite his history, not just on the printed page, but in the minds of all who were there. Help me know that we're not all going to be hammered again and again with someone else's fantasy of how the world ought to be. Help me know and believe and remember that we all saw something different in your teacher than what the TV will show us in the morning.

Come see me, honey, and show me what you've written.

Then I can sleep, knowing the bad guys won't always win.

"I don't care what she said — I already told Ryan yes!" Krista dropped her backpack on the bed and flopped down next to it, sending her rose-print comforter billowing in all directions.

"Can't you get your dad to back you up?" Hannah asked.

Krista shot her friend a "yeah, right" look. "You know my mom. When she makes up her mind, that's it."

Nodding, Hannah kicked off her sandals and sank into a beanbag chair. "So what are you going to do?"

"Whatever it takes!"

Hannah sighed. "I wish somebody asked me to go. You're probably the only sophomore in the whole school that a senior — let alone, Ryan Girardi — asked to the prom."

"I know, right?" Krista beamed. "Ryan said he liked what I did for the swim team uniform." Her smile faded. "I know it's last minute, though."

"Who cares?" Hannah tossed a stuffed panda at her friend. "I sure wouldn't."

"Yeah, but I don't know what to do about Mom. It's not about the dress — I can use my own money if I have to. It's not even about the prom — she's okay with that...sort of. It's about going down the shore with Ryan and his friends for the whole weekend...even though I told her other girls are going."

"Does he expect you to...you know?" Hannah looked down at the rug.

"What if he does?" Krista shrugged.

"Do you think he might bail out if you tell him you can't go for the weekend?"

"I'm afraid to find out. I'd rather just tell Mom he promised to bring me home Friday night, and then call her Saturday from the beach."

Hannah's eyes widened. "You wouldn't do that, would you?"

Krista stared at the stuffed panda in her lap and picked at the fuzz on its ears. "I don't want to," Krista said, "but I will if I have to."

"Are you sure?"

"Almost." Krista searched Hannah's face for a vote of confidence, but Hannah just looked back at her, wide-eyed.

"That's okay, Hannie. Don't worry. I'll think of something." Krista stood up. "You better get going. The last thing I need is for Mom to think I'm slacking off on homework."

Hannah picked up her overstuffed backpack and headed for the door. "See you tomorrow."

"Okay, bye." Krista fished *The Scarlet Letter* out of her backpack, stretched out on the bed, and started wading through the last chapters, twirling a long, espresso-dark curl around her finger as she read. *Maybe they'll let me go if I promise to wear a scarlet letter on my chest when I come back — a big red S for slu....*Krista sat up straight. *I could tell Mom it skips a generation...*

Krista threw down the book and bolted to her mother's bedroom. She dug through the bottom dresser drawer until she found the dog-eared business card she'd hoped was still there. She dialed the number. A few minutes later she made a second call to Hannah.

"I told you not to worry, Hannie," Krista said. "I think

I've found someone who'll be on my side."

"Good, because if you're going, you have to find a dress this weekend. And if you're not, you better let Ryan know so he can find..." Hannah's voice trailed off.

"It's okay. Everything's going to be just fine."

"So who's your ally?"

"Uh-oh — I hear Mom's car. Gotta go. I'll tell you all about it at school."

***

The next morning, Bill Johnson poked his head around the kitchen doorway as his wife poured a cup of coffee.

"Is the coast clear?" he asked.

"All clear," Jan answered. "I expected an argument — or at least icy silence — but all Krista did was grab a bagel and say, 'See you later,' on her way out the door."

"Maybe your little talk got through to her," Bill said, as he helped himself to a bagel.

"I hope so. She just turned sixteen. I'm not crazy about the idea that we haven't met or even heard of this boy until yesterday. What kind of guy waits till the last minute to ask a girl to the prom?"

"The desperate kind. His original date probably dumped him."

"Doesn't that make you wonder why?" Jan put her coffee mug down and looked at Bill.

"Not necessarily. Girls can be fickle at that age." Bill spread a thick layer of butter on his bagel and took a bite.

"But why Krista, all of a sudden?"

"Why not?"

Jan buttered her own bagel with short, sharp strokes. "There's no way I'm letting her go to Ocean City for a weekend — especially with people we don't know. *She* doesn't even know them. It's not going to happen."

"You're right," Bill said, pouring his own coffee. "I just hate to see her disappointed."

Jan scowled. "There are worse things than being disappointed."

"Okay, okay. Just remember — she's getting to the age when she's going to make decisions for herself. We can't protect her forever."

"And I don't want to —" Jan's voice softened, "but she needs a little more experience."

"Anyway," Bill said, "for today, so far, so good, right?"

"I guess. Chicken tonight. I'm only working a half-day today — annual audit this afternoon, so I should be home early enough to cook."

"Sounds good." Bill put his empty mug in the sink and brushed the top of Jan's head with a kiss on his way out the door. "I'll see you tonight. Meanwhile, try not to worry."

That afternoon, Jan was slicing peppers in the kitchen when the doorbell rang. She rinsed her hands and, still wiping them on a dish towel, opened the front door.

The woman standing in the doorway remained silent for a long moment. Long, salt-and-pepper curls spilled onto her shoulders. Her gauzy, russet-print skirt made her look like a faded gypsy. Lines creased her forehead and mouth, yet the years had softened her eyes. Finally, she took a deep, "now or never" breath, and gave a little smile.

"Hi, Jan," she whispered.

"Wh...what are you doing here?" Jan asked, eyebrows raised.

"I was invited. Can I come in?"

"Krista called you!" Jan said, a little louder than she intended.

"Yes — I guess she gets her spunk from my side of the family."

"Spunk? Is that what you call it?"

"It doesn't matter what you call it," the woman sighed. "We are who we are."

"Aren't you tired of leftover hippie talk, Peggy? Or do you expect me to call you Mom now?"

"Call me whatever you want." Peggy's shoulders sagged. "I probably deserve any of the choice names you can think of, but I would like to talk to my granddaughter. Is she here?"

"She'll be home from school any minute...and don't think filling her head with your free love philosophy is going to change anything. I don't care what she told you, I'm not letting my daughter spend a weekend down the shore with a bunch of 18-year-olds she barely knows!"

"Look, Jan," Peggy straightened up and squared her shoulders. "Krista called me. I could have met her someplace else. That's what she wanted to do — meet in private — but I told her if I was going to talk to her, I wanted it to be here, with you and her father present."

Jan thought for a minute, then ended up opening the door. "Come in," she said. "I'm just making dinner."

Peggy followed her daughter down the hall, getting her first look of the modest, but tasteful, home. As they passed the living room, she caught a whiff of new carpeting and glimpsed an overstuffed leather loveseat. Peggy sat down at the butcher block table in the kitchen while Jan resumed chopping peppers. Sauce simmering in the crockpot wafted fragrant tomato-richness throughout the kitchen.

"Need a hand?" Peggy offered.

"That's okay," Jan replied, chopping a little faster. "I'm good."

"Lovely home," Peggy began again, after a long pause.

"Thanks. We're comfortable."

In the awkward silence, Peggy studied the kitchen, bright with sun-friendly curtains and butterscotch walls. Her eyes caught sight of a timeworn oak plaque that hung over the doorway and proclaimed one simple word: HOPE. Peggy's eyes filled with tears as she remembered the kitchen of her childhood where that plaque had hung; how, when she was just a little girl, her own mother had brought it home from a retreat and hung it up over their kitchen doorway that same day, so many years ago.

"Grandma's plaque," she murmured.

Jan stopped chopping and looked up. She matched the tears in Peggy's eyes with tears of her own but blinked them back. "You miss her, too?" Jan asked.

"Of course I miss her. I miss them both. They were the best parents anyone could want."

"Then why did you run away from us?"

"I wasn't running away from anybody," Peggy answered. "I was running to find something. I thought it was 'out there' somewhere. I felt like I needed to leave the safety of home to find out what I was made of."

"Safety wasn't all you left behind."

"I know, Jan. I'm so sorry. I know that doesn't make up for all the hurt I caused you. I was just a kid myself. Excuses can't take away your pain, though. If I could make it up to you somehow, I would."

"You can't."

"Of course not." Peggy paused, then added, "Would it help to know that I cared about you and your well-being? I could only afford to leave you because I knew you'd get better love and attention from Grandma and Grandpa than I ever could have given you back then. How could I have taken care of you when I was so lost myself? " She rummaged through her oversized shoulder bag, pulled out a wad of crumpled tissues, and tried to rub the tears away.

"What about after you 'found yourself'?" Jan prodded. "There's been a lot of years since then. Why wait so long to come around?"

"Don't you think I wanted to come? Don't you think I thought about you every day? I spent most of those years trying to forget about you — and the only thing that gave me any peace at all over the guilt was knowing you were in such good hands."

"So you waited until their funerals to come back?"

"How could I face them and you together?" Peggy twiddled the tissue in her hands with nervous fingers. "I hoped, maybe with no other family, there'd be room for you and me to start again."

"I have a family," Jan snapped. She scooped up the chopped peppers and stirred them into the thick sauce bubbling in the crockpot.

"I know." Peggy smiled, dabbing away the final tear. "And it sounds like you and Bill did a fine job raising Krista."

"No thanks to y..."

The front door opened and shut. A minute later, Krista popped into the kitchen.

"Grandma?" It took Krista a minute to connect the aging face and curls with the younger version she'd seen in photos. When she did, Krista cried out, "Grandma!" and gave Peggy a ferocious hug. "I finally get to meet you! I'm so glad you came!"

Jan slammed the crockpot lid down, cracking it. A shard of glass plopped into the sauce. Red splashes spattered wall and counter. She yanked the plug from the outlet and threw down the potholder. "I guess we're having take-out tonight!" she spat and stalked out of the kitchen.

"What's the big deal?" Krista asked Peggy. "Why can't she just forgive and forget? Isn't that what good Christians are supposed to do?"

"I'm not the one to ask about what good Christians are supposed to do," Peggy said, grasping her granddaughter's hand, "but I don't think forgiving means not having feelings. You have to understand, your mother was just a baby when I left. Even though Grandma and Grandpa did a great job of raising her, her own mother abandoned her. How would you feel if your mother abandoned you?"

"Sometimes I wish she would," Krista muttered.

"I know that's how you feel, but feelings aren't forever." Peggy stood up and headed for the stove. "Let's clean up this mess."

By the time Bill got home from work, the kitchen was restored to pristine condition. Peggy sat alone at the table, leafing through take-out menus.

"Hi," she said to Bill. "I'm your mother-in-law."

Bill stopped in his tracks. "Peggy? What are you doing here? Is — is everything okay?"

"That depends on what you call okay. Nobody's sick or anything. Krista's in her room, doing homework. Jan's in your bedroom, I guess, nursing some very old wounds."

Bill nodded. "Okay, I get that part..."

"But what am I doing sitting in your kitchen?"

"Yeah." Bill coughed his way out of a chuckle.

Peggy let out a sigh. "Krista called me last night. I guess she got my number from the business card I left Jan at the funeral parlor. Apparently, Krista needs me on her side because she wants to spend a weekend with a bunch of kids down the shore."

"And she asked you to convince Jan and me to let her go? She obviously didn't think it through."

"Actually, I don't think that was Krista's plan. I think she just wanted my approval so she would work up the guts to go without your permission. She asked to meet me on the sly, but I told her I would only talk about it if you and Jan were in on the conversation. So Krista invited me here, and here I am."

Bill let out a long breath, like a tire with a slow leak. "I guess I'll go talk to Jan."

Peggy nodded. "But first," she held up two menus, "Chinese or pizza?"

"Pizza," Bill called as he headed upstairs. "Let's keep things as simple as possible."

Twenty minutes later, the doorbell rang. Bill paid the delivery man and put the pizza on the table. Family members came out of neutral corners and converged in the kitchen. Krista got out paper plates and napkins. They all sat quietly while Jan said grace. A tentative stillness settled in. Over dinner they chatted about Krista's good grades and swim team awards. Peggy gave a nutshell version of her patchwork career that ended with managing Rusty's Café for the last twenty plus years.

"I'd retire," Peggy wrapped up, "but they need me now that Rusty's gone. Besides," she shrugged, "it gives me something to do."

Once the table was cleared and coffee was brewing, the real conversation started.

"Thanks for coming, Grandma," Krista began. "You're the best!"

Peggy's eyes welled up — as much from Krista's affection as from seeing Jan cringe when Krista pronounced her absentee grandma "the best."

"Best or worst," Peggy started.

Jan opened her mouth.

Bill was quicker. "Maybe somewhere in between...like the rest of us."

Jan glared at him but let it pass.

"Anyway," Peggy continued, "I'm here, Krista. What's on your mind?"

"Well, Ryan Girardi — he's a senior — asked me to go to the prom with him. Of course, I said yes...I know it's last minute and everything — it's probably because he got dumped, but I don't care. Really. He could ask anybody he wants and he asked me!"

Jan stood up to pour the coffee. "Think about it, Krista. If he could ask anybody, why would he ask a barely 16-year-old sophomore?"

"What's the matter?" Krista shot back. "Don't you think a popular boy could like me for me?"

"That's not what Mom meant," Bill said, reaching across the table for Krista's hand.

"Of course not," Jan said, her voice a little softer. "I just can't help wondering why he'd ask someone so much younger than he is, someone he barely knows."

"We've seen each other around at school. He's on the swim team, too. What's the big deal?" Krista turned to Peggy. "Anyway, Mom and Dad won't let me go."

"That's not true," Jan said and faced Peggy. "I don't mind if Krista goes to the prom with Ryan as long as we meet him first. But he wants her to spend the weekend with him and some other seniors in a house they rented in Ocean City. Prom, yes. Ocean City, no."

"Don't you trust me?" Krista demanded.

"Krista, I love you. You're a smart girl and you have a

good heart — but even smart people can get in over their heads. And good-hearted people are especially liable to think — if someone does something that makes them happy — they need to reciprocate in some...special way."

Krista rolled her eyes. "Welcome to the new millennium, Mom."

Jan's jaw tightened, then softened again as she saw Krista's nose and cheeks redden — tears couldn't be far behind. Jan rested her hand on her daughter's shoulder.

Krista flinched it away and rubbed her eyes with the heels of her hands. "If I don't go for the weekend, Ryan might un-invite me and find somebody else. That's what you want, isn't it?"

Bill jumped in. "If saying no to the overnight is a deal breaker, maybe Ryan's not the boy for you."

The skirmish rehashed previously covered ground while Peggy sat quietly, sipping her coffee, waiting for someone to ask for her two cents.

Finally, Krista turned to Peggy, confident that her "love generation" grandmother would even up the battle lines. "What do you think, Grandma?"

All eyes turned to Peggy. She put down her coffee mug, looked from one face to another, then looked down at her hands.

"Well," she began, "first off, I feel lucky to be part of this at all, but I'm a guest here. You've been a family for a long time without my help. So, what I think doesn't really carry any weight, Krista, but what I think is that your folks are right."

Krista's mouth fell open. "How can you say that, Grandma? It's only a weekend! When you were my age, you hitchhiked out to San Francisco!"

"You don't know the half of it," Peggy said.

"And you did just fine. You traveled, and you met people, and you lived!"

"I did," Peggy nodded.

"And you had fun doing it."

"For a while," Peggy admitted.

"And you settled down when the time was right, after you knew what it was like to really live and love."

"I lived, all right. There were wild times and fascinating people. There were also hard times and disappointments — and lots of people full of themselves...people you couldn't count on."

"You mean like my real grandpa?"

Peggy burst out laughing. "I'm sorry, sweetie. The Danny I remember would be horrified at the thought of being called a grandpa." She stopped laughing. "I lost track of him right after we got to San Francisco. Where he is or how he's doing is anybody's guess."

Jan's cheeks flushed. She fidgeted with her spoon and stared down at the table. She'd never known who her real father was and, from what she'd heard over the years, she'd never been sure if Peggy even knew.

"Did you love each other?" Krista asked.

"I thought we did. We thought 'making love, not war' was so enlightened. Maybe it was. Maybe it still is. But what we were doing was sharing pleasure — not making love. And that can lead to heartbreak."

Jan studied the tell-tale creases around her mother's eyes.

"What kind of love abandons new life?" Peggy's voice cracked as she choked back a sob.

Bill filled a glass with water and quietly set it on the table in front of her.

Krista looked from her grandmother to her mother and

then back to her grandmother. "Things are different now, Grandma. There are ways to prevent these things."

"There were ways in the sixties, too. What do you think made us the "free love" generation? Only it wasn't free and it certainly wasn't love for a lot of us. People don't always have your best interests at heart and...things happen." Peggy took a sip of water. "Feelings come and feelings go. Consequences last a lot longer." Peggy looked at Jan, but Jan kept staring down at the table.

"I just want to go to the prom!" Krista burst out.

"I know," Peggy said. "Sooner or later, you're going to make choices that your parents can't stop. When you do, don't get pushed around by what you feel like doing. That's not freedom. Freedom is choosing, not being bullied by feelings. Think about the big picture. Then decide. I wish I had. That's all I really have to say."

Krista frowned, but said nothing.

Peggy stood up and slung her bag over her shoulder. "I'm going to get going now. Thank you for letting me be part of your lives tonight. I know I don't have the right to expect being invited back, much as I'd love for that to happen. That's up to you. If you want to get in touch with me, you have my number."

Peggy kissed the top of Krista's head, nodded to Jan and Bill, and headed for the door, passing under the "Hope" plaque as she left.

"I'll walk you to your car," Bill offered and followed Peggy out.

"Bye, Grandma," Krista finally called after her.

As the front door closed, Krista headed up the stairs to her room. "I guess I've got some things to think about," she said to herself.

Jan poured another cup of coffee and sat back down at the table. "Me, too," she murmured.

MS
Arthur Powers

(Courtney, we were awed
by your mother's courage
facing multiple sclerosis)

She types out the letters "MS."
It's no longer just an address,
she thinks, but a strange being
tearing apart her body. Not yet
thirty, she feels herself torn
muscle and mind away from bone.
Her fingers are not yet fools,
at least: in the office pool
she's still the fastest typist
— but how long will that last?
Even now, when she walks,
she's like a sailor on deck
trying to keep balance. She was
a secretary before, but
it got too much. They made
a place for her — oh, they would
keep doing it as long as they could:
even banks have hearts when one
is loved. She thinks then of Paul
and begins to sense his panic,
pledged to protect, unable to protect.
She knows he won't hang on much longer,
will leave her. She is stronger,
maybe because she has
no choice. She had one choice -
the life inside her. She remembers
her meeting with the doctor:

"There may be danger to life,"
he said.
        "Who?" she asked.
"Me or the child?"
                He looked
startled. "You, of course."

In answer, she just smiled.

The door to the penitent's side of the confessional closed with a soft thump.

Father Stephen inhaled a deep breath of warm air, appreciating the lingering scent of incense. It always took him back, reconnected him to his ordination day. He closed his eyes and fingered the beads of his rosary, interiorly praying a Hail Mary before the next penitent came to him.

The door opened and a penitent shuffled in, his lazy footfalls familiar.

Father sighed and straightened in the chair. His heart rate quickened.

The penitent's kneeler creaked. "Bless me, Father, for I have sinned." His deep voice held a note of humor.

A faint wave of nausea washed over Father Stephen as he lifted his hand to bless the man through the screen. He thanked God that St. Gertrude's had traditional confessionals, giving the penitent no option to receive the sacrament face-to-face.

"It's been a week since my last Confession. I'd have come to you sooner, but you didn't return my calls for an appointment."

Father Stephen shifted in his chair, his palms sweating and irritation threatening to shatter his peace. He shouldn't feel this way. Nothing should so easily disturb his inner calm.

"Father? Aren't you gonna say something?"

"I...wish you wouldn't come to me for Confession."

Father shook his head, disgusted with his reply. He should've left the thought unspoken, but since Blake had discovered his placement as assistant pastor at this parish, he'd come to Confession every Saturday, refusing to see any other priest and monopolizing whatever remained of the Confession hour.

Blake laughed. "Who else would I go to? You know me better than anyone."

Father Stephen could picture the look on his face, the quirky grin and the thick brows over emotional eyes that could show a man desperately lost at one moment and, at another, incredibly irate. His moods had never passed without notice.

"God knows you better than I do, Blake," Father said. "Besides, you have yet to sound the least bit repentant."

"I'm working on that."

Leaning toward the screen, Father Stephen spoke in a low voice. "Why bother with the sacrament? You know I can't give you absolution in your present state. And there's probably a line of people behind you who are repentant."

"Well, you won't see me otherwise, and I need to talk to you."

"At this point, I think you'd be better off with counseling."

"No, I need to talk to *you*."

Father Stephen took a deep breath and prayed for strength. "Okay, let's hear it. What's so important?"

"I've been in turmoil lately, not knowing what to do — can't eat, can't sleep. I'm a real bitch at work."

Father winced. "Maybe God's trying to tell you something. Have you tried praying for discernment?"

Blake laughed. "Sure. I've prayed. God's not answering

me, so I'm asking you. Figured you have a more direct line, being a priest and all."

"My advice is no different today." Not wanting to hear the sordid details and hoping to end the conversation, Father repeated the advice he'd given the previous week about listening to the voice of conscience.

"It's not my conscience bothering me. It's Robert, that guy I told you about. He's only been with me a month and already he's acting moodier than Montgomery Clift. And he's coming home late from work. You know, he works second shift, so I can't help but think he's going out after." His voice grew higher and strained. "I want us to have something together, but he acts like he's tired of me, makes me feel like I'm just his slut and now he —"

"Blake, stop." A range of emotions struck Father Stephen: compassion, disgust, sadness, anger. His hand snapped to the scars on his forearm as he prayed for the words Blake needed to hear. "You can't give in to every desire or live by your emotions. They're tearing you apart. You were raised Catholic. You know the commandments, the holiness to which each of us is called —"

"Get real, Father. You know I don't agree with that. There's no commandment that says that only straight people can enjoy love."

"That's not what I'm saying."

"Yes, you are. You're always trying to tell me it's wrong to be gay." Annoyance marked his tone, his deep voice getting louder by the word and probably carrying to the front of the Confession line. "I mean when two people love each other, why should gender matter? You think people should just ignore their attractions, their feelings for each other? It's impossible."

"It's not impossible to live a chaste life. It's the only way you'll find peace, but it requires self-knowledge and self-mastery to —"

"No, you're telling me to live a contradiction. It's in our nature to express love."

"There are other ways to love, but you're not really talking about love. Love is about wanting what's best for the other and for yourself. You need to know yourself, Blake, so you can grow into your true identity as a child of God."

"I do know myself, Steve." He pronounced the name with emphasis. "God made me this way. There's nothing wrong with it. Maybe you're the one denying who you are. You hide behind that cassock, hide in the church, denying your own desires instead of facing them."

"A priest does not deny his desires. His desire, his love, is directed to the one true Beloved." Emptiness and doubt shuddered through Father Stephen. Finding himself gripping his rosary, he relaxed his hand and let the beads fall to his thigh.

"Mm-hmm. I hear you, Steve."

***

O God, you are my God, for you I long, for you my soul is thirsting. My body pines for you like a dry, weary land without water.

A sharp pain shot through Father Stephen's knee. He shifted his weight on the prie-dieu and lifted his gaze to the golden monstrance on the altar before him, to the little white host in the center of it. One of the stones set in the intricate filigree around the host glinted in the overhead light.

So I gaze on you in the sanctuary to see your strength and your glory. He mouthed the words as he prayed. His heart ached, feeling abandoned.

Father Stephen dropped his gaze and bowed over his prayer book. *Why won't you speak like you once did?*

He struggled to maintain composure, aware that a handful of parishioners knelt in the pews behind him, not wanting to draw attention. How long had he been kneeling on the sole prie-dieu in the little Adoration chapel? He should withdraw to a pew and give another the opportunity to kneel here, but he couldn't tear himself away. He wanted nothing else to fill his sight, nothing else to distract him.

Lord, do not abandon me forever.

With all the difficulty he faced in prayer this past year, he could've been back in seminary struggling through his weekly Holy Hour. Then again, his thoughts did not turn to his schedule or obligations like they had back then. Conversations with fellow seminarians did not linger in his mind. Reflections about his past or future did not distract him today.

He simply couldn't meditate or use his imagination at all. His prayers had become dry as the desert sand and as withered as leaves in late fall.

My soul shall be filled as with a banquet...

Four years ago, shortly after ordination, he'd committed himself to daily Adoration of the Blessed Sacrament. At times, he'd struggled to keep his commitment and to remain focused on prayer. But he hadn't given up. Before long, the Lord had filled his soul to overflowing with consolation and delights he had never known. Then he'd longed for his Holy Hour, counted the minutes until he could kneel again before his Eucharistic Lord. And once there, he lost himself in prayer.

On my bed I remember you. On you I muse through the night...

Grief clutched Father Stephen's heart, bringing a tear to his eye. He buried his head in his hands. *Are You trying to tell me something? Have I made a mistake? Why do I feel this unrest day after day?*

The Lord had called him to come away and love only Him...he did not doubt that. He'd come to realize he would never find fulfillment in this world. But he had always questioned his vocation: from the moment he felt called to the priesthood, all through seminary, during his service at the parish before this one, and even today. Could he have been mistaken?

Lord, where are You? Lift this cross and speak to me again.

This past year, during Adoration, he'd watched the time more than he watched his Lord, every minute feeling like an hour. He searched for the Lord, flailing like a man in darkness, not knowing which way to turn. Still, he hadn't abandoned his commitment to a daily Holy Hour. He could not.

Give me any other cross. Take everything from me. There is nothing in the world I want. Only let me feel Your love the way I had in the past.

Impressions of thoughts that had assailed him over the past months crept into his mind: *there is no God. You have been lied to and are now lying to others. You are a fool. God does not want you. How could he, after what you've done? Your sins have built an impenetrable wall around you that no one, not even God, can tear down.*

"My God, my God," he whispered, though vaguely aware of it. *I believe in You and in Your love for me. You have changed my heart so that I no longer desire the things I once did. Though temptations flit through my mind, I do not grasp for them. I long only for You. Where are You? I am unable to find even a drop of the sweet spiritual water You once gave me in abundance. I am like a dry, weary land without water.*

Father Stephen lifted his gaze to the host again. One... two stones set in the filigree around the host glinted. Something prevented him from drawing near, as though he had somehow gone backwards in his spiritual life.

Is there a wall between us, built from my sins and imperfections or from my lukewarm faith? I don't know how to tear it down. Show me, or tear it down for me. I want nothing more than to remain in your will.

Minutes passed. Or maybe it only felt that way. A desperate plea rose up inside. *I am ready to give up everything, even what I thought You wanted of me...my vocation to the priesthood.*

***

"This is only your second year in seminary, Stephen. Don't be so hard on yourself." Father Walter, director of Spiritual Formation, gave a reassuring smile and leaned back in his chair. His white hair, smoothed back in a classic style, contrasted his youthful, clean-shaven face. The arch of his brows and the perpetual look of clemency in his bright blue eyes could disarm anyone.

Except for Stephen. Today.

Sitting across from him — on the verge of trembling — Stephen ran a hand through his hair. He'd made a mistake, had a conversation with another seminarian, and someone had overheard and reported it. In a way, he was glad. He'd put off facing things long enough, the nagging feelings that wouldn't go away. "Yes, Father, but I really need to know that God is calling me to this. I don't want to assume I'm meant for the priesthood, especially with my...well, with my past."

Stephen took a breath, willing his body to relax. He'd discussed the mistakes of his youth with Father Walter on several occasions during his first year here. Father Walter had asked many questions but without ever digging too deeply for comfort. Maybe Stephen needed to dig deeper. Maybe he needed to be uncomfortable.

Father Walter nodded, his expression serious but not judgmental. "I understand how you feel. But you need to accept that we have all sinned. We've all made mistakes." He put a hand to his chest. "I've made mistakes. Who but our good Lord and His mother hasn't? That's why He's the Savior."

"But I still struggle. I struggle here in seminary."

Nodding again, blue eyes holding nothing but sympathy, Father clasped his hands and pressed his lips together. A moment later he said, "Are you in love with Jesus Christ?"

"Well, yes, Father." Stephen answered emphatically, his heart stirring, an image of Peter and the Lord flashing in his mind.

Do you love me, Peter?

Yes, Lord. You know that I love You.

"The purpose of seminary, Stephen, is to produce priests who are deeply in love with Jesus Christ. I see that love growing in you. But you need to come to terms with your attachments, your addictions, your sins. Only then will you be ready to be sent out."

"I just don't know that I'm worthy of this calling."

Father Walter smiled. "Humility. That's a good sign you are called. I believe all who are truly called share those feelings of unworthiness. A priest who has known sin and failing is that much more capable of relating and showing compassion to others. Compassion and mercy are desperately needed in our troubled world."

Struggling to accept the words of his spiritual director, Stephen nodded. A verse from Scripture came to mind: no one, after putting his hand to the plow and looking back, is fit for the kingdom of God.

Okay, Lord, my hand is to the plow, and I won't look back. He would continue on in faith, moving forward despite his inclination to turn back.

"Thank you, Father." Stephen stood, rubbed his sweaty palms on his pants, and stuck out a hand.

"Before you go, Stephen..." Father gripped his hand, not shaking it nor letting go. "Have you considered that God may want you to carry this cross for the rest of your life?"

***

Four teenage boys performed for the parish youth group in the social hall, two zealously strumming guitars and the other two singing a popular Christian song about the light God puts inside a person. The rest of the forty to fifty teens leaned against a wall or sat on folding chairs they had scooted into a cluster near the band. A few tried singing along. Almost everyone clapped to the beat.

A group of adults stood in an open doorway on the far side of the social hall, talking amongst themselves and glancing at the teens every now and then. Some of them had volunteered to prepare snacks. Two, a married couple, planned to speak to the group about the vocation of marriage. The others were parents.

Father Stephen stood with his back to the wall and one foot propped on a folding chair, tapping his thigh and bouncing to the music. He scanned the group, appreciating the energy but unable to feel it himself. He had just said Mass for them and had witnessed their zeal in prayer. A few had gazed, trancelike and eyes glistening, at the host as he elevated it. Did they feel the love of God the way he once had?

He sighed. Regardless of the aridity in his own soul, God allowed him to be here at this moment as their priest. The teenage years had so many challenges. He would do anything to shepherd them, to encourage them on their journey, and to convince them of the Lord's deep and personal love for each one of them.

Please use me, Lord, as Your instrument.

As the song wound down, Molly, the thirty-something youth group leader, stepped away from the adults and approached Father. She weaved between rows of long tables that had gotten shoved aside to make room for the gathering, her ample figure forcing tables to scrape out of her way. She grabbed a purple plastic basket from a chair. Beaming a smile, she came up beside him.

He nodded to assure her he knew what to do. Earlier in the week, she had gone over the format several times, maybe needing him as a sounding board. She had asked for his input only once. "How would you like to take questions?"

Hugging the purple basket, she leaned close and whispered, "Are you sure you want to do it like this, Father?" Her eyes showed genuine concern.

He nodded again, trying not to look amused.

"There's no accountability with anonymous questions," Molly said.

Before the music began, he'd had papers distributed and invited people to write their questions down. "You can ask me anything," he had said, getting a few giggles from a group of girls. He wanted them to ask freely without fear of being judged. Teens needed honest answers to their questions, no matter how small or how difficult.

"I think I can handle it," Father said. Perhaps due to his young age, the parishioners at St. Gertrude's had the habit of advising and helping him with the smallest of tasks.

The music stopped. Clapping and hoots replaced it. Then everyone spoke at once.

Molly handed him the basket. Folded slips of paper filled the bottom of it. "Okay, but don't say I didn't warn you." She lifted her brows and gave him a look as if to say this was his last chance to turn back.

Father Stephen smiled, not hiding his amusement this time, and reached into the basket. He unfolded and read the first question to himself as he stepped to a table near the group.

"Okay, listen up, everybody," Molly shouted, the chatter subsiding. "Father Stephen is with us today to talk about vocations to the priesthood and religious life. He has all of your questions, and he's going to answer as many as he can, so I want everyone to give him their undivided attention."

The room grew silent and forty or so pairs of eyes turned to him.

"Before I get to the questions," he said, turning to where the teens with the guitars stood. "I just want to say, you guys rock. Let's hear it for the band!" He clapped and everyone joined him.

The members of the band slapped hands and bumped fists. One saluted Father. Another bowed.

When the applause died down, Father folded his hands and began with prayer. He prayed that the Holy Spirit guide his words and bring His grace to all in the room. Then he led them in a Hail Mary.

"Okay, we're ready for the first question." He smoothed

out the paper in his hands and read aloud, "Can priests watch TV and go to the movies?"

Once the laughter died down, he gave the straight answer and read the next question. He wanted his answers to show them a man content with his vocation, a soul in love with God. Despite the silent treatment God had given him lately, he *was* a man in love with God.

Most questions were serious.

"Are most priests happy in their vocation?"

"Do priests get paid?"

"How many years of education do you need?"

"What does the Church look for in a person who feels called?"

"What if you get halfway through seminary and change your mind?"

"What do you do all day?"

Father Stephen unfolded the next question. As he read the words, a gentle breeze filled his soul. He had hoped someone would ask something like this. "Is it hard knowing you'll never get married?"

Looking up, he scanned the faces of the teens sitting before him. "The answer to this question is close to my heart. Somewhere inside, each of us knows we were made for love. We spend our lives looking for it, with the hope of finding and living in it. God put this longing in us because it reveals something about His love."

A few had whispered back and forth while he answered other questions, but now they all gazed with undivided attention.

"Everyone is called to love, but not everyone is called to marriage." Somehow he'd always known he wasn't called to marriage. "A man called to the priesthood, or a woman called to religious life, can't imagine living another kind of life with as much satisfaction. I'd compare it to when a person realizes they've married the right person."

Father Stephen paused, thinking. He still hadn't explained it well. He needed to find other words. Glancing away, his gaze landed on a big wooden crucifix on the wall.

"A priest is called to pursue love in a way that imitates Jesus Christ, without receiving human love in return, the way spouses do. Our Lord lived a celibate life on Earth but gave Himself completely for the sake of the Church."

The words poured from him now, as if God spoke through him, giving him a feeling of satisfaction that he had not found lately in prayer.

"Marriage is beautiful and necessary in God's plan, but so are priests and consecrated men and women. They are a sign to everyone, a reminder that each of us is invited to set out on a lifelong spiritual journey. While on the one hand we are called to community, on the other we walk alone. It is in solitude that we come to know and love the person we are, the person God loves. Those called to virginity or celibate chastity live lives of deep love, but it's an other-worldly love."

Movement by the open doorway on the far side of the room caught his attention. Only three adults stood there now, the others having gone to the kitchen to prepare snacks.

A second glance drained the blood from Father Stephen's face.

Blake...what was he doing here? Dressed in skinny jeans and a faded, denim button-front shirt, he leaned against the doorjamb, thumbs stuck in his belt loops. When their gazes connected, he gave Father a crooked grin and shook his head.

Heat slid up Father's neck. He shifted his gaze to the

women arranging snacks on a table outside the kitchen and to the round white clock high on the wall. Ten more minutes.

"Oh, uh…" He searched for Molly, speed-glancing from face to face, missing her on his first attempt, then finding her with a curious look on her face. "…looks like I better wrap it up." Had he finished answering the question? What was the question?

"I think we have time for one more," Molly said, her eyes turning toward the doorway, or maybe the clock.

"Okay. Sure." Forcing himself not to glance at the doorway, Father plunged his hand into the purple basket and pulled out a well-folded paper.

Blake wouldn't shout something out, would he? Why had he come?

Father unfolded the paper and read the question to himself. His heart skipped a beat. His hands trembled. No other question had troubled him in the least. Why should this one?

"Father?" Molly said.

"Yes, um…" He cleared his throat, gave a weak smile, and read the question aloud. "How do you know if you're really called?" The words his spiritual director had spoken to him in seminary came to mind, but he didn't really know the answer.

He scanned the faces of the teens. Surely the Lord spoke to them, called at least one of them. He had to give the right answer. "If the idea is somewhere in your thoughts, in your heart, it's worth a deeper look. Pray about it. Ask God to show you His will, and find a spiritual director." He clasped his hands together and gave Molly a nod, wanting to communicate that he had to go.

Molly rose from her chair in the middle of the group.

"Oh...kay," she said, again looking at the clock. He still had five or so minutes. She turned back to him, smiling and cheerful, but the glint in her eye said she wondered what had changed. They'd discussed this. He would stay for refreshments, in case anyone wanted to speak further, then for the couple's talk on marriage. "Let's thank Father for his time with us today." She clapped, beginning a round of applause.

Father smiled and gave a nod. "Sorry I couldn't get to all the questions, but maybe Molly can get them to me."

Molly nodded.

He nodded. Then he took off for the door without looking back.

Of course, Blake still stood there, his posture straightening and his grin growing as Father approached.

Avoiding eye contact with Blake, Father focused on the workers behind the kitchen counter and on the two women that stood in the doorway. Then he glanced over his shoulder to see who watched him. A few girls did.

"Hey, Steve," Blake said, stepping away from the doorframe. "I mean, Father Stephen."

The two women, deep in conversation, hadn't appeared to hear Blake's casual greeting to Father. But they hadn't appeared to notice Father approach either, yet they stepped out of the doorway.

"Hello, Blake." Father glanced as he passed, acting as if he had no intention of speaking with him. Then he sped his steps through the hallway and to the glass doors that led to the back of the church grounds.

Outside the glass doors, moths fluttered under a porch light. One of them tapped the light and bounced back then tapped it again. A tree with a twisted trunk appeared in silhouette against a midnight blue sky.

"We're going outside, huh?" Blake caught up, grabbing the horizontal bar on the door at the same time Father did.

"Well, I am." Father stepped into the night, humid air and the chatter of crickets assailing him, instantly grating on his nerves. "I'm not sure what you're doing here. You don't have any teenage children here tonight, do you?"

Blake laughed, keeping step with Father as they crossed the parking lot. "That's a good one. No, I saw your name in the church bulletin for Vocations Night. Decided to show up, see what you had to say."

"You got a bulletin, huh? I haven't seen you at Mass."

"No, and you won't. Not until the Church gets with the times."

About thirty or so cars filled one end of the parking lot, grills and trim shining under a floodlight on the back of a church building. A hint of light reached the pavilion behind the parking lot.

Father headed there. "So why are you here, Blake?"

"Oh, you know, needed to talk."

Stepping onto the cement pad under the pavilion, Father shoved his hands in his pants pockets and leaned a shoulder against a thick post. "I'm beginning to think you're stalking me."

Blake stepped up on a bench and sat on top of a picnic table. "Maybe I am. You gonna call the police?"

Father shrugged. "Am I going to have to?"

"Maybe. But it won't be good press for either of us. You know how everyone loves a scandal."

"So what do you need?"

"What I need is your help." He paused and turned away. "I just want to talk, Steve. Don't get so uptight. If you wanted to, I really think you could help me. I'm miserable.

And you seem so...happy, content anyway."

"You know what I have to say. I don't think you're interested in my advice. I'm not going to tell you that evil is good."

Blake laughed. "Evil. Wow." He paused. "Why is it evil for two people to express their love?"

"That's not an expression of love. These guys that you see, they're...using you. Somewhere inside you know that." Father Stephen struggled to find the words. Was there anything he could say that would reach Blake? "You know you're giving away the deepest part of yourself to someone who doesn't appreciate it, to someone who can't accept it in full. That's why you're miserable."

Blake grimaced, rubbing his hand over his unshaven jaw. Then he shifted into the shadows and threw his arms up, hiding his face. He groaned.

The deep, hopeless sound, the sight of this man in agony, rippled through Father's heart. He felt like a parent watching his child suffer, unable to help. He took a breath and tried steeling himself to it.

"I don't know how to get out of this mess. But I don't want to be alone. I'm already so lonely."

Father Stephen pushed off from the pillar and took a single step toward Blake. "I understand. We all get lonely now and then. We all feel restless and driven, hungry... unfinished at every level. And we might believe that romance — that sex — is the answer. But it's not true. A sexual relationship is not the ultimate answer to your loneliness."

Another groan. "So what is the answer? You act like you're satisfied and so in control of your emotions, telling people God's rules in the confessional, telling those kids in there what to believe, but maybe you're running from something." He slid off the picnic table and sauntered toward Father, his tone accusing now. "Or maybe this is a front, and you have someone on the side. That's not all that uncommon, is it?" He stopped a few inches away.

Father shrunk back and scanned the parking lot. Someone could be sitting in a dark car, watching. "No, there's no one on the side. I take my vows seriously." He returned his gaze to Blake, the humidity and closeness making him claustrophobic. "Were you listening to me in there?" He stuffed a finger in his Roman collar and pulled it from his sweaty neck, wishing he could take it off for the night. "I don't want anyone that way. I want God alone."

"Well, I do want someone. I want to be loved. Is there anything wrong with that?"

"No, of course not." Father found himself reaching for Blake's arm. "So do I. We all do. But we can't always have that on Earth."

Blake grabbed Father's hand on his arm and squeezed it. "I don't want to wait until I die to know love. I want it now."

"You can know that love now, through prayer." Father Stephen locked eyes with Blake. If only Blake would open his heart to Christ's love. If only he would attempt to love the Lord in return.

"Right." Still clutching Father's hand, he stepped closer, every dark whisker on his jaw and the hard glint in his eyes becoming visible in the dim light. "You know what I think? You're afraid to love now, so you put on that black cassock and hide yourself away. You deny your natural desires because the Church says they're wrong."

Wanting to step back, wanting to pull his hand free, he remained eye-to-eye and accepted the challenge. "The Lord knows you, Blake. He knows everything about you, all your sins and imperfections. And He loves you, anyway. He calls you into a deep relationship with Himself, so that in heaven you can experience the fullness of intimacy with Him."

"He knows I'm gay, Steve. He made me that way." He squeezed Father's hand again, pierced him through with his gaze, then released his hand with dramatics and turned away.

"He knows your cross, Blake, and He'll help you carry it. Celibate chastity is a gift. I know you can't see that now, but virginity and celibate chastity —"

"Virginity! Ha!" Blake spun to face him, his eyes holding an accusing, mocking glare. "I heard you talking about that in there, and I had to laugh. You, Steve, are no virgin."

***

Shattered, broken, stinging with pain...

The cold, hard tile floor bit Father Stephen's forehead as he lay prostrate before the tabernacle. At 3:00 a.m., unable to sleep and weary of his thoughts, he had dressed, fled the rectory and slipped into the silent, dark church. The flame of the sanctuary lamp flickered in a red globe. A single glance at it had put him in the presence of Christ and rent his soul in two. He had flung himself facedown and groaned. Sometime later — he'd lost all sense of time — his soul had quieted enough that he felt ready to speak and to listen to the Lord, but he couldn't get himself to rise to his knees.

"Why, Lord?" he whispered. He imagined he could feel the sting of the cuts that had scarred his arm, as if the damage had occurred today and not years ago.

"Why have You abandoned me? Don't let me fall again into the sins of my youth."

Under the pavilion, Blake's touch had sent a tremor

through him, stirring memories and feelings he hadn't known in years. Though he hated them, he couldn't shake them.

***

With a surge of adrenaline, Steve drew back and swung hard.

The aluminum alloy bat that he'd begged for in grade school, hoping Dad would teach him to play ball, struck the sliding glass door with a crack. A musical sound followed as shards of chaos rained down, glittering in the sunlight.

Steve collapsed onto his knees and doubled over.

Fractured glass cut through his jeans and skin with physical pain that failed to distract him from the pain inside. Long streaks of blood blossomed on his right forearm.

As he watched the blood spread, his mind numbed.

Something thumped in the distance. Then the sound of hurried footfalls drew near.

"Hey, I'm Blake." Blake came up behind him, grabbed his arm, and yanked him to his feet. Glass shards tinkled to the cement patio. "I...live over there." He pointed to the weathered wooden fence in the backyard. "I heard something crash, so I jumped over the fence. You okay? What happened?"

Blake's family had moved into the house behind Steve's a month ago, and the two had crossed paths in high school, but they'd never spoken before. Something about Blake made Steve uncomfortable, something in his eyes.

His thick eyebrows drew together, and his mouth pursed as he looked Steve over. "You're hurt. Anyone home?"

Steve shook his head. He'd left his mother and sisters at

his aunt's house, took off on foot, and ran the two miles to get home.

"Come over to my house. I'll get you fixed up." Blake motioned for Steve to follow.

Steve stood, staring at nothing, unable to move, vaguely aware of something trickling down his shins and one forearm.

Blake grabbed the front of Steve's shirt and tugged, a flash of anger or urgency in his eyes. "Come on. Don't worry, no one's at my house."

A moment later, Steve stood with his arm in the kitchen sink, cold water running over it and stinging him. Blake paced into and out of a bathroom several times, mumbling and carrying things to the dining room table. He made Steve sit at the table and proceeded to tend the cuts on his arm with ointment and gauze.

"So what happened at your house?" Blake glanced up from his work, a bloody glob of ointment on one fingertip.

Steve averted his gaze. He didn't want to talk about it. It wasn't fair.

"I won't tell anyone." Blake laid gauze pads in a line down Steve's arm, covering long cuts that wouldn't stop bleeding.

"Think I need stitches?" Steve said, though he wasn't about to go to the hospital.

Blake shrugged. "What happened? Someone try to break into your house? Should I be calling the police?" He held Steve's gaze as he unrolled a long strip of gauze.

Steve took a breath. Why was Blake helping him? Why did he care? Taking a chance, he answered. "My dad died."

Blake nodded and wrapped the gauze on Steve's arm, his movements gentle but confident. "You two were pretty close?"

Steve's jaw tensed, resentment filling him again. "No."

Blake glanced, the emotional look in his eyes saying he understood completely — he related, he cared.

Grief welled up and spilled over, rendering Steve helpless, making his body convulse, making him double over.

"We were...never close," he said between sobs, "and now he's...dead."

Blake pulled him into his arms, and, for the moment, Steve was not alone.

Blake had come into his life when he'd desperately needed someone, starting a friendship that would turn into more, a friendship that would make Stephen question the direction of his life.

"I never knew You, Father," Father Stephen whispered to the Lord. "I never knew You." He lifted his head, then pushed himself up onto his knees.

"I've made a mistake, haven't I, Lord?" He locked his gaze on the tabernacle where red light from the sanctuary lamp reflected on its carved, golden surface. "I thought this was what You wanted of me, but now..." Why couldn't he rise above the temptations? He'd given himself completely to God and to the Church. He'd made promises. Vows.

Why had God let him come this far?

His thoughts turned to a past visit with Father Walter.

***

Burning from humiliation but determined to bring all his struggles to the light, Stephen stepped into his spiritual director's office.

"Stephen." Father Walter, never one to complain of the interruption to his work, stood and walked around his desk. Smiling, welcoming, he gestured toward one of two wingback chairs.

Stephen shook his head. He needed to get the words out before he changed his mind. "I know I've hinted at my struggles here, but I've never made it clear." He paced to the wall and turned to face Father. "I find myself attracted to one of my brother seminarians, and I recently had an inappropriate conversation with another."

Father Walter's face did not flinch. His expression gave nothing away. "By inappropriate, you mean...?"

"Yes, I...well, he made a comment with a double meaning. It took me a moment to grasp that, but then I made a lewd comment, too. And we went back and forth for a few exchanges, saying things...suggestive things."

"I see." Father Walter nodded, his blue eyes showing more compassion than concern. "Do you feel tempted to have a relationship with this or another seminarian?"

"Well, no, I — I know that's wrong." Though he'd once found comfort in his relationship with Blake, he'd made the choice to end it and move away. He believed the teachings of the Church and wanted to live by them. Realizing he could neither marry nor pursue a gay relationship, he'd found himself considering the priesthood, where he wouldn't have to worry about sexuality.

"I want to grow in my love for God by serving His Bride, the Church," Stephen said. "But I hadn't considered the temptations I'd experience in seminary."

Father Walter straightened the tissue box on the corner of his desk then looked up. "The flirting, the attraction you experience, these are little things. You're a fine seminarian, knowledgeable, charitable. Don't let these little slip-ups deter you. I think you're past that phase of your life."

Still kneeling, Father Stephen rested his chin on his clasped hands. He wished, now, that his spiritual director had given him different advice. Step away from seminary for a while. Seek counseling to get to the root of your temptations.

What emotional conflicts had caused his attractions? He needed to find out and face it. He needed to know himself, to dig deeper and try to understand the hurts in his life, especially the things that had distorted his view of fatherhood.

How could he serve as a spiritual father if he couldn't understand true fatherhood, and if he couldn't relate correctly with others, both male and female? The priesthood was no escape from sexuality. He needed a correct view of his own sexuality, so he could make a true gift of himself to God.

Father Stephen opened his eyes. Uncertainty left him like fog dissipating under sunlight.

He lifted his gaze to the crucifix over the tabernacle, seeing beyond the physical. "Lord...I know that You called me to come away, to love only You. Whatever else You call me to, I am uncertain of. But I love You and, even though You won't speak with me, I trust You. And I accept this cross, every splinter of it, knowing that You have chosen it for me."

An image came to his mind...the hand of God, holding him. And with the image, a tidal wave of peace and love. And understanding. The Lord had *not* abandoned him. He'd been purifying him and drawing him closer.

Father Stephen surrendered to love and flung himself face down on the cold tile floor of the dark church, where he prayed under the flickering light from the sanctuary candle.

***

"You may not have chosen this attraction, and you don't need to feel shame. It's what you do with this attraction

288

that's important." The speaker at the lectern, a young man in his thirties, spoke with conviction in his tone to an audience of about seventy men and women.

Stephen wiped sweat from the back of his neck and folded his arms across his chest. He glanced to either side, then behind him. Everyone else sat closer to the middle of the church, except for the few brave souls in the front pews.

No one here would recognize him. Besides, it was only an informative talk. If they knew him, they might assume he came for pastoral reasons. They might not jump to the conclusion that he had come for himself.

"This may feel like an impossible cross to carry," the speaker said, "but Christ's redemption has won the grace for you..."

A sense of urgency stirred him. He needed to make that phone call, needed to commit to attending the regular meetings. But every time he considered what he would say on the phone, the mistakes of his past and the weakness he still possessed overwhelmed him and brought him to his knees. He had to keep reminding himself that God had forgiven him and that seeking help put him on the right track.

"Come to Him," the speaker continued. "Live in Him, and you will find joy and freedom."

The speaker's words found welcome in Stephen's heart. Stephen needed to follow the advice he'd given countless penitents in Confession: let go of the past and trust God with today. This was a new day.

Stephen slumped back, unfolded his arms, and relaxed. *I leave it all in your hands, Lord.*

"What, no clericals?"

Stephen shuddered, his body tensing again. Bracing himself, he peered over his shoulder.

Blake sat down behind him, a crooked grin on his face. He leaned forward and rested his arms on the back of Stephen's pew. "You quit?" He cocked a brow, looking pleased with the idea.

"Quit? The priesthood? You can't quit the priesthood." He decided not to explain the indelible mark on a priest's soul. The thought of it humbled him. Whether or not he'd made a mistake entering the priesthood, he couldn't undo it. He'd take it with him to eternity.

"I'm on a leave of absence," Stephen said.

Blake nodded and looked him over. "I like that white polo with black jeans."

Stephen shook his head. "Why are you here? Don't tell me you're still stalking me." He had considered relocating, wanting to distance himself from Blake. But he saw this talk advertised and felt called to attend. He would need to join a solid SSA support group...maybe not one around here.

Blake shrugged. "So who is he?"

"The speaker?"

"No, the reason you're here."

Stephen shook his head again. "There's no he. I'm the reason I'm here. I'm...on a journey." A journey...yes, he needed to return to the original nakedness of man before the fall, to face and find healing for his disordered passions.

An image came to his mind, making him avert his gaze. Glass shattering. A thousand shards glittering in the sunlight, raining down on him.

He sucked in a breath. The Lord trusted him with this particular cross, knowing the trials and temptations he'd face and his weak response to them. No matter the mess he'd made with his life, the Lord could heal him, put him back together, could re-order his life toward union with

Him. Then, God willing, he would return to the priesthood.

"A journey, huh?" Blake still leaned on the back of Stephen's pew. He played with the band of his watch.

"What about you?" Stephen glanced over his shoulder to make sure no one had come up behind them, not wanting to be overheard. "I hope you're not here just for me."

A slow grin stretched across his lips. "Well...I sort of..." He bowed his head, rubbed his hair, and returned his gaze to Stephen. "I just want to be happy, Steve. I don't think I'm going to find it here." He nodded in the direction of the speaker. "I'm not ready to give up this part of me."

"Aren't you even a little bit curious?"

"Curious?"

"Yeah. Why are these people here? Why am I here? Why does faith, why does God matter to us?" Stephen smiled, the Lord stirring his heart, filling it with joy he wanted to share.

Blake shrugged and faced the speaker. "I don't know, Steve. Maybe I'm a little curious."

THE DEATH OF ME, THE LIFE OF US
Ellen Gable

"Sarah, you're too young to read the death notices," my mother always said. But here I sat at the college library, eyes focused on the obituary section of the newspaper — yes, I still preferred to read an actual newspaper rather than digital.

I also attended funerals of people I barely knew. In the years following my sister's death, I found strange comfort in learning how other people faced the death of a loved one.

What does death look like? It's a polished maple casket lowered into the ground, people in black clothes with somber faces, a granite headstone with a name etched on it.

What does death sound like? It's a priest speaking in monotone. People sobbing. Moaning. Sometimes it sounds like the silence of this quiet library.

What is grief? It's a space in your heart reserved for those you love who have died and can no longer return that love. It's an emptiness, a hollow at the base of your throat that rises up and catches when you think of the person you love who is now gone.

What is guilt? It's the realization that it is *my* fault that the person I love most is now dead. It's the dark, rigid rock that holds a conscience captive and continues to torture my soul nine years later.

The blur of the van slamming into her unexpecting body is an image that is burned into my memory. So is the screeching of the brakes and the thud of the van striking her. I was only nine years old that hot and muggy August day. But it was the end of my childhood.

***

"Let's play tag," I said to my six-year-old sister, Rosie.

"No! Wanna go back inside. It's too hot out." Her blond hair hung in wet strips, and her clothes were damp from running back and forth through the sprinkler.

"Come on. We'll play tag, then we can run through the sprinkler again." I touched her shoulder. "You're it," then I ran across our neighbor's lawn. I wasn't paying attention. I just didn't want her to catch me, so I ran as fast as I could and ran into the street. I had made it to the other side when I heard screeching. I turned just in time to see the van slam into her small body. The man behind the wheel, bigger than Dad, got out and stood over my sister's body, his mouth open. Then he covered his face with his hands and began to weep.

I couldn't move, nor could I take my eyes from her. Rosie lay on the road, her white Danskin shirt now streaked in bright red-orange. Blood covered her head like a cap, her body twisted like a rag doll. I stared, wide-eyed, unable to move as hope welled up within me when I saw her body twitch. All of a sudden, she was still.

It was quiet, the humming of the neighborhood air conditioners and the man's deep crying played like the background noise of a TV show. I heard a scream. I looked up to see my mother racing across the lawn and into the street. Bellowed sobs consumed her as she scooped up Rosie's little body. Drops of liquid trickled from my sister's bottom, creating a dotted trail on the black road as she carried my sister onto our lawn.

Mom collapsed, Rosie's blood smearing her shirt, hands and face. She screamed over and over again, "No!"

I'm not sure how much time passed, but I stayed in the same spot in the street. I wasn't able to move, so I stared at the wetness on the black street, one tiny sandal in the midst of it all.

Only moments before, Rosie was a happy girl who loved everything about life. Now she was gone. And it was *my* fault.

The squeal of sirens echoed in the distance and became louder until I couldn't hear anymore — it was too much for me to think, to hear. My eyes continued to stare, but everything became a cloud of colors moving in front of me. Flashing lights. Badged, uniformed shirts in shades of blue. A black and yellow stretcher. The shadows inside the back of an ambulance.

I felt someone's arms around me and the mumble of words. I blinked and glanced upward. It was Mrs. Grayson, our next door neighbor. "Sarah, did you see what happened?" My mouth was open, but nothing would come out.

Finally I was able to speak, but all that came out was: "It's *my* fault."

***

In the ensuing weeks and months after Rosie's death, I couldn't talk about her or her death. I couldn't even say the words "Rosie's death." At the viewing and funeral, I kept my head down as relatives and friends passed by. I couldn't talk to anyone about anything. I could hear mournful sounds coming from my parents' bedroom every night for weeks.

School and life became a fog as one month blended into the next. I stayed away from Mom as much as I could. She wouldn't want the person responsible for Rosie's death to talk to her.

Mom never once blamed me, not with words, anyway. She tried to get me to talk to a grief counselor, but I refused. All I did was wake up, go through the motions of each day, and sleep. Every night I wished that I would have a dream about Rosie. The only dream I ever had was a nightmare replaying the moment the van hit her. She was on the road, her eyes open, her small voice saying, "I don't want to play tag." I wished I could tell her one more time I loved her. I wished I could tell her that I was sorry.

If I hadn't asked her to play tag, *if* we hadn't been outside, *if* I hadn't run across the street...if, if, if. I should have protected her. I shouldn't have led her into the street. It should've been me who was struck by that van.

I didn't — wouldn't — cry, either. Every time a sob crept up the back of my throat, I shoved it back down again. I had no right to cry. I had no right to talk. I had no right to live. It was *my* fault.

We weren't much of a praying family, but I did believe in God. I tried to pray many times. How could God let her die? Why didn't *He* save her? Why didn't *He* stop me from playing tag with her? Why didn't *He* stop me from running across the street? I was angry at the birds for continuing to sing, and mad at the whole world that moved along as if Rosie had never been a part of it. Eventually, I saw that life was continuing for my parents and brothers. How could the world just continue when my world had ended?

*****

"Is anybody sitting here?"

I didn't even look up at the guy asking.

I was having lunch at the library. My preference would've been for him to leave me alone, but I shrugged. I soon would learn that Jack was persistent to the point of being annoying.

"I'm Jack." He held out his hand to me.

"Sarah," I whispered. "Be quiet. We're in a library." I shook his hand and he sat down beside me. That's when I finally looked at him. He was a pleasant enough looking boy: blond, wavy California hair, blue eyes, broad shoulders.

"Whatcha reading?" he asked, keeping his voice soft.

I answered but kept reading. "The Funeral Practices of the Ancient Egyptians."

I looked up just in time to see his eyebrows lift.

Every Wednesday after that, he was there at that same table at the college library. Sometimes he would offer to share a muffin or other snack. Most of the time I sat there, quiet, reading. He kept the topic of conversation superficial: the weather, current events, sports.

"Our baseball team is going to the semi-finals."

"Oh?"

He nodded. "I play second base."

"That's nice."

"There's a game at the college baseball field next Wednesday, so I won't be able to meet you here."

"Okay."

His eyes widened. "Hey, why don't you come and watch?"

I was never a big fan of sports, but the way he looked at me, so expectant, I surprised even myself, saying, "Sure, okay."

I went to the semi-finals and watched the game. Jack actually hit a home run, and I found myself cheering with the rest of the spectators. But his team lost. I waited for him after the game.

"A home run. Wow."

"Well, we lost, but we did our best." He hesitated. "Want to go grab a bite to eat?"

I scowled. "I thought we were just friends."

"Can't two friends grab a pizza?"

"I suppose."

There was still a part of me that wanted him to leave me alone; I hadn't really had any friends since Rosie died. The way I saw it, I didn't deserve friends.

Jack and I continued seeing each other on Wednesdays. He always did most of the talking, though. I learned that he had three older sisters and that he was attending college (majoring in microbiology) on a baseball scholarship. He liked pizza and hiking. He was an amateur photographer. We eventually began texting.

My mother pestered me about my "new friend, Jack."

"He's just a friend, Mom."

"Oh," she responded, her eyes lowering in disappointment.

Jack had come to pick me up on a warm Saturday in June for a hike in the local conservation area. I had put him off for weeks, but finally agreed to go. "Wear sturdy shoes and bring extra snacks and water," he had told me.

We arrived at the conservation area at about eight a.m.

"Take a deep breath, Sarah."

"What?"

"Close your eyes and take a deep breath. Doesn't that air smell heavenly?"

I sighed, closed my eyes and took a deep breath. The air did smell nice. But heavenly?

We hiked in silence for an hour before Jack brought me to an area with a few large rocks. He took some photos of wildflowers with his iPhone, then he motioned for me to sit down on a rock beside him. We drank from our water bottles.

Jack cleared his throat. "I know why you're so sad, Sarah."

"What are you talking about?"

"Your eyes look like they want to cry. Like you're still grieving." Then his confession. "I looked you up on Google. The newspaper article about your sister's death is online."

I pursed my lips. Jack had crossed the line. "You had no business —"

In spite of my anger, Jack took my hand. "I'm so, so sorry for your loss." He patted my back and when I looked up at him, his eyes were glistening. "You need to grieve, Sarah."

"I just...can't. I can't accept it. I don't *want* to accept it. I don't *want* to move on because I shouldn't be here. She should be alive — not me."

He patted my back. "Sarah, it's been nine years. And you are *alive*. But you're not really *living*."

My lip started to quiver, but I pressed my mouth together to stop it. I shook my head and wiped my already wet eyes.

"Sarah, please. Talk to me."

And finally, the years of holding back came rushing forward like a tsunami. My eyes welled with tears as I shared my story — not the newspaper's version, but my version. I must have spoken for an hour before I stopped. I was bawling, my eyes and nose red. He said nothing the entire time, nodding, his expression without judgment and with much empathy.

"I'm so sorry."

"Did that article say it was *my* fault? That we were playing tag and I ran into the street and she came after me? Did it say that I should've been the one to be killed?"

Jack sighed and shook his head. He hopped off the rock, my hand still in his. "Come with me." He seemed to scan the area, then pulled me to a section of grass with a bunch of dandelions.

He took my hand, crouched down and pointed. "Look."

I squinted and blinked to clear my eyes of tears. "What? Dandelions. They're weeds. So?" I sniffed.

"What's another word for these?"

"Yellow? Ugly?"

Shaking his head, he pointed. A bee was busy doing what bees do inside a dandelion.

"Well?" I asked.

"Sarah, the dandelion feeds the bee and the bee helps the dandelion. Everything alive gives something. We can't do that without others. We can't give without having others accept our gift. You've been full of grief and guilt for so long that you can't live — you can't love — because you can only see yourself."

I felt my blood start to boil. "What do *you* know about grief and guilt? Just because I poured my heart out to you doesn't mean you know everything about me!"

Jack sighed and grabbed hold of my hand. When I tried to pull it back, he held on firmly. "My brother died in a farming accident."

I gasped. My mouth fell open. "Oh."

"I know a lot about guilt and grief. I was 12. Owen was 10. My family was visiting our friends' farm. We were playing in the truck filled with canola when he slipped and went under. We had played in that truck before, but that day the grain seemed more slippery than usual. I tried to pull him up, but I couldn't because I started going under too. I survived, but I couldn't save him."

I let my fingers curl tightly around his. "I'm sorry."

He continued staring at the bee and dandelion. "I couldn't speak for weeks. My mother — a very strong-willed woman — finally said, 'Owen is safe and in heaven, Jack. It's not your fault. But he's gone. It's an awful, terrible tragedy. I hate that he died. I hate that I won't see him grow up and be a man. But we're still alive, and we need to live our lives until we see him again in heaven.' Then my mother took me back to the farm where that family's children still worked and played. And I remember thinking that there's so much death on the farm. But there's also a lot of life. My attitude didn't change overnight, but I realized that I couldn't have done anything more to save him and my mom was right. Owen *was* home, and I was alive."

He paused, lifting my chin with his finger. "So in the words of my mother, your sister's death 'was an awful, terrible tragedy. But we're still alive.'" He paused. "Sarah, you'll see Rosie again someday, but for now, you need to start *living*."

I lowered my head. I began to sob again, but I finally nodded. Jack was right. Suddenly it felt like the heavy weight of grief and guilt was gone from my shoulders.

When I had quieted, Jack said, "The first thing you need to do is to speak to your parents, Sarah. They lost two daughters that day."

"What?"

"They lost Rosie, but they also lost you. Have you ever spoken to them about Rosie's death?"

"No. My mother tried, but I wouldn't talk to her. I'm sure she blames me."

He led me back down the trail and drove me to my parents' home.

I sat in the car, not wanting to get out. "I'm not sure what to say to them."

"Speak from your heart."

I nodded, then opened the passenger door. With one foot out, I turned and asked him, "Can you come with me?"

The side of his mouth lifted in a sad smile. "Of course."

Mom was at the sink and Dad was at the kitchen table. They looked up, their eyes wide. "Mom, Dad, this is my friend, Jack."

Jack held out his hand. "It's a pleasure to meet you both."

My father stood and shook Jack's hand. My mother dried off her hands on her apron and held a hand out to Jack. "It's good to finally meet you, Jack." Then my mom sat down.

I sat in the seat beside my mother. Jack remained standing behind me. I took a deep breath. I didn't want to do this, but I turned and looked to Jack for courage. He gave it. I could speak.

"I'm sorry. I'm sorry for playing tag and running into the street and Rosie chasing me and for her getting killed instead of me. It was my fault and..." I couldn't finish. Mom pulled me into her arms and we both wept. I thought I had cried myself out when I had spoken to Jack earlier, but it takes a long time to shed nine years of tears.

"It wasn't your fault, Sarah," Mom said, her voice trembling. "It was *my* fault. I should've been watching you both more carefully." Then Mom began to weep, mournful sounds like the kind I heard just after Rosie had died.

"*Your* fault?" It had never occurred to me that Mom would think it was *her* fault. I could only see to the tip of my own nose for so many years that I was unable to see the guilt my mom was still experiencing.

A week later, Jack and I were back at the park for another hike. Jack didn't need to remind me to take a deep breath. The scent of flowers, dirt, and fresh air were intoxicating. The sky was a deep, robin's eye blue. We hiked, with Jack remaining silent and me being chatty. I pointed at what looked like a patch of beautiful scarlet red wildflowers. "What kind of flower is that, Jack?"

"*Monarda didyma*, I believe; otherwise known as Crimson Bee Balm."

"It's so vibrant."

"It is."

We reached an area with picnic tables and stopped. I took a bite of a homemade oatmeal-chocolate-cranberry granola bar that Jack's mother had made. "This is bursting with flavor!"

"You sound like a commercial," he chuckled, "but they are good, aren't they? Makes me never want to eat store-bought ones again."

I finished the bar, then lifted my face toward the sun. My grief was still there — as I knew it always would be — but the warmth of the sun, the deep blue of the sky, the flavor of the granola bar, and the vibrant red of the wildflower made me feel so content and happy that I wished we could remain there all day. "Can we —"

"Sure thing, we can stay here as long as you want. I have extra water bottles and a lot of granola bars. We're all set."

"How did you know what I was going to ask?"

"I could see it in your eyes." He paused. "This is why I come here so often."

Jack then told corny jokes and made goofy faces. I couldn't stop laughing.

"That's music to my ears, Sarah. You have an infectious laugh." His expression went from playful to serious.

"What?" I asked, concerned.

"You have beautiful eyes, especially when you're laughing."

Jack, bless his soul, was careful never to initiate any sort of gesture that took our friendship to "the next level." But in that moment, I felt so close to him and my heart was filled with love for him that I leaned in and kissed him. He returned, but did not prolong, the kiss.

***

Here at our local library, I no longer read the death notices. Now I find myself drawn to those *Chicken Soup* books.

What does life sound like? It's the roar of laughter and the mournful sound of weeping.

Life looks like an exuberant child running through the sprinkler on a summer day. Life also looks like a polished maple casket being lowered into the ground. Life is people in black clothes and people in colorful clothes.

Life is *not* me. Life is *us*. My husband Jack and I are journeying through this life together, through good times and in bad.

What *is* life? Life is a bean-sized, tiny unborn child knit together in my womb created by God from the love of Jack and me. It is the feeling of butterflies patting my stomach. Life is nausea and migraines and fatigue. Life is giving birth with the most indescribable pain. Life is holding onto our baby daughter, a girl with wispy blond hair and blue eyes we call Rosie, named after her aunt, the bright soul in heaven of a small girl who once slept in my bed, giggled at my jokes, and played tag with me.

Acknowledgments

Erin would like to thank all of the contributing authors and poets for sharing their amazing gifts of insight and truth-telling as well as their patience with the whole process of putting together a collection of this scope. To James Hrkach for the beautiful cover and the good humor.

Erin specifically would like to thank Ellen Gable for this opportunity to stretch her wings in a new direction and to see as a writer what it's like to work on the other side of the editorial desk

Scott Cupp and children for honoring this work with the tangible gifts of time, service and patience.

Ellen would like to thank all the contributors, Damon Owens for the Foreword, and her husband for the beautiful cover. Special thanks to our keen and eagle-eyed proofreaders who helped to polish all the stories.

Contributor Biographies

Michelle Buckman is the author of six novels, including the award-winning *Rachel's Contrition*. Although faith-based, her books tackle gritty life issues that place her readers in someone else's shoes to face the gravity of life's choices. Michelle's writing has encompassed an array of avenues from being a newspaper columnist to senior managing editor of a business magazine. Nowadays, she is a copy editor for a NYC-based website as well as a freelance editor, while continuing to work on new novels. Walking the Carolina beaches is both her favorite pastime and greatest inspiration. www.MichelleBuckman.com

AnnMarie Creedon has been married to her husband for almost 30 years and has five children. She is the author of *Angela's Song,* a Catholic romance novel, and is currently working on her second book. AnnMarie homeschools the three youngest of her children, sings on a praise and worship team and also in her parish choir. A native New Yorker, AnnMarie has been transplanted to the Midwest, and has fallen in love with this region of the U.S. She and her family enjoy cooking together, watching superhero movies, and chatting about fandoms.

Karina Fabian writes fiction and nonfiction, secular and religious. Her stories include spacefaring nuns, a dragon in the employ of the Faerie Catholic Church, a zombie exterminator and a mad psychic who must save two worlds. Her nonfiction varies from advice articles and writing webinars to devotionals and saint stories. She helped found the Catholic Writers Guild and has been an officer as well as the mastermind and coordinator of the Catholic Writers Online conference. Her newest book, *Discovery*, a Rescue Sisters novel, was recently released by Full Quiver Publishing. Learn more at http://fabianspace.com

Anne Faye is a homeschooling mom of three who writes from Western Massachusetts. A member of The Catholic Writers Guild, her novels include *Through the Open Window, The Rose Ring*, and *Sunflowers in a Hurricane*. She blogs at annefaye.blogspot.com and can be followed on Twitter @AnneMFaye.

Ellen Gable (Hrkach) is a freelance writer and award-winning author (2010 IPPY, 2015 IAN) and publisher (2016 CALA), editor, Marketing Director for *Live the Fast,* self-publishing book coach, speaker, NFP teacher, Marriage Preparation Instructor, and past president of the Catholic Writers Guild. Her website is http://ellengable.wordpress.com

Author, speaker, and retreat facilitator **Barbara Hosbach** has a passion for exploring what scripture means for us today. Hosbach, whose articles have appeared in national magazines, blogs about scripture at http://www.biblemeditations.net . Her latest book, *Your Faith Has Made You Well: Jesus Heals in the New Testament*, takes a down to earth look at what happened when Jesus healed and the hope it offers us here and now. Her first book, *Fools, Liars, Cheaters, and Other Bible Heroes*, invites readers to connect with a diverse assortment of biblical characters. Both books received the Catholic Writers Guild Seal of Approval.

Dena Hunt is the author of the award-winning historical novels *Treason* (Sophia Institute Press) (IPPY Gold Medal 2015), and *The Lion's Heart* (Full Quiver Publishing) (CALA 2016), as well as several short stories and reviews, online and in print, at *Dappled Things*, *St. Austin Review*, and *The Pilgrim Journal*. She also writes for *FaithCatholic*, a liturgical publication company. She is currently working on her third novel. She is the book review editor of *St. Austin Review*.

Katy Huth Jones grew up in a family where creative juices overflowed and made puddles to splash in. When not writing or taking photos, Katy plays piccolo and flute in a regional symphony. She lives with her husband Keith in the beautiful Texas Hill Country. Their two sons, whom she homeschooled, have flown the nest and live creative lives of their own. Best of all, she is a cancer survivor.

Antony Barone Kolenc has authored several published short stories, as well as an inspirational youth historical fiction trilogy, *The Chronicles of Xan* (OakTara 2013). He is a professor at Florida Coastal School of Law, where he teaches Constitutional Law. He writes a legal column for homeschooling families in *Practical Homeschooling Magazine*, and speaks at legal, writing, and home education events. He retired as a Lieutenant Colonel from the U.S. Air Force Judge Advocate General's (JAG) Corps after 21 years of service. His professional writings focus on constitutional law and military policy. You can learn more about him at www.antonykolenc.com.

Theresa Linden is the author of the *Chasing Liberty* dystopian trilogy and a series of Catholic teen fiction. Raised in a military family, she developed a strong patriotism and a sense of adventure. Her Catholic faith inspires the belief that there is no greater adventure than the reality we can't see, the spiritual side of life. A member of the Catholic Writers Guild and the International Writers Association, Theresa also holds a Catechetical Diploma from the

Catholic Distance University. She lives in northeast Ohio with her husband, their three adopted boys, and their dog Rudy.

Amazon Bestselling author **Leslie Lynch** gives voice to characters who struggle to find healing for their brokenness—and discover unconventional solutions to life's twists. Leslie lives near Louisville, Kentucky, with her husband and a rescued, feral-turned-sweetheart cat. She's written three full-length novels: *Hijacked, Unholy Bonds,* and *Opal's Jubilee*; and two novellas: *Christmas Hope* and *Christmas Grace*. She is an occasional contributor to the Archdiocese of Indianapolis's weekly newspaper, *The Criterion*. A member of Catholic Writers Guild, she posted monthly content to the group's blog for years. For more, see www.leslielynch.com

Erin McCole Cupp is a wife, mother, and lay Dominican who lives with her family of vertebrates somewhere out in the middle of Nowhere, Pennsylvania. She is a contributor to CatholicMom.com, and her books are available on Amazon. Get to know Erin at erinmccolecupp.com.

John D. McNichol was born in Toronto, Canada at the dawn of the swinging 70s. He left Toronto in 1988 to attend the Franciscan University of Steubenville in Ohio. John now lives in Vancouver, Washington, with his wife Jeanna and their children. He became a proud American citizen on September 19th, 2012. John's first book, *The Tripods Attack*, was published by Sophia Press in 2008. The sequel, *The Emperor of North America*, is available from Bezalel Books. His novel for the 9-12 year olds, *The King's Gambit*, was published by Hillside in October of 2013. He loves pizza and hates broccoli.

Damon Owens, an international speaker and evangelist for over 20 years, is the founder and executive director of joytob. A Certified Speaker for the Theology of the Body Institute, National Trainer for Ascension Press, Damon keeps a full international speaking schedule at conferences, marriage seminars, universities, high schools, seminaries, and parishes on the good news of marriage, sexuality, Theology of the Body, adoption, and NFP. Damon currently lives outside Philadelphia with his wife Melanie and their eight children.

Arthur Powers and his wife lived in Brazil for 30 years, including seven years as Catholic lay missioners in the Brazilian Amazon. Arthur is author of *The Book of Jotham* (Tuscany Press - winner of the 2012 Tuscany Novella Prize) and *A Hero for the People* (Press 53 - winner of the 2104 Catholic Arts & Letters Award). He received a

Massachusetts Artists Foundation Fellowship in Fiction and has served since 2014 as judge for Winning Writers' Tom Howard short story contest.

Gerard D. Webster is the author of two Catholic novels, *In-Sight* and *The Soul Reader*. He is the co-founder of the first local affiliated chapter of The Catholic Writers Guild, the St. Johns Chapter, in Jacksonville, Florida. His past experience encompasses a broad background—as a Peace Corps Volunteer, a soldier, an international businessman, and an addictions counselor. Most of all, he is a husband to his wife of 45 years, a father to their five children, and a grandfather. He wrote the poem, *Thou*, many years ago to honor his wife, Anne.

R. Elaine Westphal holds a BA degree in English Education, is retired from a career in supervisory management and is currently an active community volunteer. She enjoys quilting, singing, classic movies, and relaxing to classical music. Nature walks are her inspiration for her creative writing. Along with writing poetry, she also enjoys writing articles about local history and nature subjects.

Permissions:

Venus if You Do, copyright by Arthur Powers, used with permission
    Published previously in the Indiana Voice Journal

Thou, copyright Gerard Webster; used with permission

No Turning Back, copyright Leslie Lynch, used with permission

Purple Hearts, copyright by Antony Barone Kolenc, used with permission

Cries of the Innocent, copyright Karina Fabian, used with permission

Victorious, copyright Katy Huth Jones, used with permission

Movements, copyright Michelle Buckman, used with permission

Full Reversal, copyright Theresa Linden, used with permission

In the Death of Winter, copyright Arthur Powers, used with permission

Guess Who's Coming to Sunday Brunch, copyright Erin McCole Cupp,
    used with permission

Nice, copyright Gerard Webster, used with permission

My Pot of Gold, copyright R. Elaine Westphal, used with permission

Claudio, copyright Arthur Powers, used with permission

This is My Body, copyright AnnMarie Creedon, used with permission

Good for Her, copyright Erin McCole Cupp, used with permission

Pear Trees, copyright Dena Hunt, previously appeared in *Dappled
    Things*; used with permission

The Walk, copyright Anne Faye, used with permission

Two Kinds of People, copyright 2014 by John McNichol, used with
    permission

Hard Choices, copyright Barbara Hosbach, used with permission

MS, copyright Arthur Powers, previously published in Kakalak 2015

Made for Love, copyright Theresa Linden, used with permission

The Death of Me, The Life of Us, copyright Ellen Gable, used with
    permission

About the Editors

Erin McCole Cupp is a wife, mother, and lay Dominican who lives with her family of vertebrates somewhere out in the middle of Nowhere, Pennsylvania. Her short writing has appeared in *Canticle Magazine, The Catholic Standard and Times, Parents, The Philadelphia City Paper, The White Shoe Irregular, Outer Darkness Magazine,* and the newsletter of her children's playgroup. She is a contributor to CatholicMom.com and has been a guest blogger for the Catholic Writers Guild, and she occasionally blogs about year-round meatless Fridays at Mrs. Mackerelsnapper, OP. Her other professional experiences include acting, costuming, youth ministry, international scholar advising, and waiting tables. When Erin is not writing, cooking or parenting, she can be found reading, singing a bit too loudly, sewing for people she loves, gardening in spite of herself, or dragging loved ones to visitors centers at tourist spots around the country. Get to know Erin and her books at erinmccolecupp.com

Ellen Gable (Hrkach) is a freelance writer and award-winning author (2010 IPPY) and publisher (2016 CALA), editor, Marketing Director for *Live the Fast*, self-publishing book coach, speaker, NFP teacher, Marriage Preparation Instructor, and past president of the Catholic Writers Guild. She is an author of six books and a contributor to numerous others. Her best-selling novel, *Stealing Jenny*, has been downloaded over 330,000 times on Kindle. She and her husband, James, are the parents of five adult sons and seven precious souls in heaven. In her spare time, Ellen enjoys reading on her Kindle, researching her family tree, and watching classic movies. Her website is www.ellengable.com.

About the Foreword Writer

Damon Owens, international speaker and evangelist, is the founder and executive director of *Joy To Be* (joyTOB.org) a new 501(c)(3) nonprofit ministry of *Stewardship: A Mission of Faith* centered on St. John Paul II's Theology of the Body. Following four years as the first executive director of the *Theology of the Body Institute*, he served as Chairman of the 2016 International Theology of the Body Congress. He previously founded *Joy-Filled Marriage New Jersey,* and *New Jersey Natural Family Planning Association*, non-profit organizations dedicated to building a marriage culture through training, seminars, and conferences. Damon and his wife Melanie taught Natural Family Planning (NFP) for 14 years, and served as NFP Coordinators for the Archdiocese of Newark (NJ). A Certified Speaker for the *Theology of the Body Institute,* National Trainer for *Ascension Press*, and presenter at the 2015 World Meeting of Families, Damon keeps a full international speaking schedule at conferences, marriage seminars, universities, high schools, seminaries, and parishes on the good news of marriage, sexuality, *Theology of the Body*, adoption, and NFP. He currently lives near Philadelphia with his wife Melanie and their eight children.

Published by Full Quiver Publishing
PO Box 244
Pakenham, ON K0A2X0 Canada
www.fullquiverpublishing.com